Praise for TAUGHT

"An unflinchingly honest portrayal of the student-teacher relationship that reminds us that history is never finished. A must-read for educators, parents, and all who believe in the power of truth-telling and the transformative impact of education."
— DR. MICHAELLE C. SAMUEL, *Educator & Psychotherapist*

"In these pages, I found a mirror and a map—an invitation to reimagine our relationships, repair what has been broken, and reconnect with the parts of ourselves that are most alive."
— CAROLINE HILL, *228 Accelerator Founder*

"TAUGHT offers brave and poignant commentary on the continual learning and unlearning of educators, especially during a time of racial reckoning."
— LYNSEY WOOD JEFFRIES, *Higher Achievement, CEO*

"A powerful story you'll think about long after the last page. Excellent writing befitting a novel of our difficult times."
— MAT EDELSON, *Author and Pulitzer-Prize Nominated Documentarian*

"Thought-provoking and unique...there's a lot to explore here."
— NEILS RIBEIRO-YEMOFIO, *Author & Nonprofit Leader*

"These are the protagonists throughout time that stick with me. JB reminds me of a grown-up Holden Caulfield."
— RICHARD REYES-GAVILAN, *DC Public Library, Executive Director*

"TAUGHT will take you on a riveting, honest journey with Malik and JB. Their experiences challenge our notions about race and society in this fast-paced, emotionally charged story."
— JORDAN LLOYD BOOKEY, *Beanstack Co-Founder & Reading Culture Podcast Host*

"Eric Goldstein leverages his experience as a teacher, and his skill as a writer, to give us a story that centers the influential relationship between a teacher and their student—and the power of that connection to change them both. TAUGHT will surely teach you something, too: about what connects us, and what nourishes us, and why we need each other so urgently as we navigate the rough terrains of our lives."
— SAM CHALTAIN, *Filmmaker & Author of American Schools & Our School*

"TAUGHT doesn't shy away from the messiness of race and education, but it also doesn't leave us there. Instead, it invites us into dialogue, offering a springboard toward healing and understanding. Through the journeys of JB and Malik, we see how systemic racism, relationships, and the search for truth collide in a way that feels both timely and timeless."
— MARK CHABUS, *Author of Remembering Your Spirit*

"A masterful study of contrasts that define the American experience of hardship and humanity."
— DR. JESSE B. BUMP, *Harvard University, Executive Director of the Takemi Program in International Health*

"A complex story of coming of ages and of ages that are coming. Using vivid descriptive portraits of people and places, the novel chronicles lives dissolving and perhaps starting to be rebuilt. A thoughtful read that provides a final lesson to the reader: empathy lets one glance into another's life, but never truly live it."
— DR. JEANNE SIMONELLI, *Professor, Activist, & Author of Uprising of Hope*

"Laid bare the painful, complex legacy of our country's history and the virulent racism that has never gone away through characters I really cared about."
— TARA LIBERT, *Free Minds DC Book Club & Writing Workshop, Executive Director*

Published by
One Long Road

TAUGHT

Editing by Crystal Adaway, Worthy-Notes.com
Proofreading by The Pro Book Editor
Cover Design by Crystal Adaway
Interior Design by Crystal Adaway
Author Photo by Carol Clayton

1. Main category—FICTION / Diversity & Multicultural
2. Other category—FICTION / Urban & Street Lit
3. Other category—FICTION / Literary

For my mother, Sharon Sultan Cutler, my first storyteller.

TAUGHT

1

IT'S ONLY THE ILLUSION of safety, this old pickup truck that's hiding more than the past in its rusting metal. The silence is a contrast to blocks away, down 16th Street at the White House, where thousands of Black Lives Matter and Covid-restriction protesters collide at the intersection of injustice and rebellion. Both groups are surrounded by police dispatched to contain them.

Oddly noticing the white skin of my finger, I start the video on my phone and images from that infamous evening two weeks ago in early June come to life on the screen. My chest tightens as I immerse in the chaos of America 2020. Within seconds, the borders of the small screen barely contain the sea of flashing lights ripping across another volatile summer sky. An orchestra of sirens invades my ears as the camera's rapid movements try to follow the pushing bodies, pushed bodies, attacking bodies, and defending ones. Voices with uniform authority yell for the crowd to move back. At the ten-second mark, clubs start swinging with impunity. Only one's imagination, or knowledge of history, informs where they land.

Yelling enraged with civilian angst and decades of systemic injustice surges through the phone's speaker. A female-sounding voice pleads for an officer to free his tightening grip across the chest of a young man on the ground. The screams intensify as the camera rises to where people's hearts and brains should be.

More batons swing across the screen. The only indicators of their destination are off-camera grunts and bone-shattering cries. The camera ungracefully follows a scurry of indescribable activity before lowering again as the videographer zooms in to capture a motionless body lying on the ground. Someone's child or possibly someone's parent. Or worse, both.

A new circus of screams emerges from the small speaker. Several implore the sanctity of law and order, but most the sanctity of life.

I grip my phone tighter when I hear, "Grab my arm, Lew. Lean on my leg. Slide your knee forward and push up."

In the middle of those words, an explosion of purple smoke coats the small area of dominance and resistance that's so uniquely human. For several seconds the camera solely focuses on the right side of a person who I think may be Lewis, but I'm unsure. He's being dragged several feet forward only to stop, frozen in time by fate and technology, in the center of the screen at second forty-seven. A thick string of purple phlegm drips from the Black man's mouth, who I'm now certain is my former student.

My thumbs push into the peeling black plastic coating of the steering wheel and my back arches into the abused seat cushion as I pull oxygen out of the truck's stale air as if I'm rising from water. It's my first time watching the video with Lewis and Jamal, and possibly even more students, since Principal Becker shared it with the entire Biko Public Charter School, named after the South African anti-apartheid activist. Nearly everyone just calls it Biko. More than a million people have viewed the video, and many within hours of its posting. I may have been the last.

I toss the phone on the dusty dash, struggling again to find enough air to inhale. Not the kind of inhale that keeps a body living, but one that reminds us how close some of us are to not. I look out the dirty truck window, at the early morning sky above Mt. Pleasant, our neighborhood bordering the National Zoo and Rock Creek Park. A blend of multigenerational residents and gentrification have turned the homes above our basement rental into a community of million-dollar row houses and Title I schools. Hints of orange dusk create a soft silhouette around the National Cathedral to the west.

With the gearshift in reverse, I nudge the gas and think about the latest few hundred dollars sitting in the register of another skeptical mechanic. Reflexively, I slam the brakes.

What is that? Who is that?

I roll the window down with quick, circular strokes as a former student's voice lands in a tangled memory bank.

"Hey, Mr. Brown."

I rock the abused transmission into neutral, cut the engine, and slide out of the truck in one sweeping motion. The door slams harder than expected.

"You tryin' to kill me?"

The familiar voice morphs into an equally familiar, though unwelcome smile, or is it still that smirk? Pearly white teeth pinpoint the potential crash victim, and the situation instantly becomes complicated. Instead of calling him by his first name, I resort to the most tried and pointless teacher strategy I know. "Mr. Drummond."

Malik positions himself defensively. His palms face outward, his backpack is tucked under an arm.

"Hey look, Brown, you told Lew and Jamal I should be here early the morning after graduation, so..." As his words fade into the broken air, a vague memory of my walk last week with the other two members of the tight trio surfaces, then sinks.

I first notice Malik's hair is similar to the short crop of his youth, and despite the week's high temperatures and humidity, he's wearing jeans and a white tank top with a black sweatshirt tied around his waist. He holds the disconnected strap of a black book bag, preventing it from being hung on his shoulder. Another deep breath.

"What's up, Malik?"

Instantly, I remember this about Malik—how he rarely spoke at normal conversational speeds, answering questions immediately as if he planned what to say or deliberately slow as if scripting his following comments before the first. Often causing the adults around him to feel uneasy, like he wasn't all there. To others, and possibly only a few, like he was more than all there. Life made some kids have to think a few steps ahead, and Malik wore that on his sleeve.

"I'm good. I'm good."

His "good" sounds like it either has two *u*'s or four *o*'s and he bounces his head several times, and all signs point to this getting worse. *Ditch the silent gaps. Keep this moving*, I tell myself. "You sure?" I continue to guide myself with silent coaching. *Stop, JB. You're taking us in the wrong direction.* "Well, you know. You talked with Jamal and Lewis, right?"

The garbage truck passes and we move over, offering cover I use to pretend that I don't hear his response. He doesn't mention losing his uncle or grandmother to Covid or his work situation, and against all odds, it's clear that Lewis or Jamal told him to meet me here.

"How'd you know where I live, Malik?"

He smiles, but just a little. Enough to break the tension, though a damaged tension may better serve my interests. And I know from where that tension stems. After all these years, it was comments made by a fifteen-year-old Malik in my tenth-grade US History class that made me first question whether teaching was for me. Was I prepared to do the work needed for Black and Brown kids? While I'm certain he's long forgotten the incident, I have not.

"Man, after our Outings Club trip in eighth grade where we climbed that mountain. The one where we all cheered for Lewis and all. Remember? We didn't need to go back to school before five o'clock, so we came to your house and Ms. Terri got us pizzas in your backyard."

I remember this, and mainly because of the momentous experience it was for Lewis, but I don't remember Malik being there. I tap the truck's side and it makes different sounds depending on the severity of the rust underneath my fingers.

"Where are you living?"

"Oh, I recently moved into my grandmother's place while I work some stuff out."

After scanning the ground for answers, all I can find is the gumption to offer him a lift back there. Malik flops his backpack in the truck bed and walks to the passenger door, slamming it shut once inside.

I lean my arms on the ledge of the open driver's window. "Malik, you know, Lewis and Jamal think I'm taking a mini vacation. I'm not. I'm planting my tail in a campground for a few days to write letters to graduates, ya know. I think they may have misled you on what I'm ditching town for. Hear me?"

"Yeah, but…ah, never mind." Malik's lips roll inward. His eyes dart to different areas beyond the dirty windshield.

I get it. He doesn't need to say anything else. The trust placed in me years ago when he was a kid must surely have an expiration date. And Tara Becker, Biko's principal for three years, said on day one that our students didn't need any more White Saviors, a term I have despised since it crept from her lips.

I tell Malik that I need to hit the bathroom, and with him sitting in the truck, I reenter the small yard to our apartment and notice the bag of groceries and small bouquet of flowers are no longer on the stoop. The latter from the bin underneath the expensive bucket and the former with half the requested items because I skipped the last few aisles at the supermarket last night when Terri's urgent text came through. When I got home, she was on the phone nodding her head, and I heard her final words.

"I thought so. Thanks for squeezing me in."

Terri hung up and covered her face with both hands. From the stool beside the counter, I whispered, "Positive?" Her head bounced up and down as her fingers cut through her short brown hair.

A few slow seconds passed.

"I love you, JB, but you gotta not be around me, okay?"

Her words found the cracks between her fingers to reveal her beautiful lips, exposing a forced half-smile. It was the first time I thought to say, "I love you," since our wedding. I didn't and instead I walked out the door and sat on a metal chair in the yard that wobbled atop the uneven patio bricks under the constant cry of sirens and 85-degree humidity. Then the predictable text arrived from Rolando, the school's IT guru. Of the nine teachers in our 2005 orientation, Rolando and I are the only ones still at Biko. I knew what it was about, as Terri's emergency Covid test in the Metro Hospital parking lot had been at the same time as our virtual high school graduation. In the chaos of everything, I forgot to let the school know. I missed graduation. One of the most important nights of my year.

> Becker has it out for you!
> Said she didn't see you
> in the graduation ceremony.
> Asked me to confirm. You okay?
> Not like you to miss that. Call me.

The early morning sun has reached our basement windows, casting virgin light onto Terri. Still curled into the same corner of the couch with her knees pulled into her chest, coughing and drowning in what for days she's called bone aches. I didn't even kiss her goodbye when I exited last night.

For several weeks, Terri's been sharing the devastating reality of isolation that the virus is casting on patients and families. The overwhelming solitude surrounding birth and death—the two times within hospitals where you were essentially guaranteed company. Patients gripping her hands layered in plastic gloves, asking her to sit and listen. Life-long secrets, regrets, and anecdotes often followed. Then the question of all questions. Is this really it?

I watch a motionless and silent Terri through the window, realizing how much more compassion and explicit care she deserved than I was extending, but I was also sinking. Both of us interpreting the sadness of our natural and unsuccessful attempts to start a family differently. After three years of scheduled sex, glimmering streaks of light, disappointment, and thousands of dollars, we recently decided to stop trying to create what so many of my students had done almost effortlessly before finishing high school. It felt like we both swallowed the painful and oddly comforting pill of finality and only time would tell if certainty would bring us a level of comfort that hope had not. We still had each other, but whether there was enough love to rebuild with, neither of us had the courage to say.

I whistle into the outer door that despite its white steel bars, we still refer to as the screen, and Terri moves in front of the open window and turns around, having not seen me. She cuts off the Public Radio and I begin to hear her softly singing. It's that song. The one from the mountain roadside. The one she's gently sung and hummed every few years over the two decades of our living beside each other. First as a college couple, then young professionals, engaged, married, and somehow to this strange junction that I think neither of us completely understands.

The serenity in her notes, and with so few words, its own elegance. Those simple lyrics, "life is people," could feel like finding wings in midair. And still, all this time later, I don't really know what it means.

Terri stops when she notices me through the window. "Oh, I didn't see you there, JB. Thanks for the grub."

I foolishly point to the grocery bag that's since been moved to the table and she nods, mouthing, "I know. I put it there."

Through the subtlety I hear, *I love you.*

"I thought you planned to leave already. You're still going, right?"

I focus on the lines in her forehead, telling myself they're the signs of age, wisdom, and patience, but I fear it's something worse. I touch the screen where Terri placed her hand a second before and when I lower my fingers, she whispers, "Wash your hands."

"I'll be back in a few days."

"Call every day, JB."

"I promise."

A minute later my door closes more quietly than Malik's and we drive toward what's most likely the farthest place from someplace better for him. *Protect boundaries,* I tell myself.

The parkway beside Rock Creek is bare because the pandemic has emptied roads, offices, schools, but not the streets around the White House. Where we merge onto Interstate 395, helicopters and patrol vehicles grip the Capitol perimeter. Malik places the top seatbelt strap behind his back and leans half his body out of the truck like a child, and per his request, I drop him at the back entrance of the Oxford Manor Apartments.

Malik steps out of the cab and leaves the door open, moping the few feet to the truck bed where he retrieves his backpack. My phone on the dash flashes a text from Terri, thanking me for the flowers. Malik returns to the open doorway and looks down, both of us wishing the other would say something profound and hopeful, although only one of us should be expected to do so.

Malik is about to say something, and it sounds like "Well…," but he turns to the side.

I look into the rearview mirror to see what's making the piercing screech of skidding wheels. Suddenly a car slams to an abrupt stop in front of the building across the street.

POW, POW, POW, POW. The unthinkably loud, unmistakable, and all too common sound of gun fire rips through the air.

Instinctively I cover my head and shrink down in my seat. From the corner of my eye, I see Malik duck, now guarded by the open passenger door and his head level with the base of the seat cushion. Two, maybe three seconds pass and I start to slowly lower my hands as three more shots in quick succession whiz around the truck.

Malik jumps into the seat and yells, "Go, go, go, go!"

I jerk the truck into first gear, and within twenty feet, we pass the car I think the shots were fired from, but I can't be sure. We roar down the road as Malik yells, "Shift up, shift up!" and I realize I'm pushing twenty in first gear. I slow for the stop sign at the corner of Bowman Street when I see a car spring forward behind us. Second gear. Third gear, and I swerve onto McDaniel Boulevard and then Interstate 295 as Malik sits with his bag on his legs, looking out the window, but less like the child he appeared to be minutes earlier coming from the other direction. We pass the Capitol, which feels less dangerous than on our approach.

The same choppers and sirens surround the National Mall as my ears ring with the thunderous mixture of metal, powder, and friction, and if Malik is talking, I cannot hear him. I haven't been that close to gunshots since I moved away from the farm. *Was Malik the target? Was anyone hit? Is anyone dead?* None of these considerations register in a haze of robotic lane transitions and gear shifts as we pass the memorials and Potomac River before entering the Northern Virginia suburbs.

I lose sense of time and place until I realize that I haven't taken a deep breath in what feels like a longer time than a living being should, and I reach into the gulley of my chest for air. Confused about where I am, who I am, and who is now beside me, we pass the sign for Dulles Airport some twenty miles from DC, as a deep snore rips from the passenger seat. Asleep, Malik's head leans on his right shoulder, and I follow the road west.

2

THE ROUTE 66 SIGN conjures a split-second fantasy that we inadvertently landed on the iconic American road anchoring song, story, and travel lore. Main Street of America, though I'm unsure if the good part kicks in before or after the next Walmart.

Malik is silent and motionless, staring out the window. Possibly lost in the rodeo of time. In a haze of confusion and ringing ears from the gunshots, I intermittently forget he's here. Instead of curving around to the south, I abruptly head north, and two things become clear. First, I need to talk with Malik. Actually, I need to get Malik to talk to me. Second, considering what's taken place over the last hour, if the day is going to bring us this close to death, why avoid getting further in its way. My phone vibrates and I see Terri's text.

> Talked with guy on stoop few hours ago. Said he was a former student. Said he knew you were leaving. Told me he walked across city cause Metro is down. He was kind.

Malik turns his head, but with his eyes closed I'm unsure if he's awake. He didn't mention anything about walking across the city, a seven- or eight-mile trek by any measure of the shortest route and two more things become clear. While a lot of Malik encounters involve laughter, and mostly his, this is not going to be one of them. I quickly forget the second, momentarily consumed with a faint memory from years ago, during one of the first weeks of the school year when Malik and his friends were in my classroom after school. A safe space for some kids to avoid the large crowds and obstacles that arose within them. Tonia Howard, the eighth-grade Math teacher across the hall, stormed into my class as Malik, Jamal, and Lewis sat scattered in the otherwise empty room. She made several ninety-degree turns around rows of desks, and when she reached Malik, she grabbed his ear and twisted his head upward to the sky.

"I see you goofing on the great Lawd during Sunday service again, and I'll patiently wait in line behind your grandma to personally slap me some righteousness into your boney Black ass, you hear me?"

Howard's lip movements, hand gestures, and pronunciation were impeccably in sync. Though not her target, I also stood a few inches taller. I'd never seen a teacher grab a student before, and certainly never like that. Was this legal? Was she allowed to do that because she knew his family from church? Because she was Black? There's no way that could happen if she wasn't. Aside from those questions, it was hard to deny a heavy dose of love infused into her threat to whoop the Sunday gospel into Malik's backside.

Ever since, Jamal and Lewis joked about this every time we were together. But then and there they stood in silence, though maybe without the same degree of shock as my own. When she released his ear, Malik sank a few inches toward the desk, making it hard to determine whether his descent was the work of gravity or relentless theatrics. Then that grin appeared—Malik's signature smirk. Half-rounded cheekbones and raised eyelids and shoulders that moved by the same lever.

Howard gracefully walked toward the door, but just before leaving she turned to Jamal and Lewis and pointed. "Don't. Do not. You hear me," she said at nearly the same volume.

It was the most legible unfinished sentence ever spoken. She looked like Aretha Franklin with her eyebrows nesting in her forehead and chin bent forward, looking over her projected fingers. She twisted her body and left the room.

Malik then pointed at his friends, fake laughed, and with an elevated voice anchored in embarrassment said, "Ha, she told you guys."

That was Malik. Other flashes of his eighth-grade year filled with frustration, humor, and distraction consume my mind. Mirroring messages from other teachers, I told him that his advancement to high school was a gift. A poor choice of wording after a decade of reflection. An even worse promotion strategy. Malik sidestepped assignments and completed just enough work in each year's final weeks to move on to the next grade.

In front of his small groups of friends, which shrunk as the school year progressed, he was a practical joker and impractical tough guy. He excelled in neither role. Laughter ensued when he'd recite Muhammed Ali quotes down to the word and mannerism, and while most fists swung before fights even started, his classmates gave Malik warnings. Pointing at the other kid, he'd often call the school guard over to "help him before I show that I don't play." Adults and students shared a universal eye roll. Alone, or around Jamal and Lewis, he was kind and desperate to be recognized for doing something right. It was too hard to not like him then and nothing at his graduation made me think that I'd see him again.

But that thirteen-year-old Malik isn't sitting beside me in the truck right now, and it's unclear how much I'm about to learn of who he's become. I figure he must be around twenty-three, and the last time I saw him was inside a car I walked by downtown, smoking a blunt. I looked over, noticing his familiar smirk through the car window. Seconds later the car door opened, followed a boy-man cough, and he yelled, "Mr.

Brown." Cough. "You remember me, right?" I kept walking. I doubt he remembers, but now I'm remembering last week's walk with Jamal and Lewis, and Malik's presence in the truck is becoming more clear, though not more navigable.

When Jamal decided to become a teacher a few years back, he reached out to observe some classes, request a recommendation letter, and solicit help assessing teacher training programs. His correspondence picked up within weeks of the pandemic, asking about virtual instruction and how I was teaching about the Black Lives Matter movement and police brutality. He should have started with *if*.

For Jamal, the protests ignited a quietly brewing purpose. My mistake was thinking that it was at odds with his naturally calm demeanor. He spent years listening and absorbing the world around him, whether at home with five older brothers and sisters or at Lafayette University, a mostly White school where he graduated with the support of an academic scholarship and job at the school paper. When Jamal was home, Lewis was always by his side.

Many of my former students were attending the Black Lives Matter protests downtown, but Jamal was on a mission to film them. Last week I texted Jamal after word of his video going viral, though at that point I still hadn't seen it, and several days later Jamal, Lewis, and I walked around the flat Capitol Reflecting Pool. Neither asked if I saw the video, each probably assuming I had.

"Mr. Brown, we capturing a necessary record of history."

The conversation continued, though I wasn't sure it was moving forward. Lewis was expectedly quieter, responding on cue with affirming nods to Jamal's, "You feeling me, Lew?" and "You know we setting the story straight, right, Lew?" As I've always done, I monitored the patterns of Lewis's legs and arms as he maneuvered through his twenty-third year of life with Cerebral Palsy, his condition since birth. He was now taller than Jamal, and his arms were thick with new muscle. With that newer confidence.

I wasn't sure why I hadn't watched the video until this morning, and even without the actual vision as a reference, I thought about Lewis struggling to get his right hand, the one God locked in place, outward to balance himself upward as a purple cloud of tear gas thickened around him. One teacher wrote, "It took several views to realize it was Jamal's left arm hooked under Lewis's armpit as he held his camera in the other hand, yelling, 'Lean on me, Lew. Use your knees, Lew. Close your eyes, Lew.'" Then the video cut. Just like all the emails said it did, but I'd soon learn that my colleagues' narrative was wrong.

We walked in front of the Lincoln Memorial, thinking of the young men less as former students and more as modern civil rights leaders, or so I wanted to believe. But I was still missing a lot. This wasn't a social reunion. I had written to ask how I could help while at the same time not knowing what help looked like.

"Mr. Brown, safety means different things to different people, and my safety isn't my top priority. We need to confront and document everything. If not now, when?"

Thoughts that it wasn't documentation that was in short supply sprinted in my head. And as our conversations continued, I figured we'd possibly come to the end of a line, or was it the end of a lie. Maybe Jamal, and possibly even Lewis, slowly, or not so slowly, realized there's too much history I didn't teach them. Too much I left out. Too many perspectives I didn't present. Too many lies I unintentionally disguised as truth. They'd be correct if so, but there's more that they couldn't know. That we were both victims of my early teaching years. I wasn't ready. I wasn't prepared to teach students whose lives were proof that I misunderstood history, and what I did understand was incomplete. When this became clear, it was only clear to me, and Jamal's and Lewis's positive reflection of class showed how we can sometimes shine in our blindness.

We walked toward the Washington Monument beyond the eastern boundary of the Reflecting Pool as helicopters circled overhead. I arrived with an open mind and a clear mission to explain that this moment didn't need more martyrs. Fifteen years working in Southeast DC offered enough evidence that the senseless loss of life of so many young Black men for all the wrong reasons won't extend a unique set of condolences when someone dies for a more righteous cause. I knew it wasn't right to link the honor of protest to the pervasive community violence, but somehow the media and Jamal's videos showed how similar the results could be. Both men looked like they hadn't slept in days, and the energy and anger in the air was palpable. I directed my attention to Lewis, who was chronically overlooked when he was with Jamal.

"Lewis, tell me about the video," I reluctantly asked before remembering my plan to first ask about his new job at a video game production company.

Lewis lowered his head, making it clear that the widely circulated video wasn't what he wanted to discuss. He turned to both sides slowly and said he had to sit down. "Still sore from the incident," were his exact words, the last two barely above a whisper. The scars on his right arm were easy to see because it was always in front of his body.

I felt Jamal looking at me, like my inquiry about the video was directed to the wrong person. I tried again to get him talking. "That must have been scary."

Lewis didn't initially answer or respond, and I wished that I had said something different.

"I'm just glad Jamal was there to help you up. Everyone's talking about seeing you knocked over and him pulling you up."

Lewis quickly pivoted, appearing to jolt upward to his feet, but after several elevated inches, a shock of pain brought a cringe to his face and he guided his body back to the bench. "Yo, that wasn't Jamal liftin' me up," Lewis grunted with what I hoped was temporary discomfort. "That was Malik."

I was caught off guard, having not thought of Malik in a while. Then I remembered the many years of never seeing them apart. A friendship bonded by church, disinterest in sports, fascination with video games, and the early sense that navigating the obstacles of becoming a man in their neighborhoods would be easier together.

"You know, Malik ain't been right for a while," Lewis said, gently shaking his head side to side. Possibly one of his few pain free movements. "Malik stayed over for a few weeks after helping me move, and he still got too many stories of him doing stupid stuff. And by that, I mean stuff he ain't even tryin' to do. Stupid stuff just happens to Malik. You know, his uncle retired a few years back from Andrews Air Force Base where he was a mechanic. He took Malik with him to a garage in Upper Marlboro. He barely lasted a semester at UDC."

Jamal was about to speak, but Lewis, in a gesture I hadn't seen from him before, put up his hand to Jamal, who reluctantly restrained himself.

"But his uncle got Covid in April and died weeks later. His grandma, who Malik was real close with, probably got it from him. She died too."

"See what happened was," Jamal clarified, "his grandma was in Prince George's County Hospital on one of those breathing machines."

"A respirator," Lewis interrupted, but Jamal basically ignored him.

"His cousin worked at the hospital. She told Malik that his grandma wanted to see his auntie. Asked Malik to get her up in

Baltimore and bring her to the hospital and be snuck in to say goodbye to her moms. She thought Malik had a car, but he ain't tell her that he sold it."

Lewis started shaking his head.

"So, what Malik do," Jamal continued, "he left the shop in a customer's car and drove to Baltimore. He thought he'd have it back in a few hours, but this dude ratted him. Malik already been in trouble with the garage owner. He said he felt real good an' all getting his aunt to the hospital and when he was leaving with a broken taillight, the car came up as stolen. The city's finest had their guns drawn. Face down on the ground. You know the rest."

But I didn't. I didn't know the rest. I'd never know the rest, but it was clear that Lewis and Jamal knew the rest and for now their story was done. Lewis pushed himself up and the three of us continued on the gravel path, not necessarily in silence but not contributing to the surrounding noise—a blend of sirens and anticipation. Then we reached the Lincoln Memorial.

"So, what's new with you, Brown?" Lewis asked.

"Nothing really," I said after an awkward pause.

I didn't want to tell them about the letter from the doctor, if you'd even call him a doctor. I didn't want to tell them about Terri's secret, or was it a lie? Or that the principal requested detailed communication records of my tenth-grade students after she claimed I had the lowest online attendance rate at the school since virtual teaching started.

And in the silence of self-pity, Jamal said, "Wow, still rocking that wild life, Mr. Brown."

We all laughed, but it didn't last more than a few seconds and we may have laughed for different reasons. At the bottom step leading up to Lincoln's feet I told them the only thing on my radar was leaving town for a few days to write my senior letters.

"That's when you go to the mountains and sleep in a tent and make a fire, right, Brown?" Lewis asked.

"Yeah, something like that."

We looked at each other for a long moment. Not uncomfortable, just longer than most moments.

I said goodbye and felt proud about who Jamal and Lewis had become, though less confident in the decisions they'd make and the choices being made around them. I was a few feet away when Jamal yelled out.

"Mr. Brown, ya know who needs to get out of town?"

"Who?"

"Malik."

I was surprised but not shocked, and because the odds of it happening bordered on nonexistent, I yelled back to the young men, "Sure. Tell him I leave the morning after graduation. Early." And within seconds I forgot the cheap and untrue words were ever spoken.

With Malik no longer snoring but possibly still asleep, a buzz from the phone brings my attention back to the road. I glance at the small screen that has only brought dread since its first view this morning, and a name I'm not looking for tightens my gut. Tara Becker. With empty road in the rearview mirror, I slow down to read Becker's note. I know it isn't safe, but I'm sensing that neither is what she's written.

Subject: Thursday Meeting at 12:00 p.m.

Mr. Brown:
Missing last night's graduation ceremony
without a reason or communication is highly
offensive to our community. Needless to say,
attendance was required. I would like to talk
with you about this. Please use this link for a

> video conference on Thursday at noon. We may
> be joined by members of the school's Board.
> Principal Becker

I toss my phone on the dash, wanting to build on my negative thoughts of the woman, but her note is another example of her ability to communicate complete ideas with few words, a skill I admired. Rolando's text was helpful, but it didn't reveal anything new. This has been brewing for several years, and I don't see it improving despite thinking of ways it could. Keeping my head down and focusing on teaching students and essentially ignoring her is appearing to make it worse. In the end, our relationship will be bad for students, as most contentious adult relationships are for the children around them.

We pull into a convenience store lot, and the roar of wind ripping through the open windows for the last hour settles into virgin silence.

"Where are we, Brown?"

"Just crossed into West Virginia," I say, facing the back of Malik's head as he looks out the window.

"Wow," he says, turning to me, rubbing his eyes.

I'm not sure if he's talking to me or himself.

"Where are we going?" he asks.

I don't immediately respond, but then, "Not sure. Want something to drink or a snack? I'm starving."

I raise the green bandana from around my neck, and Malik enters the store with a white makeshift mask that at first glance looks like a sleeve ripped from an undershirt. An older man wearing a NASCAR shirt several sizes smaller than his large belly sits on a stool behind the counter. I greet him and a second later realize that the man's shirt isn't the only thing too small. Malik flips the hood of his black zipper sweatshirt over his head and walks by the counter, and whatever benign or friendly energy we entered the store with evaporates.

With the pandemic and protests happening not far away, everyone is on pins and needles. A small TV on top of a cooler displays a muted Fox News broadcast of riots in Portland, Minneapolis, and DC. Ironically, the NPR station Terri played in the apartment this morning reported these events as protests. Malik hands me two bags of chips and a soda and walks out with his hands on his head. An already tense situation amplifies.

The man looks up from the screen that shows Malik exiting the store as I grab *The Winchester Record*, a regional paper off the stack. He follows my eyes from the paper up to him, and I follow his eyes from the same paper back at me. "Black Lives Matter Riots" reads the top headline. Our wordless conversation comes to an end, and I exit without saying thank you, which I rarely do. The warm early morning air is sticky and hot.

"Were you cold in there? I saw you put up your hood," I murmur, barely out the door.

"Why would doing that mean anything other than me being cold, Brown," he fires back. He couldn't even take a breath before responding, and I realize that while Malik was a kid I knew well, as an adult, he is practically a stranger.

"Why I got to show my face to a racist, Brown?"

"How do you know he's a racist, Malik?"

We hop back into the truck and continue driving north. Looking out my window, I'm thinking it might've been easier to say nothing. Did I need to say his name? A habit, I tell myself. First at the beginning of the year to remember names, and later… I can't remember why I did this later, but now it feels condescending.

Malik rubs his eyes, exhales, and lowers his hands to his lap. "Brown, you just know," he says, his volume and tone quieter.

"You just know," he repeats, and another exhausted exhale reflects something I've rarely seen in Malik. Calmness.

And I know that he's right as I ponder my ability to understand how the fatigue created by years of passive racism can be draining. This exhaustion reads in large font across Malik's face. His relaxed and confident tone say as much as his words. He's right. Sometimes you just know.

Despite being a weekday, there's traffic leading down the hill into Harpers Ferry. Malik's eyes widen at the row of nineteenth-century architecture as we park at the bottom of the road. I snap open the tailgate and it thunderously drops, bouncing a few times before settling into place. Malik and I are both around six feet tall, but as I hop up a few inches onto the tailgate of scraped white paint, Malik's feet never appear to leave the ground to sit beside me. I think about how I've sat more in these metallic grooves than maybe anywhere, and in another few minutes of direct sun, the metal will be too hot to touch.

"We going back?" Malik asks, looking out to the river beyond the railroad tracks.

I don't know the answer to that.

Neither of us speaks, and the rivers' singing provides a temporary respite. A few birds fly by. An occasional car passes. Several cyclists pedal past us. The late spring rapids of the Shenandoah River rush over the final rocks before rushing into the larger Potomac.

"Not this second, but yes."

Malik looks down, but I'm not sure exactly where.

Should I ask him about the morning? The shooting? What did it have to do with him? Was he in trouble? Was he running from something? Asking if he needs to go back is about all I can muster. I hop off the tailgate, and Malik and the truck rise an inch or so, and on my mental truck repair list, I note the rear shocks. *I hate this truck.*

We walk past the historical markers telling the story of John Brown's raid to the town's northern access of the Appalachian Trail, the winding and wooded footpath passing through the village. From here it's around a hundred miles north to the trail's halfway point and several more months of hiking to Mount Katahdin, the trail's most northern point in Maine. Few who start in Georgia make it there, and I was one of those who didn't.

We pass signs slow enough to read their titles but little beneath them. Near the edge of the river, the trail transitions from gravel to dirt, and despite trying to create distance between us, Malik is right behind me at the first switchback and we continue up the mountain.

Forty-five minutes later we reach a clearing that overlooks where the two mighty rivers collide. I don't remember any of this. Wasn't I here before? I was, but I wasn't, and the sense of new agony refreshes a thousand miles of unhealed memories. The mountains of Maryland, Virginia, and West Virginia surround us.

"Remember when we climbed that trail? Had *goat* or some other farm animal in the name, and Lewis made it all the way to the top?"

I should get behind his new dose of optimism, but I find it unwelcome. "Yeah, I sure do, but honestly, Malik, until this morning I didn't remember you being there."

"Stop playing, Brown. I was standing a few feet behind Lewis when he walked across the steep ridge. You's was cheering as I stared into that fool's ass praying his crooked grip held."

I walk around Malik whose lightened energy helps the mood but not us moving forward, and like a child unsatisfied with an answer, he steps in front of me.

"You being for real, Mr. Brown? No way. Ah nah. No way. I remember Ms. Terri yelling, 'Stay right behind him, Malik. Stay right behind him, Malik.' Back at the van, she pulled me aside and said that if it weren't for me standing within reach of grabbing Lewis, she would've had a heart attack. She gave me a hug."

Of course, I remembered Terri being there, as it was her idea to start the Biko Outings Club. The Billy Goat Trail hike in Maryland was our first trip, and I awarded extra credit to my eighth graders who attended our Saturday adventures, though only a few did. I remembered Jamal at the top, looking down at Lewis with encouragement. That memory was easy—the hero up top extending his hand to raise a friend to safety. I'm also starting to vaguely remember another student beneath Lewis moving step-by-step with no attention to their own safety, but I never placed who that was. Lewis's accomplishment that day was heroic to his peers. For Terri and me as well. Though it took a few years for him to admit it, it also had a powerful impact on Lewis. Apparently, Malik too.

"Man, that was a day I'll never forget, and while Lewis and I been in some tough places, and I knew his, well, you know, his condition, I'd probably not been as scared with him at any time before or since. I remember thinking how I'd grab him if he fell, and well, you know."

"What about if *you* fell?" I ask.

Malik lowers his head. "I ain't thought of that." It appears he's lost in his thought. "Man, when Jamal's mom picked us up that afternoon, I told her that we climbed Mount Everett, and even she knew that was dope."

"You mean Mount Everest," I say with the impression of a smile.

"Is that the largest one? I remember you saying that in class," he replies, presumably referring to my eighth-grade World Geography. "Yeah, I mean, I probably told her that we climbed both of them, Everett and Everest." And he smiles, possibly joking, though I'm unsure.

I walk on, thinking about the vivid memory of Jamal on top of the cliff, offering loud encouragement to Lewis. Fitting that the one lowering his hand from the top is remembered instead of the one pushing someone up from the bottom. Like Malik risking himself to help Lewis when he was knocked over during the protest while Jamal's glorified because he kept filming.

After several minutes of Malik walking too close to my heels as we descend, I let him pass as an eerie feeling sinks into my legs. Then it creeps up my body. The gaps between the trees expose the river. We're almost back at the trailhead. The sound of the rapids is melodic except for an otherwise pounding heart. I avoided this spot for twenty years, and I walk past Malik, who leans on the North sign. Pause. In front of me is the footbridge that carries hikers across the Potomac River and I direct my eyes to the exact spot. Painful muscle memory. Malik keeps walking toward the village, and I stare out over the footbridge and no one is here. Just like the last time when no one was there. The first time. When it mattered. His promise that come hell or high water, no matter what, that we'd meet at the bridge. Now the water is not only flowing from all directions through the mountains, it's pouring from my eyes, which I mask from Malik's view.

Malik stands beside one of the historical marker signs as I discreetly wipe the blend of sweat and tears off my face, and when I reach him, he turns toward me, hands on his hips.

"You ever teach us about what happened here?"

I walk past him, concealing how few things boil my blood as much as this question. A student asking if we covered a topic that we explored in great depth. The significance of John Brown's raid in Harpers Ferry was one of them. I don't answer him, instead insisting that he wander around. That we'll meet at the benches by the old railroad depot, and I consider writing some letters, feeling consumed with the irony of being in a place with a historical stench of racism so similar to what thousands around the country are protesting against now. Malik walks toward the armory. Winding through the thick brush toward the river, I barely miss stepping on a small brown snake that weaves into a rock pile.

The moving water feels soothing around my feet, and I splash under my arms and douse my head into the shallow current. My thinning curly hair feels oily, and the cold water relieves the pain of the scab behind my left ear from wearing too tight of a mask for the first weeks of the pandemic. The water gushes up my shorts and around what I now consider my lifeless prick.

First the years of indecisiveness. That was fairly easy, as I've always been that way. But the fear was real. At thirty-five, Terri claimed to be in the modern woman's sweet spot. Whatever that meant, it sounded encouraging. Thirty-seven sounded like a fine age to become a father, if one had to be, and months of formulaic sex followed. On one or two evenings, Terri surprisingly referred to it as making love, though I felt like I was continually underperforming at both. We interpreted the results as nature's slow and crooked path differently.

A year or so later, in one of our meetings with the maternity counselor, I learned that Terri's doubts set in quickly. Against her sister Cassie's guidance, or my own had there been any, Terri turned to the internet. New pillows, schedules, and an altered diet followed. The light that had briefly shined on our excitement to create a family dimmed with excessive structure and cautious optimism.

The topic of starting a family went quiet for almost a full year, but within days of learning that Terri's mother was showing aggressive signs of dementia, Terri suggested we seek more formal help. And by 'we,' we both knew she would seek more formal help. I shouldn't have been surprised that her gynecologist focused on her. She was her patient. It was almost an afterthought to be checked. For time's sake, which were her exact words, the doctor advised us straight toward IVF. After a thorough consultation, we silently left the office with the brochure outlining the process and cost, but secretly, I didn't know if it was worth it. There were things Terri didn't know about me. What I've seen parents endure. No cost was worth the risk of history repeating itself.

Around the holidays, I heard Terri on the phone with Cassie. "I know it's not cancer or like that, but the whole thing is causing so much anxiety, Cas. I don't…"

Terri stalled her dialogue when my footsteps made it clear I was approaching. You could hear anything in our small apartment, and if I was bent on listening, I should have stayed put. She stopped until I turned around, not remembering what I walked into the kitchen for in the first place. A minute later I heard Terri say, "No, JB hasn't seen a doctor yet. He never says anything. It's gotten worse, Cas." I walked the remaining few steps from our bedroom to the bathroom, flushed the empty toilet and stood in front of the mirror. In February, I went to the clinic and gave a sperm sample to the young receptionist behind the desk.

In early May, I conducted virtual office hours for our seniors from the couch after Becker canceled their last semester Sociology elective a few weeks earlier. Our seniors needed to check off too many boxes to graduate, and Becker designated non-essential classes optional. It was the right call, so I mainly chatted with Ja-Quea Norris, Antoine Evans, Darrel Jenkins, and Neville Jones, or Nevy, their new name after publicly identifying as gender fluid, a term I first heard months earlier.

When Terri walked out into the small backyard to chat with our landlord who lived upstairs, I long-stepped a few feet to the kitchen, touching only certain of the large foot-by-square-foot floor tiles like a wall-to-wall board game. Unintentionally, I glanced over to Terri's computer, something I rarely did. An email from the fertility clinic was open on her screen. It was from mid-March, almost two months earlier. The email said that the results from the lab indicated my sperm count was so low that I was clinically infertile. Momentarily stunned, I returned to the couch with a fresh coat of shame for giving the clinic Terri's email as my own point of contact.

That night, Terri asked to talk. Actually, she asked if I was busy. We had already taken a silent walk around the neighborhood. At first, I didn't answer, like often. Terri opened the fridge and the small mirror on the door reflected the new light blond hair growing on my cheeks. *Still too patchy to be considered a beard,* I thought, which would be my first. But it wasn't the hair on my face that I saw, it was the masks. The mirror and door closed, and Terri walked past me to the couch and closed my laptop. She'd never done that before.

"Thanks, JB," she said.

"For what?"

"For being there for me. It means a lot," she continued, with love and care in her voice.

I lowered my eyes and felt new levels of shame because she didn't know that I already knew. Really knew, or so I thought. I watched her eyes move around the room, possibly contemplating how she would break the news to me gently. But the real shame was not being able to give Terri what she wanted, like before, or since we met, before the first conversation about children. It was my condition and not hers that prevented everything. Everything except the pain.

"Listen, I want you to know that although it took some time, your test results came back, JB." Her smile was unwelcomingly warm.

I wanted to say, "I know, I know, you don't have to tell me." But I didn't.

"It means a lot to me that you got tested. You did that for me…I mean, for us. While there was doubt before, there isn't any longer. Your test results were fine. They confirmed that I'm infertile."

With my eyes fixated on the dimple in Terri's chin, I watched her tilt the corner of her lips upward. A more optimistic person would have mistaken it for a smile.

"It just is what it is," she continued, then leaned forward and gently kissed my forehead.

Like before, I didn't say anything, wondering if there was another note or why Terri was doing this. Why was she not telling me the truth? What purpose did this serve? Her words elevated the confusion and sadness to a new level. I was already silent, and then I was silent and emotionally absent. A husband who truly cared at the level I aspired to would've extended his hand, held her, hugged her. But with every second, I became more frozen, unable to be that person.

Malik rises from a bench some thirty feet away beside the armory and strides toward me with a seriousness that I'm capable of matching. "So, Brown, let me get this straight. This White dude John Brown, who appears all dope and righteous with the Lawd and all, took it upon himself to end slavery by attacking an armory that stood right here?" He points to the crumbled structure of what's now a historically protected monument.

I'm not sure if his time alone while I was in the river was ten minutes or an hour, but he's summed up the big picture before he interrupts me.

"Wait, wait, wait." His hands wave in the air like it will impact my listening.

All I notice are his skinny arms. More so than that, I wonder if he has another shirt in the broken-strapped backpack he tossed in the truck bed.

"So, if this brotha marches around the country building an army for his big battle, how's he only rolling into town with under two dozen men? Really?" Whatever word Malik planned to say next is never said, and he shakes his head, turning his gaze to where the rivers meet. Possibly unaware that the frustration he feels now pales in comparison to that of John Brown and his cavalry for the exact same reason more than a hundred years earlier. "I thought around half the country was against slavery. What's not adding up, Brown?"

My mind sinks, or maybe it's my heart. There's just so much to learning. A journey at times so peaceful and raw leading to inspiring discoveries and then utterly endless mistakes, pain, and letdown. Malik must know by now that being against something and willing to fight for it are painstakingly different battlefields. I think of Mr. Grupp saying that if the kids graduate full of unanswered questions with the will to keep searching, then we've done more than our jobs. But I'm unsure if this moment is an example of what Grupp had in mind.

I move to the concrete bench Malik just vacated. More questions I cannot answer. Maybe in some ways it's a win. He gathered information from multiple sources. He critically analyzed the information. Maybe a hypothesis is near. *This can turn into a proud moment,* I tell myself. But the sinking inside me is taking on water and I'm back in the well. The rope isn't reaching low enough to grab.

Malik walks away again, and I sense that he's not walking away from me. He's moving to think and a flashback surfaces of him doing this routinely a decade ago, and it wasn't just him. Then the shame returns for repeatedly failing to grasp how young boys needed to move. Their need for mobility to be at peace with their bodies and minds. How it resulted in endless redirections and detentions. The inability of adults to understand our students' primal needs—and I was one of these misguided adults. I hear Malik's voice rise again.

"So why didn't more people join him?" he asks. His hands since moved behind his body.

I'm about to answer. No wait. I mean respond, but he speaks before I do so.

"So let me get this straight. He has five or so brothas, right? Why didn't more Black people join him? Wasn't his cause their cause?" Malik makes two fists and squeezes them into the air and then releases them. He follows the deflation of muscle with a deep breath.

I look back at the bridge, still waiting for someone who will never arrive. Malik appears to be looking there too. The rapids shine as they flow over the rocks. Both of us grip the metal railing that stretches the perimeter of the river overlook.

"I can't imagine what life was like back then, Malik," I say softly. "Sure, these buildings reveal a little, but the limit of resources, the separation. The racism. I just can't imagine its potency during this time." I finish my sentence, realizing the time I'm referring to may not be that explicit. Whether he feels I'm talking about now or nearly two hundred years ago isn't exactly clear, and Malik doesn't seek clarification.

"Why didn't more people join? Shoot, if I were a slave, I'd join that crazy muthafucka in a heartbeat to earn my freedom."

Malik stares out over the river, and I tell him that joining John Brown's brigade must've sounded like a trap to some. A certain death sentence to others. He kicks a small rock, which flies off the bluff and ricochets off several boulders before splashing into the water. He turns away from the river and looks over my shoulders to the nineteenth-century buildings as I search for a legible thought.

Learning can be an emotional and angry exercise, I think to myself. "You're right, Malik," I say, speaking to his back. "You're right about more than you probably even realize." My voice is now as calm as his was before. Unfortunately, the thoughts that accompany it are less so.

"Oh, about this, yeah, I'm damn right," he says, swinging his arms around, accompanied by a volume that straddles yelling.

Malik turns back to where the rivers merge. He places his hands on his head like he did in the store this morning, but nothing else is similar to then. That was an act of defiance. What's happening now is different. Possibly surrendering to the limitations of what we can know. What we can understand. How we make sense of a history overflowing with more hate than any history should contain.

"Brown, seeing what's happening now, I just…I just…I just don't know what I think." Malik swipes his hands in the direction of the monuments and historical signs.

I think how the pathway toward understanding our history is a cruel one. I want to praise his pursuit of learning. Reinforce that his tough questions will lead him somewhere profound. But the words I say out loud sound something like, "You thirsty? We still have sodas in the truck."

He looks at me. No, he's looking *through* me. While at first I thought his look was one of feeling sorry for himself, I now sense that he may also be feeling sorry for me. For being unable to move us forward. For not knowing where to go or what to do. Possibly sensing that I may be much more of this person than what he envisioned, or mistakenly what he remembered. If so, then for the first time we may be on the same page.

"Malik, I hear you," I say quietly. I want to tell him that I'm learning silence is complacency, but I'm concerned that he might ask how I was allowed to be a teacher without knowing this before. To tell him that sharing his emotions is a good thing. That his confusion is a good thing. That finding fury in understanding history is a good thing. But I say none of this, thinking about how I've always found a false safety in silence.

"You know what?" Malik says. His tone balances anger and wisdom, a potentially dangerous cocktail of emotion for a young Black man from the perspective of many White people. "All these signs talking up history and this shit happening in all these different shapes and sizes since the beginning of America, but what it don't say is that all this shit happened then and happens now, because White folks can't stop hating on Black people. Ain't that it, Brown?"

In the strained moment of silence I ask myself if I can nod my head and we can all go home, but my inability to seize the moment has nothing to do with Malik, or so I think. I'm drowning in my own complicated, death-filled history, and I'm starting to think I'm not gonna make it out of here much better than him.

"But as small a crew attacking the armory as this was, that's some authentic soldier shit right there, Mr. Brown." Malik points to the stone perimeter of what remains of the long-fallen armory. "One of those signs over there"—he throws his arm in the other direction—"talks about how John Brown's raid was an early step in the Civil Rights Movement. You get that, Brown?"

I don't answer him, silently wondering whether he's shared a statement or question.

"You even hop forward a hundred years to when our history books love to highlight how White people stood up, but really, how many? Two percent, three percent? Shoot, maybe even five percent of all White people. What's that make the rest of 'em? Complacent? Racist?"

"Whoa, whoa, whoa. Wait, Malik. There's other ways to stand up for people, right?" I shoot back. "I haven't gone down to the protests. Terri hasn't gone down. We've been busy working. We didn't know about them in advance to take off work. Are we racist or complacent?" I let it sit for a moment. I wish I had a script. "Plus, is protest the only tool to fight injustice?"

I don't intend for that to be answered, and it isn't. He pushes himself from the top bar of the railing, keeping his arms extended, when I tell him it's time to go. The walk back to the truck is silent, and we race to roll the windows down, the doors ajar to let the built up heat out of the truck's cab.

"Ya know what it all comes down to, Brown?"

I again don't answer, feeling he's delivered a few other points under the umbrella of what it *all*—whatever that means—comes down to.

"It comes down to what we're willing to risk for someone else to be free."

I repeat the sentence in my head, wondering if I've heard this somewhere else, by someone else. He opens the soda and plops his right arm out the window. The hot and sticky air, if it can even be called air, shifts from pleasant to angry, and I want to tell Malik that what he's shared is profound. Instead, I wish Malik would tell me that I'm a waste of his time. Rip himself from the steaming truck and head to the train station at the bottom of the village.

"Well, let me get something else off my chest," he continues before licking his lips. Both of us border on dehydration despite the soda. "Ya know, believe it or not, I remember some stuff from your class."

I perk up, longing for reflections like this, and I assume what comes next will follow suit.

"Even Jamal and Lewis remember you speaking about people around the world who were persecuted. For real, I thought some of that was powerful. Ya know, eye opening. One group was like, what do ya call 'em…oh yeah, like the Dali Lama Crew in China, and a group in Chapas, Mexico. Yo, did I say that right?"

No. He didn't. But I nod approvingly.

"Some group in Peru called the Shining Path, which I remember because Lewis and I used it in our comic strip."

Silently I'm amazed by how much Malik remembers. A total win. We close the doors at the exact same time and the smash of old metal in unison has a unique and shallow grandness to it.

"But that's not it, Mr. Brown," he continues. "I remember you talking up all these groups around the whole world that got mistreated, except the ancestors of the students sitting right in front of you."

3

I MET TARA BECKER the first day of teacher orientation three years ago, in 2017, after a ten-year principal stint by Andrea Zodd. The only qualities the two women had in common were that they were White, loved kids, and both signed emails with only their initials. Oddly, they both sometimes even referred to themselves using them. The differences were stark.

Zodd was beloved by just about the whole Biko community. Her farewell notice at the all-staff meeting the morning of graduation left few dry eyes. She spoke about missing almost every recital, soccer practice, and field hockey game of her own children to be sure she was present for the same events of Biko's students.

"When my youngest daughter told me her friend had asked if she had a mommy, part of me broke. My husband attends our girl's events. It just didn't feel right that my own kids could have the support of two parents when many of Biko's kids only have one." The parents in the room nodded the fiercest. Like Zodd, Biko's teachers offered endless amounts of attention to our students, and sometimes that attention was at the expense of providing the same to their own children. I wonder how they did it.

On the first all-staff day that August, we all wondered who was going up to the makeshift podium in front of the bleachers. Then a pair of high heels clicked across the polyurethane-coated wood floor and Tara Becker introduced herself as our new principal. She was younger than I expected, especially since the two candidates I interviewed as part of the hiring committee were significantly older. The email introducing Tara reiterated that our staff had interviewed all three candidates, though everyone I spoke with also said they'd participated in interviews with only the other candidates: the Latina lady from the Bronx who'd been a principal for almost twenty years and the Black guy from Richmond who'd been an assistant principal. Other than my tenure, I wasn't sure why I was on the committee in the first place.

Less than a moment after telling us about her two-year teaching stint with Teach for America, and as if possible, a briefer impact as the principal of an all-girls private school, she announced her mission to uplift the lives of our Black children. Nearly everyone sat up straighter. She had the room's full attention. The moment's seriousness was undeniable, and not only because it was her introductory remarks as the school's new leader, but it was the first time the Biko community was explicitly talking about race. In hindsight, maybe that was the problem.

I sat behind Howard, who clapped when Becker said this, and she was the first to stand when Tara solicited questions. When Howard clapped, everyone had to join in, though it didn't occur to me that everyone would want to. From where I sat, all she did was explicitly refer to our students as Black. We've always discussed how to uplift our students, but Howard thanked our new principal "with a capital *T* for her honest talk." The moment had greater implications than I realized.

"We need to do a better job understanding the lives of our Black kids," Howard continued. "This honest talk is exactly what we need." It was her response rather than the comment she responded to that initially confused me. I thought the unwritten rule was not to explicitly refer to our kids as Black kids. For more than ten years, I thought our goal was to not describe our students in any way that distinguished them from any other group of kids. I thought that even referring to our students as Black was off the table. It was ingrained in my head that doing so was taking us, and them, backward to a time when skin color mattered. It felt like overnight our students went from African-American to Black. When I think of it now, I wonder what prevented me from seeing the power in this transition. Sadly, in some ways still.

Howard's words that day to our new principal still ring. "The challenges to deeply and authentically engage in this work as teachers is nowhere close to the challenges that Biko's students face beyond our walls." Teachers approached Becker after her remarks to introduce themselves. Her smiles looked fake and ceremonial, or maybe I hoped they were. They weren't.

Following Becker's introduction, I walked up the stairs side by side with Allen Byrnes, one of Biko's two physical education teachers. I'd been meaning to ask him for years when it had stopped being called Gym class and maybe this was a good time for that.

"I'm over it, Brown," Al said. His navy blue jumpsuit made swishy sounds every time he moved.

I considered asking him what he was over, as it wasn't as implicit as he intended.

"What was that, Brown? Like thirty minutes, and my White guilt is spent. Know what I mean, JB?"

Big Al, as he referred to himself, spun around the banister where the narrow staircase changes directions like our students do and stopped. It was then, but not in the steps before, that it became clear Byrnes was asking me a real question. His position prevented me from passing, and I looked to the other staircase to assess if moving there was possible, but the transition felt awkward.

"Am I wrong, Brown?" He placed his hands on his hips, and for a few seconds I watched the whistle around his neck sway back and forth until the friction of his shirt held it in place.

What should I say? No one's around. *I can tell him that he's not wrong,* I thought. *Maybe he'll then move aside and I can keep walking. Isn't that the path to least resistance?*

"I don't think so, Al. I mean, Big Al."

This satisfied him, or at least it made him reposition his body so I could walk by. "See ya around, man."

"Yup." I double-skipped the remaining steps to the second floor.

Becker wasn't easing her way in, and my inbox awaited with several community emails from the new principal elaborating on her mission to lead us to be a community of antiracist teachers. I silently repeated the new term several times—*antiracist teachers.* She was planting her stake in the ground, and it felt like she was intentionally throwing fuel on the small candles that lit our collective understanding, that for some was a complicated topic. Becker wanted us to address the most powerful limitations to our kids' future, starting with our own community as a microcosm of a society rooted in blatant and systemic racism. I wasn't ready and I had no direction on where to start.

Becker's case was that breaking the cycles of systemic racism was as critical as teaching academic skills and content knowledge. Even without thinking this through, I wholeheartedly disagreed, though I couldn't explain why. In her closing comments that morning, she called our work a journey to becoming antiracist. It sounded messy and uncomfortable, and those were places I avoided whenever possible. When the day started, I was professionally comfortable. Then I wasn't. For a moment I considered which was better for my students, but I then quickly dismissed the comparison.

Wasn't my instruction, student learning, and results enough? I thought other people would address the explicit ugly racism part. Why did Becker's call for a community centered on racial equity feel threatening? I didn't dismiss it, but how I wondered, could I deal with the messiness of racism comfortably? Becker wasn't going to make that possible.

Zodd spoke about "our kids," and we all got it. We knew what she meant. We all believed that our ideas and intentions were in their best interest. Becker wasn't starting with this premise. She understood this was going to be a long, bumpy, and unpleasant process to transition what we all knew was implicit to explicit. There was no longer a distinction between being on the front lines of our Black children's education and being on the front lines of addressing the racial inequalities that limited their education. That's where my struggles started. I didn't make this connection.

The rush of 100 new students could make you forget almost every adult relationship, and I didn't think about Becker during the first days of the school year. Two weeks later, she shared an email with the subject: "Continuing the Conversation." It included the first of regular articles on antiracist teaching, and the articles spiraled into her purchase of a popular book about antiracism that every staff member received before the Christmas break.

That January, Becker invited staff for an early morning coffee once a month to discuss the articles she circulated. I appreciated the gesture and thought her strategies contributed to a unique exchange of ideas, and I read the articles Becker disseminated. I even thought about them, but I didn't want to discuss them. Zodd hosted a few happy hours that were memorable because of how the karaoke provided a musical backdrop to several younger teachers' drunkenness. This was a different kind of community bonding.

The only discussion group I attended was for the article about the benefits of Black teachers educating Black students and the challenges of Black teacher recruitment. Selfishly, or for other unknown reasons, I didn't want to participate in the discussions that felt like I had to accept a conscious role for history, and that concern was enough evidence that I didn't understand the work on our plate. For the first ten minutes, one of our science teachers shared how another high school principal asked her how her PhD in biology would transfer into the high school setting. "I knew that if I were a White academic with that level of degree, a high school principal would gush over having me on their staff."

Howard then spoke about how her niece, a six-year-old kindergarten student in a predominantly White public school, was suspended. Then she paused before repeating, just short of yelling, "*Suspended* for grabbing her jacket out of a classmate's hand who teased it away from her. Would that have ever happened to a White student having done the same?" she rhetorically asked.

Becker shared data about teachers without a lot of experience with Black students who often mistook Black preschoolers' talking for chronic chattiness and frequent mobility for hyperactivity. Other stories followed, though none of them seemed to be in response to the circulated article. When the first period bell rang at 8:15, I departed the library feeling emotionally drained and entered a room full of rambunctious eighth graders. The timing of the discussion group also stood out as it felt like the first of several events that would lead to my downhill spiral at Biko, or should I say, with Becker.

The day we returned from spring break the following week, an email from Becker landed in everyone's inbox sharing that she'd gotten married. A beautiful picture featured her eyes locked into those of her groom, a muscular Black man with a wide smile who stood about the same height as her tall frame.

She looked happy and proud, and what more could anyone want from their wedding day? But at the same time, I wondered if she'd send the wedding pic if she'd married a White guy. I'm pretty sure she would if she'd married a woman, but a White man? I wasn't so sure.

That afternoon, Jim Cooper, who was our Social Studies Department Chair, and Rolando stopped by my eighth-period planning block. Our annual jaunt to the Pit was that afternoon, where Winston, the school's janitor held his fraternal court of booze and banter in the toolshed nestled between the boiler room and gymnasium. My memories of sitting in the dark red leather chairs crowded around the wooden table, under the low-watt light bulb inside an old milk container were never fond. The year before, I sat in front of the industrial fan that rotated in the corner, making it impossible to read about the missing child pictured on the back of the milk carton. The light's small radius lit the pile of old scratch-off lottery tickets piled on the table. The gathering was a blend of cross-cultural immersion, humor, gossip, and artificial machismo. The Pit Sessions, as Winston called them, were always well beyond 5 p.m. on a Friday when every child, parent, and most teachers were long gone. I promised myself a short and liquid free visit.

Winston was a large man with a huge belly and balding gray hair, and I figured the extent of his exercise capped at pushing the large broom across the school entrance atrium, one of the campus's smaller flat surfaces. But Winston was more than Biko's maintenance director and chief repair dispatcher. He was a community anchor, greeting every student by name, flirting with mothers, joking with grandmothers, and regularly helping kids in trouble. Everyone knew Winston, and you weren't somebody until he knew you.

I first saw Winston's assistant, LaVar, as I approached the Pit. He had the exact opposite body shape as his supervisor, paper thin and muscular. Almost on cue as I leaned in the doorway, neither about to enter or to signal that I wouldn't, Winston said, "Boys, you see the pic of Becker and that brotha? I knew when I first seen her that she was into, you know, that dark meat. Knew it. Knew it like I knew it."

Winston didn't need an audience, but he adored one. His own laughter would suffice, and it was often overconsuming. LaVar lightly chuckled. Rolando immediately took a sip of his drink, possibly disguising his discomfort. I could never read Cooper, who started to read aloud a weeks-old headline about the Redskins' new coach. Multiple attempts from both men, albeit shallow ones, tried to change the topic.

"How long she gonna last? I mean, this gotta be one year and done, right fellas?" Winston barreled.

In that moment I realized the smartest thing I did all day was not enter that room, although the doorway now felt closer than I preferred.

"Yo, Brownie, I bet you a bottle of whiskey she ain't here next year," Winston yelled across the room. He was the only one who called me that, for which I was thankful.

Winston was the kind of guy in need of a bet to track, to joke on, to measure progress against, to win, and ultimately, to rub in when he did so. It's what he did, and if he liked you, he offered you a bet that was too hard to refuse. While I didn't want that level of engagement with him, dismissing his offer would cause more disruption than the wager itself, though I later wished I'd negotiated other terms. Winston sat back and slammed his cup, one filled much higher than the others.

Still in the doorway, my mind wandered, thinking that although I didn't understand Becker's language of charts and graphs to connect observations and assumptions to data, I knew Biko was years behind other schools in leveraging research to advance our work. Becker was showing us the correlation between our students' confidence and social and emotional wellbeing with their ability to read, write, and execute simple and more complex math skills. Education research wasn't only out there in abundance within our city and beyond, she was bringing it directly into our community. She presented on topics like the importance of student sleep and eating habits. The need to pay greater attention to our students when they were not in our classroom, and even after thirteen years of teaching, these were new ideas to me.

We all knew that many of our students lived in single-parent homes, but Becker's data was the first time we saw the correlation between living arrangements and students' likelihood to graduate. With Principal Zodd, our job was to show enormous amounts of love and build our students' confidence in themselves. Yes, we focused on test scores too much, and in the latter years, Andrea presented internal data on class disruption, student removal, and suspension rates, but their approaches were profoundly different. Becker was introducing new ways for us to see our work. Why did I find it so annoying that she constantly snacked from a Tupperware container of raw vegetables?

"You got it," I said to Winston and turned around as the disgruntled men cursed me for leaving. I didn't think much about Becker's wedding photo, the Pit, or the bet for the next six months.

My second year under Becker's leadership kicked off without fanfare. I'd had a similar teaching schedule for around ten years. Two preps of eighth-grade World Geography, two preps of tenth-grade US History 1, and a Sociology elective for seniors, but it was the middle schoolers that occupied most of my thinking. I was drawn to their rawness and rampant confusion. Fascinated with the messiness of their thinking and ability to process ideas with so much changing in their minds and bodies.

When I talked with students who I thought were on a path to success after graduation about their most defining school experiences, most of them reflected on their high school years. When I presented the same question to students who weren't in great places, most of them pointed to things falling apart in middle school. That scared me.

Unfortunately, the optimism that carried me into the school year grounded in its third week. I was late, again, to my new weekly double cafeteria shift—my first double in ten years. I double-stepped the staircase, something I made kids reverse and repeat one step at a time when I caught them doing the same. Like them, I felt the risk of being caught was less than the risk of being late. Tanya Robinson, our wonderful college and career counselor, moved in my path as I fast walked through the hallway. I was surprised when she didn't move and placed her hands up, palms out in front of me.

"What happened, JB?" Robinson asked, concern etched on her face.

I wasn't aware of anything having happened and to fulfill the request to reach my table post before the students, I replied, "All good." As I politely walked beside her she extended her arm.

"Chris Gaskin is in Becker's office. Is he okay?"

I had no clue what she was talking about, and my blank stare possibly prompted her to continue.

"JB, this is serious. Chris is a good kid."

I stopped and looked at her, my expression only frustrating Ms. Robinson more until she walked away. I started walking away too, albeit slower.

"Brah!"

I turned around as Cooper reached within an inch or two of my personal space, something he too often did. "What the fuck, JB?" he whispered.

"Stop. What's everyone talking about?"

My voice was slightly louder than Coop's whisper. He pulled up his phone, looked down, swiped his thumb a few times, and turned his phone around to face me. It was a picture of Chris Gaskin beside my desk, holding an upside-down bottle of Jim Beam with the cap on over his open mouth and the caption:

Getting R Us History on in Brown's class. How we do it.

I froze, shocked equally by the dangerous image and confused by how such a photo was possible.

Cooper noticed a group of seventh graders being escorted back to class and nodded at me to walk outside.

Then I remembered. An hour earlier in the waning minutes of third period, I had heard student voices I recognized yelling in the staircase. After several seconds of it escalating, I'd excused myself as the staircase beside my classroom had unfortunately become my de facto responsibility. The group of freshmen boys quit horse playing in my presence and explained that their substitute dismissed them early. Being trustworthy students I knew well, I passed on challenging their response and directed them to the cafeteria. Within seconds of returning to my room, the bell rang and my students departed, though in hindsight there was an energy—*Or was it laughter?*—in the air. Cooper explained that when I'd stepped out of the room, the photo was posted on Instagram and had circulated widely and quickly, followed by a flurry of emails between staff.

"What the fuck, Brown?" Cooper repeated, then he looked down at his phone, walked away a few steps, and turned around. He exhaled from his lower lip, sending his bangs in the air. "Just got a text from Winston. He said he placed the bottle of booze in your drawer over the summer. Said it was from some bet."

Over the summer? A bet?

Cooper walked away but not before patting me on the shoulder.

I needed to do something and still didn't have enough information. I walked to Becker's office and knocked on the closed door. She responded to come in, but when I did, I wasn't the person she expected. Becker and Nicole Burton, our new assistant principal, were leaning against separate walls. Chris was sitting with his hands balled under his chin.

Unsure what to say, I whispered, "Chris, you okay?"

Becker responded for him, which none of us appreciated. "We've been better, Mr. Brown," she quipped.

Burton looked at Becker after glancing down into her phone. "It's received more than 400 views," she stated.

Only at that point did I understand the depth and embarrassment of the situation.

"Thanks for stopping in, Mr. Brown, but can you leave us for a few minutes and wait outside my room. I'd like to speak with you next."

I gently closed the door behind me as an older Black man walked into the admin office and announced his name to the receptionist. He sat down a few seats from me. I said hello, and he nodded.

The door to Becker's office opened. Chris walked out and passed me with his head down. Chris, like all my students, was allowed in my desk drawers. It's where I kept extra snacks and pens and school supplies. I figured that he'd opened the wrong drawer, and his decision was impulsive, conducted in the name of humor and completely absent from considering any consequences.

At the same time Becker walked out of her office and stood with her back to me in the doorway of Leroy Roberts, Biko's Director of Culture and Community, the administration suite door opened again. A familiar face entered, a White woman, though I did not remember her name. Becker called me into her office, and the older man and woman followed. I sat down first.

"Mr. Brown, this is Dr. Johnson and Ms. Pinsley, members of Biko's Board of Directors. They're here because of the serious nature of what occurred today. While Chris demonstrated extremely poor judgment, I've moved past his unfortunate action. Kids make stupid decisions."

I nodded because I believed what she said was right, but also because I hoped it was a way to not let this evolve into a contest of wits. I would surely lose that.

"I am now in the awkward position of writing to Biko's several hundred families to inform them that their children are safe and that our community is the best environment for their academic and emotional wellbeing. Despite a terrible photograph that was widely shared on social media of a student in one of our classrooms, your classroom, holding a bottle of alcohol that he found in your desk. Mr. Brown, do you know how writing a letter like this goes?" Her pause and darting eyes illustrated the rhetorical question.

Had I said anything, I would've said that she summed up the situation accurately. Naturally, I said nothing.

"Do you have suggestions about what we should do, or what we have to do? What if this photo reaches the Charter School Review Board, City Council, or press?"

Then it hit me. This really did put her in a terrible position. There was a moment of silence, and I'm not sure what she sought in her question. An answer, guilt, blood?

"Let's get right to it, Mr. Brown. Why was there alcohol in your desk?"

I was totally caught off guard and couldn't argue with the validity of her concern. I wish that I had the courage to say it, but that was too much to ask. I had seconds to respond. What made this worse was that the truth didn't work. I was a terrible liar. Some people lost their cover through wandering eyes, twitching hands, or bouncing feet. On these rare occasions, I was a circus of all three. With every passing second, it was clear that I was buying time.

Do I tell her the truth? That I didn't know it was there. I never open that bottom drawer. Tell her that it was given to me? If so, by who? Share that I won it as part of a bet? Or worse, reveal the nature of the wager? Rat on Winston? My head spun one bad option after another. Could I say that I didn't know how it got there? What surprised me most then, and still today, was how quickly and easily these ideas arose. Around students, my mind flashed between ideas and concepts quickly. Around adults, I often froze.

I'd had a lifetime of not knowing what to say when something needed to be said. Even when Becker talked about how Biko's teachers needed to be bold for its students, I knew she probably wasn't talking about me. I wasn't bold. I wasn't decisive. Actually, outside the classroom, I didn't talk or do much at all, often afraid to stand up for what was right if there was any sense that my safety or comfort were at risk. I had to get myself out of a stupid situation without making it worse for myself, for Chris, for Winston, and ultimately for Becker. The only way to do that was to lie, or mostly lie.

"A few weeks ago, Ron Grupp called me to say that he wasn't coming back to Biko." I knew Becker would know this was true as she was the reason he wasn't. "He asked if I could help pack his room." I looked up and at each of them, as everything I shared up to this point was true. I had a grip on a story that was as boring as possible. One which left little room for blame. It just might work, but it wasn't the story of how the bottle got there.

Ron, who Rolando called Old Man Grupp, would cover for me if needed, or so I thought. Grupp had shared that Becker told him we needed younger teachers who looked more like our kids, and that she wanted to open his position to someone who could grow with our community for years to come. Though he understood, he was stunned, and it was only through his sharing the year's lab ideas that I understood how hurt he was. As I looped bubble wrap around glass vials and other lab tools that he'd personally contributed to Biko, I wondered how I'd feel if the same happened to me. Then Ron told me to calm down with wrapping. "We're not chucking them off the building," were his exact words.

Grupp was also an outlier in the Biko community as a Vietnam War veteran. He took up teaching when he was sixty-five and this would've been Ron's fifth year at Biko, his first high school teaching position. I wasn't exceptionally close with Ron for a few reasons, but mostly because I wasn't close with anyone. His room was on the first floor in the back of the building, and he entered and exited through the rear parking lot, where I rarely ventured. He had a calming presence and skillfully communicated complex scientific theories in simple language that our students grasped. Our kids loved him, and he loved them back. It felt like he'd finally found meaning in his work, and it didn't happen until his thirty-year military career ended, though that's all speculation.

"I drove over and helped him for a few hours"—*still all true*—"and in the fall, I received a note from Ron, thanking me for his help. He shared that he'd left a small gift of appreciation in my bottom drawer, but I never checked." I raised my shoulders for a moment. "I haven't gone into that drawer in years. All my students can access my top drawer. It's where I keep extra snacks and school supplies."

I paused and moved through some facial expressions that I'm not sure had purpose, then continued. "That's all I got. If this didn't happen, I may not have known there was a bottle in my drawer for months, or years."

Ms. Pinsley broke the silence, and I was glad it was her. "Mr. Brown, this is a very unfortunate situation and from your story, the string of poor choices extended far beyond your involvement."

I could see Becker's face shift from anger toward me to the same emotion at her. Seeing that, I nodded at the older lady, affirming her assessment.

"I'll add," Pinsley continued, "you may not remember, but I've been in your classroom before, Mr. Brown. Your teaching speaks for itself, but as I said, this is a highly unfortunate situation."

I had the exit ramp I needed, and more so than feeling a dose of relief from her comments, I was shocked for having the courage to get myself out of a situation I didn't need to be in. I had a track record of doing the exact opposite, but I felt like I storied my way out, or so I thought. "I agree with you, Ms. Pinsley. There was a string of unfortunate decisions that led to now, and I'm genuinely sorry for my unintentional role in why we're here."

The bell rang, and I informed Becker and her guests that I had my fifth period class arriving within minutes. She was in deep thought, looking at the wall. Pinsley and the gentleman looked at her and then back at me. No one said anything.

Becker looked up from a deep thought. "Sure, yes, you're right." She then stood and said, "Mr. Brown, we're done with you here, and we'll speak with you again if we have any questions."

When I walked out, Winston was standing beside the athletic trophy case in the atrium, leaning on his broom handle. We locked eyes for a second, though for him it may have been longer. The next class was slow and uneventful, and I kept my eyes away from the vertical rectangle window above the doorknob. The feeling of people staring inside my room was overwhelming, and I was nervous to jump into the sea of email I was unfortunately linked to.

Winston and I never spoke about the incident. I never knew what happened to the bottle. I never saw a community email. And I never spoke about it with Chris Gaskin. But everything changed that day. I opened the top drawer to grab a snack and something hooked on the bottom drawer, making both drawers open. A yellow sticky note fell to the ground. It read, "You won. She's back!"

4

THE MORNING AFTER THE last day of third grade, our family headed north on Interstate 93. Within the hour, the only home I'd known on the south side of Concord, New Hampshire was a relic from the past. The long and snowy winter that had recently evaporated seventy-five miles south hung to life up north. After passing the Lakes Region, the White Mountains came into view. The rivers, or the few we saw from the car, rushed with spring melt. Mountaintops hid in the clouds. It was mid-June and other than going to Darren's hockey games, I couldn't remember the last time the four of us were in the car together. My birthday was in a few days, and I repeated what my teacher said about me turning eight in the eighth year of the eighth decade, but no one in my family acknowledged Ms. Gepse's brilliant observation.

Our mother, Sara, turned around from the passenger seat every few minutes to point something out to my older brother. Both parents were concerned about how the move would affect him. The previous evening, I'd overheard her on the phone telling someone that he was upset, though it felt like Darren, who was thirteen and five years older than me, was often that way.

"Sara, tell JB about the mountains too. There's two of them back there," Father said, maintaining his gaze on the road.

But I didn't see Mother soliciting only Darren's attention to the mountains that would neighbor our new home as an oversight of my existence. Or maybe I did and over time found ways to relish in the comfort it provided. In the end, I had little choice.

Until Father, who was rarely called Frank, acknowledged my mother's singular focus, I wouldn't have noticed.

"And you too, JB," Mother said with rapid precision, barely turning around. "Darren, look, I mean Darren and JB, look. The snow-capped mountains over there." She pointed out the right side of the station wagon, though there were just as many outside the left window, where I sat.

As our mother decorated her narration of the passing land-scape with vivid descriptions, I listened to the radio news. My focus required attention as the reception weakened north of Plymouth, a college town we'd eventually visit often as Father's business grew. Compromised by low volume and a choppy signal, the report was about the Supreme Court upholding a law that made it illegal for private clubs to discriminate against women and minorities. Several years later when our parents gifted Darren an encyclopedia set, I referenced the date and read every word I could about the case.

We passed the exit sign for Jasper and our mother turned almost fully around. "Darren, our new home is in the next town of Dalmaqua."

Like clockwork, Father said, "Sara, JB's back there too. Talk to them both." His deep voice was deliberate and assertive, and considering these characteristics, also often ignored.

Father neglected to significantly slow down on the exit ramp and the sharper-than-expected turn in conjunction with slamming the brakes caused several boxes to topple behind us in the station wagon. A rare demonstration of aggressiveness for an otherwise calm and risk-averse man. In what may have been the first question I ever asked both parents, and certainly the first I remember, I leaned forward just barely able to grip my fingers around the sides of the front seat's headrest.

"That story we just heard, right? The Supreme Court"—and I may have called it the Superhero Court—"it was a good decision, right?"

I had recently learned about the judicial branch in school. I even knew the names of two or three justices. A few months earlier, our third-grade class had taken a field trip downtown to the state's Capitol building. I certainly knew what a woman was, but I wasn't sure of the other term. "What's a minority?" I asked.

Darren looked at me and with his left hand gently pushed me back in my seat. There was no immediate answer, and I debated if it had to do more with the question's content or who was asking it. Our mother was a junior high school art teacher and outwardly liberal, although I didn't really understand what that meant for years to come. She briefly looked to her left at the man she more often referred to as our father than her husband, possibly waiting to see if he'd answer or if she should. Maybe to see if she was allowed to. I sat back, trying to remember where our mother last directed Darren's attention and I named the colors from the sky downward: white snow, green trees, brown soil, gray rocks. I stopped there, stumped by the color of water.

"Of course it's good, JB. Everyone needs to be treated fairly. Discrimination of any kind is wrong," Darren said. He was so matter-of-fact, and with the tips of his fingers he scratched the top of my head and pushed my chin away from him with the same hand. I wished he'd do that all day, but when I turned back, he was already looking away. Beyond his window had so much to offer.

"That's right, Darren. You're one hundred percent right," our mother quickly followed.

She turned around and smiled at him, and my heart warmed. By the time her head rotated the several inches where her gaze passed me, I remember her eyes being closed. Her smile was gone. She peered back at our father. It was an angle only I could've seen. Her look was part affirmation and part declaration of independence, but I could have been wrong about both. When it came to the dynamics of relationships, I often was.

"It's complicated," Father said softly, possibly talking to the steering wheel. He was a large man, and in the past year, a round belly had appeared under his shirt.

"Not really," Mother retorted, eyes forward.

Darren wasn't paying attention, or so I thought, but to me it was the first time I ever heard anything that sounded this notionally defiant. Embarrassingly, I felt proud for her, or maybe that's part of the story I made up as I got older.

I wondered what Father meant when he said the situation was complicated. Over the years, I replayed and analyzed the conversation in my head countless times. While time and reflection often lead to clarity and resolution, it was not the case when it came to our father. Did he disagree with the straightforward declaration of our mother? Did he not agree with the court's ruling? Was it about the possibility of having to explain what the Supreme Court was? Was it because he didn't want to talk? Was it because he was stressed about moving into a new home? Why didn't he simply state that the news was good?

Mother narrated our way down several miles to the end of Herb Ross Road, where our house was the last before the river. Only then did it become clear she had been here before. "Almost there," she said, this time not specifically identifying Darren as her audience.

I pretended that she spoke to us both. Father would have wanted it that way.

In a land that minutes before felt like endless mountains, the valley floor was flat. Over several fields, large groups of brown cows swished lanky and wiry tails over their backs. We passed goats and a chicken coop, then suddenly were overwhelmed by a horrible smell. Father slowed as we approached the farmhouse and barns. Then he slowed down even more, but I wasn't sure if it was because of the Animal Crossing sign or that he wanted us to fully absorb the welcoming experience. Either way, I was starting to feel carsick. The pristine landscape from farther back felt like it was pulled from a catalog, but here felt different. Enormous piles of poop, that I later learned was from the cows, lay plopped in the middle of the road. Tractors, some of which appeared to be inoperative, dotted a large field beside several house trailers. Random machinery, some of which took years to identify, sat in between.

Near the end of the parking lot, two rotting posts held an uneven board painted white. In green letters of nondescript font, it read: Welcome to Mountainbrook Farm. Behind the words was the outline of the Old Man of the Mountain. Father drove a few hundred feet beyond the sign where a row of what looked like newly planted trees lined a small grassy bluff. He turned into the dirt driveway on the same side of the road and toward our new home.

Within seconds of the station wagon making a complete stop, the four of us went in different directions. In hindsight, it was symbolic of how life would be in our new home. Mother walked into her new house. Darren, who exited the car holding his hockey stick, immediately heard the yell of two similarly sized boys holding hockey sticks and after a brief discussion with the two teenagers, Darren told our mother that he was off to play. From that moment forward, Darren and our neighbors, Timmy and Trevor, would be inseparable. Until what pulled them apart could never reconnect them.

Dad popped the hood and, for all practical purposes, also disappeared. There must have been a sound he didn't like. At that time, I believed that if something was out of the ordinary, Father would investigate. I believed he approached trouble head on, and I valued having a parent like this. It took years to learn how misguided my inference was.

For as long as I remember, I did the exact opposite. If something felt wrong, I turned around. I walked away. I learned that if you were quick—contrary to the conventional wisdom of others—trouble rarely followed. I engaged in helping someone if it was easy, or dare I say, unavoidable.

Left without directions or invitation, I walked past the house to a small trail leading to the Dalmaqua River. Its movement was slow and constant, like I later learned was how everything moved around here. It was the first time I remembered standing beside a river alone. There was grace, and even as an eight-year-old boy, I felt peace. The river would serve that purpose for many years, and the serenity it offered was cherished. But these cherished offerings were temporary.

On that first night when I heard Mother's call for Darren, no one could've known that such a sight and sound would be commonplace for years to come. Darren and his new friends slammed electrical tape rolls against one of the back barn walls where three painted lines marked hockey goal posts. I watched them from the bluff after walking a few hundred feet from the river beside our property. When I came into the house, I dodged my parents who were blinded by the large boxes they carried.

Like Father, our mother was short on benign conversation. I remember her saying multiple times that her last task before moving was cooking our dinner casserole. Father didn't say anything at the first meal in our new home except to ask for the salt, which our mother retrieved from a box of unpacked items. Darren was a fast eater, and I marveled at his efficient use of utensils. How he used his knife like a goalie stick to navigate the peas and potatoes onto his fork before crushing our mother's homemade crust. Everything he did was interesting. Before going to bed, the four of us stood on the fully screened back porch where our mother hung one of her paintings. One that had never covered the walls in our old home.

Darren's shirt was stained with sweat and dirt, and I studied the way it molded to the muscular shape of his back as he stood in front of our mother's artwork. Over my brother's shoulder I could only see what looked like clouds, and when I moved to his side, instead of looking at the painting as I'd intended, I faced Darren who stared forward with such intensity that his mouth hung open. When he noticed me, I turned to erase the moment's awkwardness, though willing to repeat it a thousand times over if I could. In the painting's center, a young girl hopped across a field. Her light blue dress blew in the wind above the high grass, more brown than green. Two adults watched from their horse-drawn wagon. One of the characters, maybe the girl's father, wore a large hat.

"Where is the girl running away to, Mom?" Darren asked, possibly more softly than I ever heard him speak.

"Why is she running away, Darren? Maybe she's just running," our father replied surprisingly, as he often avoided conversation with his family. Then, as if the interaction was over, he walked a few feet away to open and close the screen door several times, noting out loud his intention to oil the hinge.

"We're all running away from something, Darren," Mother said, just as quietly.

I wondered if her words were purposefully whispered so our father would not hear. Her shoulder-length brown hair showed new streaks of gray. Had I been any further away I would not have heard her myself.

She kissed Darren's shoulder and then whispered in his ear, "But we don't always have to."

They held each other's eyes for the shortest and strongest of moments. Maybe she knew what would happen. Maybe it was the look of impossible love that a parent has for a child.

Either way, those seconds contained a million messages, and unfortunately, just as many warnings. They were connected in that way, and it was a beautiful bond I never understood.

We headed back into the house and when she walked by her husband, she placed her hand on his shoulder. Unwise to the emotions partners sought in each other, it felt more like a gesture to maintain her balance than a show of affection, and I don't think he noticed either way.

Before climbing into my new bed, I hung my body out the window and looked up at the sky lit with stars, more than I had ever seen before. When I laid back down, I'd switch senses and close my eyes, trying to identify the different sounds, intrigued and confused by the valley's symphony. That sound I later learned was nature, and I tried to keep it close to my heart in the years to come when the fears set in.

Our parents' and my brother's rooms faced the river on the west side of our home. My room, a smaller version of Darren's on the other side of the mostly symmetrical house, overlooked our neighbor, the Mountainbrook Farm. Twenty feet below my window, healthy grass covered the small bluff that rose no more than fifteen feet above the surrounding valley floor. The colors faded from rich green to brown as it sank on the other side. The bluff was the first spot where you could see the farm from our home, except from my room where one could see almost everything, or so I thought. Over those first few evenings and endless nights thereafter, I sat on a flipped milk crate in front of that window watching the farm move and grow and die and start again in all its predictable, chaotic, and wicked ways. On the rarest of occasions, I'd watch it be still, or at least appear to be still, and those peaceful intervals were bliss.

The next morning, I came down the creaky staircase as foreign voices spoke from our kitchen. Seconds later I met our new neighbors, Kent and Dina Simonelli, owners of the

Mountainbrook Farm. They sat around the table with my parents enjoying coffee and pastries, talking about their boys and the weather, and from the few minutes I listened, not much else. We were neighbors on a large property in a valley ending at a river where approximately 600 acres belonged to them and ten or so oddly-shaped acres between them and the river to us. We shared the land and borders of a dead-end road. From this first conversation through the last, their relationship was built on two foundations: proximity and necessity. I never saw the four of them sitting at a table together again.

For the next few hours we toured the farm, starting with a formal introduction to their sons, who Darren had spent most of our waking time with since arriving. Trevor was Darren's age, and Timmy was three years younger. Other than a lukewarm greeting, they didn't say much to me for several months, which didn't bother me.

As we walked over the different fields, I stood a good ten or so feet behind the adults. Trevor, Timmy, and Darren ran off beyond the greenhouse and somehow I don't think anyone was surprised. I heard tidbits of their banter while awed by every sight and person we crossed. Like our parents, Kent and Dina had married young. Each family had two sons. The similarities for the most part ended there. The Simonellis' desire in largely unpopulated New Hampshire was to live off the land, continue a life committed to social justice, and when able, be a profitable farming business. By all accounts, the first two ambitions became their DNA.

Dina's family moved to New England from Norway when she was young. Kent's family had farmed these valleys for generations. The only outlier to farming was Kent's father, who was the sheriff of the most northern county between us and the Canadian border. When Kent's younger brother inherited the job after their father's death, their relationship was strained and leveraged in desperate ways for years to come. But Kent was determined to return to his grandfather's roots as a farmer.

In the late 1970s, Kent and Dina had borrowed to the bank's limit and their parent's patience to purchase a 500-acre swath of valley land so far north that Kent's brother asked if they were becoming Canadians. Eventually, they'd borrow again to purchase an adjacent 100-acre lot by the highway. The only problem, or the only one they were aware of, was that previously their new oasis was the fertilizer testing site of a large international agricultural firm.

By non-scientific accounts, and a few that claimed to be, the land was chemically contaminated. It was unusable. It would not suit their vision. It's why it was so inexpensive. But they were young, determined, and naive, and Dina and Kent had seen this recipe turn dreams into reality before. In the two years before welcoming animals and planting their first harvest, they worked the soil tirelessly and prayed. They also applied lessons from Kent's family farm and the years he and Dina had lived and farmed among the Maasai tribe in Tanzania, where they had met in the Peace Corps in the late sixties. They turned a nutrient-free patch of abused land that every sensible farmer in the region had passed on into a thriving agricultural hub serving central and northern New Hampshire, the Connecticut Valley into Vermont, and parts of eastern Maine. A portion of the land had been so intentionally rehabilitated that within two decades it produced certified organic vegetables. Nothing short of a miracle, according to some. To those who knew Kent and Dina, and the loyal few who stayed with them under storm and sun, it was less shocking.

A consistently healthy herd of cattle, hogs, goats, chickens, and other animals routinely rotated pastures with the seasons. The farm distributed its year-round CSA boxes to restaurants, retail stores, farmers' markets, and at times, people's homes. I only remember these facts because of my frequent reading of the brochure, which Dina insisted I do after every edit starting in junior high school. She declared I was a good writer, but all I did to earn the title was pointing out once that *hogs* had been written as *hags*.

The static brochure presented the farm like a brick-and-mortar operation, though to my knowledge, nothing on the farm was as durable as either. It was so much more than a menu of services and products. It was a community created with intentional diversity, and this was possibly the most organic element of all its ingredients.

For the vegetable team, work was an annual cycle of seeding, watering, weeding, and harvest. For the livestock team, it was always more complicated. Between Memorial Day and Labor Day, the community tripled in size. The farm was a chaotic and rhythmic movement of people offering their bodies and souls to something beyond themselves and on some days it felt like both would break. Evenings were a party, a celebration of life, where the same bodies sore from labor would dance for hours under the night sky to the radio or live music played beyond the back barn. In other months, the farm could become a cruel place where limited daylight left less time to accomplish the same responsibilities. By December, everything was frozen.

While some of the Farm Store's regular customers became frequent people in my life, a staple of the farm's residents became more family than neighbor. During my second decade, it felt like every adult I knew came to the farm. Our teachers, doctors, and Mother's colleagues at the regional junior high school were regulars. Most of the staff were seasonal, and the dozens who returned for more than two or three seasons were few. A good chunk were Peace Corps alumni, as the institution's alumni newsletter was the only place Dina approved of posting job and volunteer opportunities. It took years for me to realize that more than half the staff were exchanging work for a place to live, learn, and grow.

What made the farm additionally unique was that most of the workers were connected to Mountainbrook from Dina's work with the refugee resettlement program in Concord. A few years before we arrived, she had welcomed several families from Ethiopia who had relocated during the country's widespread famine. While Dina and Kent sometimes disagreed about the endless issues navigating daily operations, they were aligned with making Mountainbrook a place where all people could live, work, and thrive regardless of origin, creed, race, sexual orientation, or any other distinction, though in those years these were the only ones I knew of. I had not seen any place like that before and few, if any, since. I'm not sure by what and whom they were both shaped to this belief, but it was a foundation that was never compromised. Even while having nothing to compare it to, I knew it was a special place.

The farm could also be an intolerable environment. Folks with a weak work ethic or flawed character were doomed, and the only thing between these traits and leaving was time. Like anywhere, occasionally there were problems. Most worked themselves out, but Dina and Kent had a short list of nonnegotiables. Those who came with hard drugs found scant people to enjoy them with. A few men turned out to be sexual predators, but they encountered women strong in their conviction, voices, and when needed, their fists. The same wasn't always the case for the young men lured with similar tactics, though only one such incident reached Kent's and Dina's attention. When it came to the people and markets at Mountainbrook, Dina was in charge. For everything about land and machines that crafted it, there was Kent.

The first time I walked over the bluff, it felt like we were entering another world, and part of that spark lit my soul every bluff crossing thereafter, except maybe the last time. The farm was magnetic. By the end, I had encountered around 300 different people from all over the world. It was life-giving and life-sucking and most of all, it was transformative. Every person left different from when they'd arrived and their presence, whether valued or dismissed, shaped those who remained.

On that welcome tour with Kent and Dina, we met some of Mountainbrook's most influential residents. Within a hundred or so feet of the bluff, Kent removed his hat, making us feel that this first introduction wasn't the one he preferred. We followed his gaze to a skinny man reading over a clipboard in front of a house trailer as he leaned back in a folding beach chair. He wore faded red shorts, a short sleeve Hawaiian themed shirt with the top few buttons open, and a white beach hat. In his large open palm he rolled what I later learned were Chinese meditation balls in a hypnotic, circular motion.

"Greetings, neighbor," the man said with a joy that exceeded the energy of the man who introduced him. His metal glasses slipped down his nose as he stood up, and Kent appeared to roll his eyes.

Father's expression was stoic and unimpressed. Mother looked right past the man to the trailer itself, as did I.

"Guys," Kent said, slightly less than enthusiastically, "this is Professor Farace, or Matt," his voice trailing while saying the man's given name. "He helps with the vegetables when he's not teaching in upstate New York at Oneonta State College." A place none of us had heard of. The professor volunteered a bit of his story, but the only part I remembered was that he drove a four-hour, one-way commute on Tuesday mornings and returned on Thursday nights for his farm work.

The professor led the weekend market in Manchester, which was Mountainbrook's most lucrative. When I overheard Dina telling Kent that all new hires should shadow the professor at the market to learn best practices, Kent slammed his hat on the side of his blue jeans and spat, "The last thing we need is another know-it-all telling customers about the righteous divinity of our cows and goats."

"He makes the farm money, Kent, and that's more than some of us around here."

Her words carried consistent warmth and little room for misinterpretation. Shortly thereafter, every farmhand Dina considered for a market post trailed the professor for several weeks. They always had stories about his conversations with customers and his packing strategies aligned to the theories of the great philosophers. Over the years, I'd say there was never a benign conversation with the professor. He answered simple questions with unnecessary complication, and his questions were often worded with greater sophistication than the answers they sought. Few things were easy with him, and I kept my distance unless I had a question about our crops or packing for a market, which he knew everything about.

On the table beside his trailer door sat a box of books from which he encouraged the farm's staff to borrow. A sign above the box read: "post-reading discussions available by appointment, or spontaneously with Merlot."

From the location of his trailer, the professor saw a lot. I'd learn a lot from him, although most of these lessons were upon reflections of earlier discussions I hadn't understood. If he wasn't off teaching, he was either in the fields, at a market, or in the warm months, sitting in the same chair he now stood beside. Several feet away was his friend, Tessa, who greeted us while bending over in a strange triangular motion that I later learned was a yoga pose called Downward Dog. She was quiet, kind, and in the summer months, wore loose fitting shirts with no bra and her breasts were the first I saw beyond the pages of a National Geographic magazine. Tessa's beautiful blend of French-infused English made you wish her responses were longer, but she rarely spoke or asked anything of anyone.

The Simonellis and the professor, who Dina and Kent only called Matt when they weren't around other people, were an odd but efficient team. Kent was serious to his bones. The only sarcastic comment I ever overheard him say was, "Every farm barely making money should have an on-site philosophy professor instead of a dependable bookkeeper." That was just after the professor had handed him a large envelope of cash from a farmers' market. The professor was reliable and honest. Kent may have even cracked a smile. The professor was rarely without one.

Over the years, I slowed to listen to his conversations. The nuance of his explanations and curiosity were distinct. Oddly, in as much as he spoke, he spent most of his time listening. He was always asking questions while he worked, which he once said helped turn the monotonous routines of harvesting vegetables into interesting episodes of what he called "mundane meeting magic." Nothing was ordinary about him. He made people feel in a strange way that their lives were fascinating, and to this day, I've never met anyone like him.

As we continued the tour, Kent rattled off several names of folks working in the fields. His subtle waves were met with equally non-enthusiastic waves in return. We stepped over a few puddles before standing in front of an open industrial garage that closed in November and reopened mid-spring. Father asked our mother in a whisper if it had rained recently. It took years to learn how his mind worked. He saw everything through the lens of risk. If it hadn't rained, the large standing puddle would be alarming. I'd know from my summer with him several years later that standing water was a sign of questionable operations. Farms should drain if properly designed, he'd tell another farmer. While his customer base slowly grew throughout the state, our first tour of Mountainbrook infuriated Father. To him, it was one preventable accident after another just waiting to happen.

Kent wiped his brow with the rag that always hung out of his back pocket. Moving from the bright sun to the shaded garage, he turned his head a few times, squinting to identify the several men hunched over machinery with mechanical optimism. He assessed who might be worth an introduction, but his work was made easy when a door was kicked open by a young man who walked through and dropped two large pipes on the concrete floor, creating a thunderous sound. Even Kent covered his ears. The rest of us thought it would be too rude to do so or weren't quick enough to react accordingly. Our eardrums temporarily rattled.

"Russ, come over here for a sec, will ya?" Kent said, making two full revolutions with his arm.

He looked around the same age as Darren but was several years older. Russell Burke was minimally polite and tipped his cap, the most curved I'd ever seen. For years I wondered how Russell ever saw anything coming from his sides. Despite Kent introducing him by name, Russell repeated his full name and the name of the town where he lived, though talking only to my parents. With pride, Kent shared that Russell's family had farmed and forested the surrounding valleys for generations, and that the farm was nothing if anything without him—a comment Kent extended toward several other people over the next hour as we continued the tour, crossing fields identified by their harvest.

"Ah, here he is," Kent said with relief at the sight of a large Black man carrying a pig over his neck.

I later learned its weight was several hundred pounds. The man's ability seemed effortless, and his tucked-in T-shirt didn't appear to even slightly budge. It was obvious Walter knew that an introduction would follow as chefs, restaurant owners, market managers, or individual customers sometimes requested tours that were led by Kent or Dina. Everyone had to meet Walter. As the professor said years later, Walter was the heart that pumped the farm's blood.

Walter waved the little bit of arm not occupied with the large animal. "One of my girls needs to see the doc," he said, his voice muffled by the weight on his neck.

Colonial French fused with proper English beautifully blended into his words. Even Father showed amazement as Walter carried the pig with both care and ease and stopped at the back of a dark red pickup truck, gently lowering the animal onto a mat. The veterinarian placed a stethoscope around his ears and to the animal's underbelly.

We followed Kent to within a few feet of the truck and listened to Walter and the vet, who Walter thanked for coming while on vacation. The gilt wasn't eating and her stool contained blood. Walter's attention to detail and compassion for the animal made us instantly like him, though I think we already did. He ran every aspect of Mountainbrook's livestock from birth to slaughter. His body was wide and neither skinny nor heavy, as his round and solid belly was still years away. He had a large head and patchy beard, and within those few minutes, we had all seen an impeccable display of the man's strength and gentleness. Kent said that Walter's energy with the animals was part of the reason why people traveled hundreds of miles for the farm's products.

Everything I knew about people on the farm was from what I saw or heard. Walter's story before the farm was all the latter. I may have been around ten and stocking the Farm Store, which was as labor-soft a job as the place offered beyond the small office room where Luca Lucano made sense of Kent's piles of orders, invoices, and receipts. Luca came and went as he pleased, answered to no one, and not once did I ever see him step foot in a field. The next room over was the Simonelli's kitchen. Kent was on the phone telling someone about how he met Walter in Quebec.

Shortly after Kent and Dina's purchase of the valley, minus our ten oddly shaped acres between the farm and Dalmaqua River that were now our home, Kent had traveled the region in search of equipment. He became a gracious customer of a farm in southern Quebec, whose aging owner was selling machinery on the wind down to retirement. Walter helped load items no longer of use but full of potential into Kent's truck. When Kent had asked on a following trip for loading assistance, the old man with broken English told him Walter was gone, that he regularly went away for weeks at a time.

Kent learned that after serving in the Ghanaian military, Walter worked for a private French military company out of Quebec City. Kent had no idea what Walter did or where he went but saw him a few weeks later. When Kent offered him work on his new farm, Walter explained that he had a year of service left on a contract. But he wasn't referring to the farm where they first met. A year later, Kent received a letter in the mail from Walter asking if his offer held and saying he could meet at the border with his papers. That was 1980, not yet one year into the farm's shaky start, and the year I was born.

While family was at the center of Mountainbrook, I never knew or heard anyone ask about Walter's. When Mother once asked Darren to write a Father's Day card, he sarcastically replied that he didn't have time to write to his father, or the others like Kent and Walter. Mother stopped what she was doing and asked how he knew Walter was a father.

Darren looked up from his book with a confused expression following our mother's second request of the same question. He then shared that he had once chased Trevor in a manhunt game through the back barns and come across Walter's apartment. He looked inside and saw a picture of what he was sure was a younger Walter with his arms around a woman, with two girls sitting with smiles in front of them. Mother looked perplexed, and thinking the conversation was over, I left the room.

Back on the tour, Walter extended a courteous greeting in English infused with French sophistication once the vet drove off. He politely offered his services if the need arose, and Father expressed an interest in getting to know him better, which Walter reciprocated. Oddly, they did.

Ironically, I had the longest conversation with Walter just before leaving the farm for the last time, and in those ten minutes I learned more about him than in all the decades before. Then as I drove away, Russ was the last person I saw, standing in the parking lot holding the master clipboard. Although I didn't know why or how, I was pretty sure he wasn't spending half his day leaning over broken tractor engines anymore. While his responsibilities had evolved, his expression had not. His straight eyes told neither the truth nor lies. He stared at me, and I briefly stared back at him. By then, there were hundreds of reasons, or one terrible one, to look away, but I didn't. To do so would have meant I cared, and all too often, I didn't do that either.

Timmy, Trevor, and Russell were different in a lot of ways, but they were all cut from the same cloth, born mountain boys at a time when the mountains were a way of life, unaltered for tourists and adventure sports. When they weren't decorated by urban lore, sleep away camps for suburban Boston families, and the *Sunday Times* travel section. These boys' families lived here before the ice cream parlors and T-shirt stores. The mountains were part of their fabric, and somehow Darren found himself right at home among them. They welcomed him as one of their own, but he had to earn his place among the boys the hard way.

Dina's and Kent's boys lived the farm life while also embracing their parents' cultural affinity and lifestyle. Russell was all country. Farming was his family's roots and their mission to overcome the land with machines perfectly suited him and keeping those machines working was a full-time job. I never heard Russell ask a question, offer help, or extend an opinion. For only a few people is this a recipe for getting by, and he was one of them.

Russ never went out of his way to blend into the intentional design of the farm's community. He worked closely with Kent and Walter, and like both men, was quiet by nature. I once heard that he acted noticeably cold around Zoya, Kami, and some of the other foreign women who managed the dairy operations with Dina. In his defense, these women may not have known that his affect was nearly as identical among the men with whom he shared the garage. The farm let everyone know that people were all different.

Russell put off the energy that years later my students would say was of someone they knew was racist, though their claim wouldn't be supported with evidence. To some of us, over time the evidence became clear, or so we thought. Darren worked with Russell on and off for several seasons. They were an efficient and effective team. Their strength and endless energy bundled hay, stocked freezers, loaded trucks, and provided Walter and the professor with muscle. Darren never raved or complained about their work, though one time he told Imre, a Hungarian doctor who returned to the farm for several seasons, that Russ was a dick, which I only remembered because it was the first time not hearing him called by his full name. But Russell was reliable if anything, and that's a trait Kent couldn't pass up even if it came with questionable character. Over time when doubt and then logic obscured Kent's loyalty to Russell, his family's prominence in the region always forced Kent's hand.

Darren rejoined Kent's guided tour as we walked through a small stretch of shin-high grass covered with disconnected hoses, wheelbarrows, a trampoline, wiffle ball bats, hockey sticks, and a half dozen snow shovels. The burst of cool air reached our hot faces as Dina, holding a crate of jars, kicked open a door and Kent reached to open it. No one exchanged greetings. It was all business. We entered what may have been the cleanest part of any area we'd seen on the farm, the Dairy House.

Dina reentered the room holding the same crate, now empty. As Kent stumbled on his words, she interjected and insisted Zoya meet her new neighbors. The woman had a small frame and wore what looked like a long white lab coat. A net covered her black hair. She removed her rubber gloves and walked to the sink where she washed and dried her hands, then placed her left hand on her right arm while extending her hand to my mother.

"It's so nice to finally meet you, Sara. I'm Zoya."

Dina smiled. Zoya was everything she could want in a partner and friend. Her affection instantly warmed the cool room.

Zoya greeted Darren and Father as one, an odd grouping to anyone who knew them. She then turned to me. "Do you like cheese and yogurt?" she asked, looking right into my eyes. She placed her hands on her hips, her complete attention on me. "Do you know how they're made? Would you like to learn? Have you ever milked a cow before? Would you like to learn?"

I did not answer with words, or to my understanding even without them, and Zoya continued before I even could. This felt like my first introduction to the farm's fast pace. Even the sweet Zoya had zero time to coddle indecision.

"Let me find my dear Kami," Zoya said as she walked out of the room.

Before our gaze covered the enormity of the metal tanks, she reentered, holding the arm of a girl with a striking resemblance to her mother. Kami smiled and extended her hand to my mother, holding her right arm with her left hand. The same gesture as her mother. It was my first lesson into a world of traditions and customs that I'd learn from Zoya. She was her own classroom of knowledge, and her teachings made traditional classrooms pale in comparison. When Kami and Darren locked eyes for the shortest of seconds, something happened. And even if it didn't, I'll always believe that it did.

In two or so hours, we had covered Kent's estimation of the farm's important areas, but now it felt real. It was accessible. Upon meeting Zoya, we went from living beside a farm to living within it. Part of that energy remained vibrant every day thereafter. But the menu of choices she offered wasn't extended to solely build our depth of experiences. She needed help. Mountainbrook needed help. And it was always that way.

That afternoon, I sat on the bluff as Darren walked past holding a sandwich our mother had hoped he'd eat at the table beside her. He walked to Kami, who I hadn't seen in the field. She steadied a cello next to a folding chair facing the river. I'll never know what they talked about, but I watched them for what felt like hours.

This pattern continued for days, weeks, and years. I'd sit on the crest of the bluff with comics or books or model airplanes or nothing at all and watch them. Not in a creepy or obsessive manner but in an adolescent-bored-with-time kind of way. Over the years, I watched them sit in silence and read, leaning against the large maple or back-to-back, or eventually with Kami's head resting on Darren's muscular leg. Her long hair never missed a chance to blow with the breezes the mountains sent to the river. They laughed, threw blades of grass at each other, and read aloud passages of the novels that intrigued them. There were many.

On one of the first evenings in our new home, Darren rushed into the house as we sat for dinner. Father noted that he seemed to have made two great friends in Trevor and Timmy and then he added Kami's name. Mother smiled at what I thought was Darren's blushing. If I wasn't shocked by the question following the recent string of outbursts, I was caught off guard by Darren's response. He appeared happy. It felt like he was at peace.

"Did you know Kami's real name is Kamali?" he asked our mother. "It stands for the African spirit that protects babies from illness. She said that if she were a boy, her name, I mean his name, would've been Kamal, which is one of the ninety-nine names for Allah." There was inquisitive energy and innocence in his voice, which were two traits nearly erased from Darren altogether over the past year.

I didn't know who Allah was, and when I realized that waiting wasn't going to inform me, I tabled my curiosity. The previous week's car ride to our new home had made clear how this works.

In that first summer before the culture shock of a new school set in, Darren ate, drank, and slept four things—working with Kent and Walter, playing hockey, swimming with Trevor and Timmy, and spending time with Kami. Trevor and Kami became his closest friends, and Darren would be the same person and totally different for each. But the relationship with Kami was the most fascinating, one I couldn't have known about so deeply had I not secretly spied on them with every opportunity.

From what I remember, our tour ended at the industrial cooler that stored thousands of pounds of packaged meat. Kent rattled off the names of familiar cuts, but the freezing air made focusing on anything besides the temperature near impossible. After stepping over a bouquet of wires and extension cords, Father asked about the electrical hookup, a question we knew had no suitable response. Kent looked around as if unaware where the hookup was and quickly moved several crates into another configuration, equally as unorganized.

"We'll cross that bridge when we get there, my new friend," Kent said.

With his back to all of us, Father compared the mental map of where things should be with where they were. Sadly, Kent meant it. Mother and I looked at Father, knowing Kent's response was a recipe for Father's blood to boil. Father may have sensed it first, but it became clear at that moment the Mountainbrook Farm was significantly underinsured, if insured at all. To Father, who was growing into one of the state's leading agricultural insurance agents, that came with too many risks to reconcile.

The transition from the freezer to the outside air zapped the energy straight from our bodies. As the door closed, Mother and I noticed a blinking red light on the thermostat outside the cooler door. She knew from her husband's compulsive awareness of lights on his truck that orange signaled an approaching problem, but red signaled that the problem had already arrived. Like her, I'd heard the same sermon dozens of times, so I was surprised when she asked Kent about it. Though our time together that day was brief, we weren't surprised by his response as he waved us along.

"Ah, I guess something ain't right. I'll look into that later."

As if the tour was more prescribed than we thought, we followed Kent to our last stop at the Farm Store before returning home. For the next ten years, until I went off to college, I'd see that light blinking from my bedroom window every night. Over time, I realized it signaled exactly what Kent said it did.

5

THERE'S ENOUGH LIGHT TO see that no other cars are in the campground loop and Malik is snoring in the tent. It will be awhile before the morning dew that coats the truck's rusting metal burns off, and even covered with the thin camping mattress, the grooves of the truck bed make for a terrible night's sleep. My eyes sting from the smoke of last evening's fire, where Malik and I sat on opposite logs around the flames that burned a whole lot more than wood. We exchanged a flipped frisbee with cheese and crackers and occasionally looked in each other's direction, but neither of us offered anything to really see.

Now a semi truck in front of us on Route 340 claims the one-lane state road to itself as we maneuver a series of turns onto a smaller road on the west side of the Shenandoah Mountains. I reason it's too late to suggest that Malik wear a mask. We've been within a few feet of each other for a day, windows down, no masks. It's hot and the A/C is busted anyway. I look over the wheel and out the window.

"So let me get this straight, what ya think people out here think about Black Lives Matter?" he spouts. "No really," he continues before I can respond, though I certainly didn't plan to in that short a time.

"Why do you ask?" I say, wondering which response will end our conversation the quickest.

"The Black Lives Matter signs are everywhere in the city. You could believe they were beyond it too. That's all, I guess." His volume fades with each word.

Does he believe that? I'd have to ask to know, but I reason that Malik's time in rural America is limited. While I couldn't think of a more engaging topic than travel and exploration with a former student, right now it feels like a trap and I don't think anything can change that. Oddly, more so than my interest to not talk with Malik, is my interest to know what he's thinking.

"Ya didn't answer me, Brown. What do people think of Black Lives Matter out here?"

"I'm not sure. I can't tell what anyone thinks about it back in DC unless I see a sign or a shirt, right? And honestly, I'm still confused. I think I get what being against Black Lives Matter means more clearly than being for it. Make sense?"

The silence blends into the heat-stained wind. *Am I making sense? Have I asked him once if he's okay? If he needs help? What if he says yes?*

"Why do you ask?"

"Why do I ask?" Malik fires back, and I think the question is another set up. He's waiting to trounce. "Geez, Brown. People out here ain't afraid of signs, but none of them raise awareness to what's going on. Ain't that enough of a reason?" His tone rises with each word.

I wish we weren't having this conversation, like the last conversation about race, or the one before that, or the next one.

"It's only been a few weeks since Breonna Taylor been shot eight times by police while sleeping. You know about that, right?" Malik says.

I don't answer. He knows I know about it. Or maybe his question is impeccably valid.

"Shit like that don't happen out here, and sure as those cows gettin' milked, it definitely don't happen to White folks, right, Brown?" I don't follow his pointing to the cow herd on the passing field.

Everything Malik has shared, albeit still not much, is true. But there are more versions of the truth than ever before. We're all listening and seeing a limited collection of voices and scenes. Our interest to hear views and perspectives other than those we already agree with continually fades. I think that while some people out here see the same videos of police brutality people in the cities are protesting, other videos and other narratives are sweeping the attention spans of people out here. For every scene captured on video, another happens before and after it. Someone else's video. Sometimes we're watching the same videos, but often we're not.

Maybe Malik understands these polarities better than me. Maybe he comprehends how the president uses the Black Lives Matter protests to enhance his mantra of law and order to roaring crowds before and even during the first months of the pandemic. Branding that order will keep the protests that shake the cities from reaching White suburbs and beyond. Like leaders before him, fear is a tool, and a dependable one. But I don't say any of this out loud. The recent wave of racial injustices and protests in response to them have led to intense conversations with students. Fortunately for me, none of them in person. Luckily before now, none in my truck.

Sure, teaching history opened continual doors to conversations about the White landowner, or the White slave trader, or White political racist, but I felt desensitized to them. I never felt Black, but even more so, I never felt White like the people we spoke of. Other than a shared skin tone, I was just as foreign to those people as my students were, or so I thought. But over time, I realized that the distance I associated and what they associated between me and the villains of history weren't as great as I imagined.

It took years to realize that my life was offered opportunities, or privileges, because of the actions of those people. Like almost all the valuable lessons, I didn't realize this on my own either, and with Malik's anger ready to spill, I wonder if the safety of engaging in difficult conversations about race, White privilege, and injustice in the classroom was yet another mask for steering away from the same discussions beyond it.

"Honestly, and don't take this the wrong way, Brown, but White people love signs. They love wanting people to know what they're thinking."

In his pause, I realize that I'm silently calling a play-by-play of his actions and comments instead of engaging with him. *What did I ever do on these long drives alone?*

"And if I can ride this out," he continues, lightly tapping his hand on the thin metal of the door's exterior, "I think some White people feel it's their darn responsibility to let me know what they're thinking. They're so confident in themselves."

He exhales out the window like he's smoking a cigarette as a large truck rides up on my bumper. I swipe the pile of empty chip bags on the seat between us and feel for the atlas, which I plop on Malik's lap while mumbling something about needing to find another road.

Malik stops talking and of course it's right at one of the few times he has more of my attention than I can muster on anything else. His finger traces a section of smaller roads in southwestern Virginia, an area we'll avoid at all costs. I bite my tongue and look out the window to the valley as a sweltering wind whips through the barren landscape.

"I always think of scary ass muthafuckers as dudes from the city, but my uncle told me that some of the most danger-ous men in his unit were country boys. Some of his friends, ya know, guys he served with, would come into the garage and talk about their tours. Crazy really, but the same small yard behind the garage where my uncle meditated was the same place hours later where these men sat around on folding chairs and cussed the afternoon into night, flipping drinks and stories about their time overseas. I'd make sure I was near the back door working on engines, or cleaning mostly, just to hear 'em."

He loosens the red bandana from his neck and wipes his brow. It's the first time I hear of his uncle. *Is this who Jamal and Lewis said died of Covid?* I tap the wheel, restless with uncertainty as several engine lights flicker and I smack the dash a few times. They chaotically blink before disappearing.

"Ya know, you may have fooled Jamal, but not me, Brown. I'm onto you."

I regrip the wheel with both hands. Tighter. This isn't worth it. Malik doesn't know what he's talking about. While expressing bursts of sensical thinking, it's clear that he's an angry young man. The minuscule sense that I could help his situation, or maybe even his bruised ego, evaporates with every turn and I tell myself that Malik is an immature, overgrown kid, not smart enough to follow the guidance of the caring adults who've bent over backward for him. And there's relief in confirming the situation.

Deep breath.

"You said it yourself. Don't we value the same things? I mean, wasn't that the main theme of eighth grade?"

Before I can see Malik's face, we're both distracted by a red barn with a huge TRUMP painted in blue letters on its side.

Caught between the gratitude that a former student can identify the main theme of a class from years ago and the current moment, there's nothing I can think to say. He didn't ask a question. How did this happen? Yesterday morning I almost hit him behind my truck and now we're driving in the middle of nowhere, stuck in each other's heads.

What happened to him? What is he running from? Is he the only one?

I set the questions aside, knowing I should use my limited time to prepare for meeting with Becker in two days. How many letters do I need to write? I think about Terri. I should've called her this morning to see how she's feeling. Instead, I'm here with Malik, and he exchanges the road atlas for one of the newspapers off the dash. Both sides of the windshield are in desperate need of cleaning and when the paper moves under the glass a clear reflection shows my face. I stare at it for a few seconds as sickness takes hold in my stomach and I slide the atlas to cover the glare's image.

"You cool, Mr. Brown?" Malik calmly asks.

The frustration mounts. *Am I trying to loathe him? Accept him? What do these considerations even mean?* Sadly, I fear it's something worse. I may actually need him.

"Ya know, when Jamal told me and Lew about becoming a teacher, Lew asked him who he wanted to be like. Now, you's was on the list, Brown, so I'll give you that, albeit not very high on it. And so, well, after talking about other teachers, he said he remembered how you opened our eighth-grade class telling us that although we were all different, we all sought the same things." He waits, occasionally glancing toward me.

We pass another ramshackle barn. While not the first of its kind in the thirty or so miles since Harpers Ferry, this Confederate flag is by far the largest we've seen. I don't say anything, debating whether to solicit Malik's attention or feel relieved that it's temporarily directed elsewhere. *Do I truly believe that we all value the same things? What's his point?*

"Safety." Malik nods his head, like he's speaking to the both of us. His voice is evenly pitched and softer than before. "It's safety why Black people join gangs in the cities and maybe just as much why Whites join militia groups in the country. How the things offering some people safety are what threatens others."

My left leg starts to bounce, a nervous habit for someone so relieved by motionlessness. What he's just shared is profound, but I won't tell him this. Instead, I repeat it to myself, knowing I've rarely made points this clear to students.

"It's true, Black people reaching greater heights than ever before and that shit, I mean, progress." Malik arches his back outward, stretching his spine. "This progress for some reason is threatening to a whole lotta White people. That's a conversation I ain't hearing."

I stagger my fingers to fiercely regrip the wheel, hoping to squeeze the conversation from the truck. "There's a lot of conversations not happening," I blurt, wishing I hadn't responded so quickly. It's almost one hundred degrees, and the humid sheet of air under the grayish blue sky is sucking the wind out of the cab.

"Shoot, Brown, how can you talk to people with all of 'em flaunting their guns? They ain't looking for a conversation. These muthafuckers are looking for war, or as all these Confederate flags show, want to reup the one they think ain't finished. Yeah, lots of conversations not happening." Malik takes a momentary pause, which I think will last longer. "Like in the hood, people with guns often remind themselves, and then you, of the gun they carrying when they hear views not so aligned with their own. Just sayin', Brown, I've been told of one rule: avoid people with guns. And if that can't happen, do whatever you need to do to not piss 'em off."

I think to tell Malik that this sounds more like two rules, albeit an appropriate addition, but I don't, wanting to move our conversation away from him referencing his hood, or any hood, but it's unfair to prefer he not speak his truths. I know this. I don't want to think about how half of DC lives with endless access to all the amenities of a top rate city and a portion of the other half refers to their community as a hood. And for the first time I consider that this stupid old truck in need of endless repairs might be the easier fix.

Malik knows that most White people are good people. He also knows that enough of them are not. Slowly, or not so slowly, Jamal and Lewis have also realized that too many White people are still too happy to march in a parade for equality as long as they return to the comforts of their communities, ones often shaped by systemic racism. I guess by now Malik knows I'm one of them. The dashboard lights flicker again and I'm about to slap the dash, but Malik beats me to it with a short, four-hit drum roll. The lights flash a few times before dimming away.

"Man, I know people are struggling with, well, basic needs in the city. C'mon. 'Course I know. You saw where we were just… Yo, Brown, when did we leave the city?"

"It was yesterday morning, Malik," I say, frustrated by the sense that only I feel it's been longer. My hands slide over the sweat on my face. "I don't speak from experience, but I know a lot of White people. They're struggling too, ya know?"

But the real struggle is with my words, searching for something profound, or at least something not completely redundant to say. I stumble over a series of sentences about how with all the opportunities offered White people at the expense of those not offered to others, we still can't completely align privilege with prosperity, though layering capitalism into a conversation about racism isn't exactly a recipe for lightening the mood. Malik spares me the embarrassment of calling my idiotic thinking by name.

I think of telling him it's not a new notion that folks out here think they're taking society's second fiddle to folks in the city. They see their brightest leaving for better jobs in the cities, often returning home to visit with more progressive views than with those they left with. They see money invested in cities, but their papers highlight our city's failing schools and impoverished neighborhoods. This narrative, and maybe rightfully so, casts fear. That fear is then manipulated by politicians and others who show the city as home to an elite wealthy who control the corporations' puppet strings that close the rural factories where they work. A fascinatingly sad cycle of endless half-truths. Then I stop, thinking that Malik's not paying attention, and I reason that I can't blame him as he surfs his arm out the window in circular shapes that tease something beautiful dancing around the obnoxiously warm wind. It's clear we're not talking against each other, or over each other, or despite each other. We're talking right *through* each other.

I return from the momentary distraction to an unexplainable frustration, which I'm pretty sure is Malik's tapping right heel, a movement that otherwise wouldn't bother me except for the empty bag of chips under his foot. The remaining crumbs left in the bag create a crackling sound in its own category of annoyance. I want to ask him to stop. The sound booms in my head, which in his defense, may be the only place it's heard.

The closest feeling to anger surfaces in my chest. A rare emotion connected to the mistakes we can't correct. It's always about Darren. So many years of knowing I had to go to the bridge in Harpers Ferry, but why?

"Yo, Brown, you're due for a breath, a'ight. Ya turning red on me."

Malik's words break a spell only Darren is capable of casting. With seconds as hours, weeks as days, months as years, I loosen my grip on the wheel and stretch my feet, following Malik's suggestion, realizing the easiest move is to return to where we last were.

"You're right," I say, realizing that I've said these two words quite often to someone I've cast as not making much sense. "You're right," I repeat, more softly. "For the last few decades, people in rural America are seeing people who don't look like them succeeding. Out here, the economic foundations are crumbling. In some cases, the government is paying farmers to not grow crops. Factories are closing because people don't realize their interest in cheaper products means goods are made elsewhere. No one wants to accept this. The systems we thought would work forever are splintering. Others are no longer functioning. Suffering always finds a culprit."

Malik nods his head, and I'm not sure if it's because he agrees with me or he's pretending to make me feel heard when he's not listening.

"There's real fear, Malik. Some of it I understand, most of it I don't, but whether you understand it or not, whether it's valid or not, we have to be attentive to people's fear." Then I remember the most important part. "And the news, the politicians, they stoke that fear. They feed it, right? If you're afraid, you pay attention. That attention creates engagement."

"That engagement creates donations and votes," Malik throws in as if we're playing a game. "What are White people afraid of, Brown?"

My eyes wander from the road to look for an answer, any answer, but I can only think of my own high school experience of learning about slavery and the civil rights movement. I kept telling myself I must have missed a major chunk of instruction, but I know that's not true. I never missed school. The civil rights era, what it was like to truly live as a slave, how people lived in the age of Jim Crow. At best, the topics were narrowly covered. It's only years later that I'm seeing how their absence, or intentional neglect, left a prominent stain of illusion.

Sure, there were isolated lessons on King, Tubman, and mention of Marshall, but without the larger context to how people lived, how Black people were forced to live. There weren't a lot of Black people in northern New Hampshire, besides on the farm. The first memory of being academically introduced to slavery was horror. The second, shame. I didn't blame my parents. I felt relieved to know the truth. I felt a matureness for being included in what I thought was shaping into an honest conversation about our nation's historical messiness. Before that it was Pilgrim potlucks with feathered Indians swapping dishes from the microwave.

"Ya know what I'm thinking? Can something like what happened at Harpers Ferry happen again?" Malik rhetorically asks, moving his hands like a DJ scratching a turntable.

"Like what?"

"Like a group of people taking over an armory to overthrow a government."

The Harpers Ferry reference feels so distant though we only left there a few hours ago.

"I don't know," he continues, exhaling at length to possibly smooth his frustration.

"Ya know, peeps out here…" And I pause, thinking why I said "peeps," remembering how Terri occasionally joked that I never utilized my urban dictionary daily allotment. "I'd say that some people out here watch the Black Lives Matter protests, wondering if they want to take over the cities."

Malik laughs, thrusting his arms outward like the orchestra conductor so fed up with his musicians that he throws his baton into the audience. "Now, what in gawd's name does that mean?" He swivels his head on his neck without turning his upper body. "I've been at the protests. Have you? Wait, you already said you hadn't, Brown. They been passionate, full of love, and dare I say it, beautifully Black and proud. And yes, many of those steps are fueled by generations of anger, and I can't think of one Black person who sees how Black people walking forward wouldn't be."

My cell phone beeps and vibrates an alert that it's overheating and will soon shut down so I take it off the dash and slide it between the seats. Then I reply, "I just don't think there's a reason for that, Malik." And I wonder if he'll infer that I'm talking about a repeat of what happened in Harpers Ferry almost two hundred years ago. "John Brown and his ragtag crew thought they would recruit a lot more people willing to fight. In the beginning they thought the problem would be to secure guns. In the end, they lacked soldiers to use them." It's all I can think of to say.

"There's no shortage of guns. Heck, people out here got more guns than the militaries of small countries. Brown, you saw my dumb ass reading the signs back there. And I ain't trying to move on from my earlier point. Why aren't people more worried about all the guns people out here already have?"

I'm saved from trying to respond when Malik interrupts my short-lived response, again.

"Yo, I know there ain't no recordkeeping here, but for the record, Black people aren't interested in taking over anything. What would we want to take over? There's a reason for that shit happening. I mean the protests. Are people out here seeing what we're seeing?"

"They are," I quickly say, then realize I have no evidence to support this. I'm not so sure, but I don't want to admit this. *Just move forward.* "But people, and I mean people everywhere, can only see what they witness or what they're shown. Overwhelmingly, it's the latter. What you and what others see is sometimes…" I hold off, waiting to see if Malik will interrupt me again—almost baiting him to do so, which he doesn't.

"Yeah, I get it. Windows get broken. Cars burned. Sure, some wackass ni— I mean some pepped-up people throw shit in the face of police. But shit, White people do that same stuff when their hockey team wins the championship, right?"

I silently repeat what Malik just said, ensuring there isn't a question.

"Ya know, wasn't it only a few years ago where a bunch of White dudes took over some sort of, what da ya even call it, a, a…what is it? Yes, a wildlife refuge in Oregon. Didn't the sheriff offer them lunch or some shit? Imagine if that was a bunch of Black people." Malik stretches his arms and flips his hands in a motion like Terri's yoga practice, calm when the energy around us is anything but and I'm taken by this ability, considering the tension I can't escape.

"I heard you, Mr. Brown, but you didn't answer my question."

I tear at a piece of the rubber coating slowly peeling off the wheel, thinking it will help me remember what he's referring to. I'm just not sure, and the path of least resistance is to say that he's right, but for some reason I don't.

"Ya know, our city messes with the minds of Black people 'cause we don't interact with poor White people. I know they're out here. I know they be living in some poor ass shit too, but it looks different."

We pass what feels like a quarter-mile stretch of trailers mounted on a swath of overgrown fields. Expired machines dot the land. Redneck utopia was what the professor called similar areas. Malik has a fascinating manner of speaking with pauses. Small and unnecessary pockets of space and silence that reinforce or contradict his message.

"At least poor White people ain't all living' on top of each other. They get to spread out their twelve half-built lawn mowers and three and a half pickup trucks all over big yards," Malik says, chuckling. "I wonder what kind of whack shit you'd see if poor Black people spread their stuff all over the yard?" He lightly taps the metal beneath the outside of his window, loud enough for me to wish he weren't but not loud enough to reasonably ask him to stop.

We pull into a gas station since I only purchased half a tank Monday night before Terri and I returned from the hospital. The old-style nozzle feels like a relic of the past and an index card taped beside the gallon meter informs me they only take cash. I give Malik five dollars for sodas before he heads to the bathroom around back. I walk inside and place a twenty on the counter.

"Pump two," I tell the shopkeeper, an older man not wearing a mask. I think about my promise to Terri to not go inside anywhere.

The sound of petroleum gulping through the old black rubber hose is hypnotic. I'm tired after a terrible night's sleep in the back of the truck. The side lot contains three dirty pickup trucks that don't make me think they belong to people who ran inside for a quick purchase. One is raised without front wheels, and there's subtle joy in seeing a truck in worse shape than my own. The difference is that no one's trying to drive these. The crackling of dirt and small rocks under my old sneakers sounds western.

The pump slows to a crawl when the meter reaches $19.00 and to offset the moment's boredom, I track my payment numbers, blinking my eyes to guess when the number will change. It feels like a whole second passes before each cent of gas registers.

The creaky store door opens and the shopkeeper leans out of the doorway with his hand on the handle, yelling, "I'm gonna make it easy for you to get out of my store, and if this doesn't work, I'll take matters into my own able hands."

Malik tosses two soda cans and a snack bag onto his seat through the open passenger window. He grabs the door handle, and I see his eyes momentarily close. When they open, he looks unrecognizable to the person I barely knew minutes earlier. He releases the handle, walks by the back of the truck, and keeps walking. I stare into the older man's angry eyes and contemplate whether I'm more surprised about Malik's incident in the store or that he's heading toward the road.

More so than seeing Malik walk away, I'm frustrated by investing so much time in my gas counting game only to release the lever short of a full purchase and stumble to align the pump in its holster. I follow Malik toward the road but stop within a few feet. *Should I move the truck? Get in it to drive after him? Get in and go in the other direction?* Reluctantly, I continue walking after him as he disappears along the wide, dirt shoulder.

When I finally see Malik, he is farther away than I thought. There's real distance between us, and it dawns on me that he's not blowing off a little steam or stretching his legs. He's walking away. I turn and see the old man, hands across his chest, now a few feet from my truck where I left my phone and keys on the seat. I contemplate going back to ask what happened, but every second I don't walk diligently after Malik, he gets farther away. I start jogging to keep pace.

"Yo, Malik, *stop!*" I say, finally yelling by the last word.

He turns, but I realize seconds later that it's less about me than to distance himself from the thick brush consuming the roadside. He walks into the middle of the broken country road. With no oncoming traffic, I increase my speed, springing forward to get beside him. I peek over my shoulder every few seconds to check for traffic, concerned he's not doing the same.

"What happened in the store?" Quick glances at his face reveal nothing but hopelessness.

Sweat pours off my head, and our steps on the blistering asphalt become a synchronized messy pattern. Four legs moving in unison with no purpose other than to get away from the previous step. One rumbling car and then another with a screeching motor round the bend ahead of us. I grab Malik's arm and pull him to the side of the road as both vehicles get as close to us as they can without their wheels leaving the road. A cloud of dust and exhaust engulfs us as a barrage of pebbles strikes our bodies. Malik throws his hands up in the direction of the vehicles, now out of view.

He curses out loud into the air, broke of compassion, then veers onto the cracking concrete footpath leading to a small one-room church. Heavily-chipped and stained white paint cover the building. The church marquee displays the name of

Pastor Kyle Harrison above the message: "IF YOU ARE NOT WITHIN, YOU ARE WITHOUT." Malik sits on the second to bottom step, and I stand a few feet back, silently reading the message several times while rearranging the comma.

"Malik, you came to my house. I didn't come to yours, so, so, so, so what gives?" I wish I felt enough energy to scream or throw something or do anything for once that isn't passive or that actually expresses something to someone, but I don't. Instead, I walk in a small circle around the overgrown grass that bends to the concrete walkway.

"You think I need you, Brown? You think Black kids need you?" He barely looks up, his volume now at the leveled tone I wish I'd used.

His soft and harmless words strike like…I don't know what. *Why would he say this?* I restart my circular steps but now in the opposite direction. I think about what Malik just said. Repeating it to myself, again moving commas around to see if a less demeaning message could be constructed. He has no idea how much I haven't been needed.

"What happened in the store, Malik?" I say not so much whispering but not matching his volume either.

"Nothing. I got our stuff and then asked for a receipt like like I always do, but—"

"Nah, I'm just not buying that, Malik. You just asked for a receipt and that resulted in him and you storming out of the store? Possibly getting some stupid hillbillies to nearly run us over? C'mon, man." I instantly regret cutting him off.

Malik rests his bent elbows on his thighs and arches his back, straightening his posture. "Ya know, Brown, you can walk in that store and your only thought is whether you have an extra dolla for a lotto ticket. Whether you sippin' Coke or Pepsi. Every time I enter a store with White people, I think about how much discomfort I'll have to embrace while being watched for the next ninety seconds. Racist motherfucker."

"Not everyone you meet out here is a racist," I say, throwing my hands in the air like a drunk referee signaling an unsuccessful field goal attempt.

Malik lowers his head, shaking his skull side to side. His face then lowers into his hands. "Right. No, you're right."

Despite mumbling under his breath, his words are deep, calm, and clear. Then the clearest of thoughts surfaces. We did it. Progress. We made it to this point. The rope has reached the bottom of the well and I'm confident that the muscle of logic can pull us both upward. I nod my head, certain I understand the lesson he's learned. His misunderstanding. How I helped him see it.

"You're right. That man ain't no racist. He's a fucking hero! Standing up for…ah, forget it." Malik looks both ways as if there's something to find, but it's just us.

I don't know what happened in the store, or before, but for the first time I recognize that something is broken. Maybe it's what Malik has felt for a long time, or maybe just now. In his hanging head I feel something I've ignored for a long time. Something potent and unforgiving. Something unlike other pains but something still unnamed. It's what we run from. What I run from. I realize that no one, including Malik, would come to me for help. Then why him? Why me? Then my pause turns into being stuck. Being stuck turns into being frozen. Being frozen turns into realizing something, and possibly for the first time. All my years working with Black children and young adults, and we've never been in a store together.

He looks up at me, then away.

"C'mon," I say, stepping back a few feet after seeing sweat roll off his forehead onto his shoe. It doesn't dawn on me that it's not sweat. "Listen, maybe we should go back to the city. C'mon, let's go back to the truck, okay?"

Malik nods his head and then wipes his brow, or possibly his tears. I'm not sure. We walk back to the gas station, which is farther away than I thought.

"Brown," he says, and after a few seconds where he appears to be waiting for me to recognize him, I nod. "Do you believe there's a lot of racism out here?"

I raise my sweat-soaked bandana and wipe my lips. I'd rather not think about his question. There's no easy answer, or maybe there is, and in return Malik only receives the silence I wish he'd offer me.

"Ya know, Mr. Brown," Malik says calmly, "sometimes when you don't say anything is when I hear you the loudest."

6

OVER A DECADE LIVING beside the farm, I saw hundreds of people come and go. At times I was shocked by the professional careers temporarily stalled or suspended to pitch a tent or trailer in exchange for meals, minimal payment, and an opportunity to live and work as a farmer. Lawyers, doctoral students, teachers on summer break. The occasional professor, though the only one I can pin down was the eccentric resident, Matt Farace. Most workers were students and specifically ones in graduate programs at the University of New Hampshire where Dina guest lectured on agricultural sustainability and migratory studies—two oddly connected areas of expertise.

Regularly I heard Professor Farace say the farm had more degrees than cows. "More culture than any farm in the valley, and I'm not talking about our yogurt," was a joke on seasonal rotation. The professor would then push his glasses up his nose with his lanky middle finger. Skepticism of his sarcasm and possibly his PhD in philosophy were the only things Kent and Father likely agreed on. Occasionally, the professor's antics became community theater. An intentional act to lighten the mood created by relentless work and nowhere was this more evident than the farm's summer morning meeting.

Dina, Kent, Walter, the professor, Russell, the farm boys (Trevor, Timmy, and Darren), and a host of seasonal employees would start working the fields by 5:00 a.m. to capture a full day's productivity. Optimizing daylight was key, but I was rarely part of these early morning assignments. By choice, Darren was. For several years, he was probably the only person who routinely floated between Walter, Kent, and occasionally Dina's team. Everyone wanted him by their side. Everything about him was effort, and when Darren worked with a team, their work was completed sooner. He was a great asset to Walter because he was strong and attuned to the livestock schedules. He was the perfect complement to Kent's inability to foresee risks. With millions of dollars in machinery, crops, and livestock, they were everywhere.

At 7:50, the morning bell rang. The crew had ten minutes to assemble beside the back barn where Kent and his clipboard awaited. To my knowledge, I was the only person to show up and start at the bell, but I wasn't a formal part of any team. I was just there.

Everyone gathered in a large circle. By then the sun was in full ownership of the sky. Sweat dripped from every face and body from what already felt like a full day's work. Walter said this was the most productive block of time because what followed sunrise was people. With them came distractions. Kent would extend a proper Mountainbrook Farm greeting and a quick prayer, though it was never made clear to whom we prayed. Walter read off a list of to-do's, like where Kent was haying, parts arriving for Russell's repairs, fields the professor's team were planting, then harvesting, and so on. Dina, not holding or reading from any clipboard, listed the farmers' market schedules, crews, and packing teams. Kent concluded every meeting with another prayer—"Praise for sun, rain, health, and the grace that brings us together to strengthen our Earth." With his last word, but not a second before, everyone sat to eat.

From Memorial Day through Labor Day the community meal was my favorite part of the farm experience. Under several canopies were two tables, and in front of each person's chair was their own cutting board that served as a plate. A rotating kitchen staff set out hefty cast iron bowls with around five pounds of bacon and sausage, dozens of scrambled eggs, trays of fresh biscuits, seven or eight mason jars of yogurt, bags of granola, and multiple loaves of freshly baked bread. Several pots of coffee and water pitchers scattered the tables. It was a scene I could watch over and over. A mad, chaotic, and oddly synchronized passing and dishing of plates for approximately two minutes. Then for seven to eight minutes it was only the sounds of hungry men and women fueling their bodies with the freshest food on the planet.

By the tenth minute, the cutting boards were nearly as clean as when they were set. That's when heads started to lower. When the heavy breathing started. When I watched the faces of the men and women, some known well and others strangers until their last day, contemplating what their bodies were capable of beyond the moment. I watched them breathe, think, forget, feel, question, and ultimately rest their muscles after three hours of intense movement that was greater than what most people exerted in a whole day. I imagined their conversations with their souls, possibly asking themselves if farm life was for them, or if they had another seven or eight hours left in the tank. This minute or two of downtime became dangerous when it got comfortable, and those with experience would pep up and drink mason jars full of water. Walter would rise first, and there wasn't one backside seated seconds later.

On occasion you would hear the professor perk up as the staff dispersed. "I noticed someone borrowed Plato's *Republic*. When you're finished, please bring a cheap bottle of Merlot to my trailer with a chair and several hours of unoccupied time." Once it was something like, "To whoever has Nietzsche's *The Birth of Tragedy*, be ready to feel inner pain like your soul has never experienced, and please return it. It's been ten days." Farm vets, as Dina called those who'd spent several seasons, would smile or laugh, a subtle appreciation for his contributions and awkwardness. Farm life was hard, and his antics had meaning that few understood to make it less so. I was one of them.

The professor was oddly approachable and it was hard to avoid his long, lanky legs and tall frame around the farm or sitting on the chair beside the trailer. He was the only adult I felt comfortable walking over to if I was just walking around aimlessly, wonderingly. Anyone else would've directed me to do something, as walking the farm without a task was a privilege not offered to many. He was a machine of answers, but what I most appreciated were his thoughtful questions. He asked about my interests, track practice, and school, though it was hard to know if he was being condescending when I shared what I was learning.

I wasn't the only one who responded to the professor's approachability. Darren scurried through his book box almost more than anyone. Over time, our mother became friends with Tessa, who she once described into the phone as a strong, independent mountain woman and fellow artist, though I never considered with whom she spoke. Our mother was raised on the outskirts of the conservative Amish countryside in Lancaster, Pennsylvania. The values of her large family were a sharp contrast to her appreciation of wine, museums, and galleries, which she attributed to four years of college in Boston, where she met our father. Albeit decrepit to the eye, the professor's trailer was also inviting and a congregation spot for the farm's older folks who outgrew or intentionally avoided the younger staff gatherings behind the back barn where they listened to the Grateful Dead and smoked pot.

Our mother's engagement into the professor's and Tessa's inner circle was at first measured, but in time it became a place she sought for calm and artistic comradery. One spring season she was invited to join their small community circles. They held hands and softly sang songs with words I struggled to comprehend from the bluff, but "solstice" and "peace" sounded overused. One of those warm weekend afternoons was the first time I saw Mother and Tessa look around and then walk inside the trailer holding hands. That evening at dinner, Mother was more relaxed and happier than I had ever seen her before.

We hadn't moved into a new home at the end of a secluded road. We'd moved into a new life. One physically, emotionally, culturally, and spiritually absorbed by the property beside it. For Darren and our mother, the draw to immersing themselves within its mysteries was immediate. He saw exploration and adventure. She saw escape from a marriage stale of love and void of maintenance. For me, our oddly-shaped patch of earth nestled between hills and river was an endless maze to wander, occasionally stopping at different places and groups of people, wondering if this could be the kind of place where I fit in.

Many workers were young couples eager to wet their agricultural feet. There were also single men and just as many women, some of whom wore headbands with names like Dakota, Yael, and Spirit. Professor Farace called them Gypsies. Others called them loners. One fellow left in the middle of a team meeting after telling Kent that the farm was a dismal labor camp. I found that interpretation mind blowing. One or two people covered their mouths to hide laughter. The farm was anything but funny. When someone arrived looking for a vacation, they rarely lasted. The days were too long, the work too hard.

People liked Kent but no one overly much. The exception to that may have been Darren. Kent was always moving but never with urgent steps. He listened but only for the information he needed. He knew how to respectfully, but not always politely, end a conversation. Having a farm with as many inoperable parts as those functioning gave him a bible of reasons to limit every unnecessary interaction, and he often did.

Darren could see Kent's work, but seeing our Father's work was less clear. He couldn't see insurance. He couldn't hold a policy. He couldn't see the result of a responsible protection plan. He saw the farm as work and was drawn to its lifestyle of endless labor and reward, though neither of us understood at that time the real hardships Dina and Kent endured to believe that this endless valley of struggles was really their dream.

Darren's strength and ease with which he soon mastered the farm responsibilities caught everyone's eye, especially Kent's. Within a few months, when he whistled for Trevor and Timmy to hop in the back of his pickup for a delivery or chat with someone up the valley, Darren hopped in too. It didn't take long before newcomers asked Kent and Dina about their three sons. While it felt like Dina's responses were direct and factual, it sometimes looked as if Kent wished Darren was one of his boys. In the years to come, their bond strengthened and time would tell that their relationship saved Darren the most when he may have deserved it the least.

That first school year in our new home was uneventful, like the others. Ms. Irom was my fourth-grade teacher. Some students didn't even recognize me as the new kid, and I wondered if it was worse to be a new kid who knew no one or mistaken for someone who'd been beside their classmates unnoticed for years. Darren's first year picked up where the last left off. Despite an ability for school to be an easy academic experience, he was starting to act up in class. For the first time, he struggled with hockey. Contrary to his former coach's style in southern New Hampshire, his new coach wanted his players to fight. They were going to play Canadian schools, and there, fighting was as true to the game as ice.

Fighting wasn't hard for Darren but learning who his opponent was would soon get in the way of playing time. Trevor and Timmy weren't troublemakers, but they didn't steer clear of boys who were. Soon Darren found his way into a group of boys with a clear pecking order, and he accepted the notion that to be with them, he'd have to catch up with his fists.

In school there was one space where Darren was not only different but a whole other person—the French class he took with Kami. There, he was a model student. He and Kami walked the farm practicing conversational French. On several weekends, our mother took Darren, Zoya, and Kami to Montreal to visit the city's museums. Tessa even joined them once or twice. Beyond a near fluency in French, Darren learned to also speak Amharic, which impressed Zoya almost more than her daughter.

Kami was well liked but had few friends in school, which probably had to do as much with her being brown-skinned and African as with the obscure location of her residence. For Kami, Trevor and Timmy were more like brothers, and it was evident Kent and Dina treated her like a daughter. When you lived on Mountainbrook Farm, you didn't really need to look elsewhere for community. Despite Kent and Walter routinely redirecting his strengthening body to occupy more labor-intensive tasks, Darren used his extra time to help Dina and Zoya in the Dairy House.

Over a few years, Darren's and Kami's relationship evolved, though to my knowledge there was no intimacy between them. On the picnic table where Kami, Darren, Trevor, and Timmy did their homework in the warm months, I heard Kami and Darren promise to attend the senior prom together, even though for weeks they'd been joking about how pathetic the drama surrounding junior prom was with other people.

"Let's roll up in a tractor," Kami quipped.

"No, we can do better. Let's ride up on horses right beside the limos," he replied.

The sound of the brothers' laughter increased with each proposal.

"Yes, that's it," she said, playfully punching Darren's shoulder.

While her swipe was endearing, I couldn't help thinking it probably would've hurt me. They'd high five and say something in French I couldn't understand, but when Kami repeated it, flipping her middle finger to the air, I felt like a clue was revealed. Darren then said something in Amharic when Kami bent over in hysterical laughter, a snort on the short horizon. Then Zoya surprised them both when she exited the nearby Dairy House. They both straightened up as she shook her finger back and forth.

"You naughty boy, Darren. Those words are for the peasants and street beggars of Addis. Plus, how did you so quickly master my language?" Zoya said, reluctantly smiling. She loved Darren.

I'd say the most significant gift Kami gave to us all was balance. Around Kami, Darren was calm. He was comfortable. Subsequently, her presence brought calmness and comfort to our family. When Kami was in our home, she enlivened our mother by asking about her paintings. She structured inquisitive questions about insurance policies to our father. Darren's tone was softer, and we all found quiet joy when upon his initial refusal, Kami would jokingly demand that Darren let our mother kiss him goodbye before leaving the house.

It could have been easy for someone not watching them closely to think Darren's bursts of erratic behavior, occasional nights drinking with friends, and not returning home were a stress on Kami, but I never saw her show it if it was. On the farm, everyone was hiding something. Darren listened endlessly as her cello training evolved from the simplest of practice exercises to first chair in the school orchestra. He never missed a performance. When she played in front of the professor's trailer, the rich sounds of wood and string floated over the farm. When she played alongside the banks of the river, the deep sounds of thunderous serenity trailed through the valley. The only time, or rather the second time, I ever saw Walter not moving was when he leaned against the grand chestnut listening to Kami stroke the bow with her head down, her chin pressed into the top of her chest. It was mesmerizing and I believed that the river's water conformed to the music she created, spelling a sense of stillness over a place in constant motion.

Darren consoled her when she bared her deepest fears that the rude, under-their-breath remarks from other girls had racist undertones. He'd remind her of her intellectual and artistic beauty and throw in a "cutest girl in the valley" comment, which made Kami blush before playfully punching him.

"Hey, tough guy, did you forget that our valley is overgrown with testosterone?" she'd respond.

Real friends know how to replace sadness with love. They laughed for hours, listened to each other's stories, and removed the doubts they placed on themselves. Darren routinely told Kami she was the smartest person he'd ever known. She told him he was the kindest person she'd ever known. Their bond evolved through peaks and valleys like the land that surrounded us, and to this day, I want to believe something that pure can never truly be lost.

The hundreds of small jobs that Dina, and on occasion Kent, assigned me offered the opportunity to work with hundreds of different people over long days, weeks, and seasons. At the time, I didn't realize the education it provided. My first summer job was an unexpected one in the Dairy House, where I cleaned the cheese and yogurt production areas. It started a few days after I finished fifth grade, coincidentally on my eleventh birthday.

Initially, I was disappointed about spending a chunk of the day inside, but this changed during the sweltering August heat. This was Dina's domain, and she was mostly accompanied by staff who had joined Mountainbrook as part of the refugee relocation program where she volunteered in Concord. Between conversations about food, traditions, music, dance, and the lives and customs of the people who worked there, a daily overview of the world's happenings created the most fascinating classroom.

That winter as my sixth-grade teachers covered ancient civilizations, fractions, and short stories, I listened to the Dairy House women talk about the flaming streaks of Scud missiles flying through Iraqi skies, trailed by Patriot missile interceptors as war waged through our television screens. Months later it was the riots after four Los Angeles police officers repeatedly beat a Black man named Rodney King. Then came the assassination of India's former prime minister, Rajiv Gandhi, by a suicide bomber. On one quiet afternoon, Zoya turned up the radio to hear the press conference about the remains of eleven men and boys found in Jeffrey Dahmer's apartment. I listened to everything. The world's news spun in the Dairy House. None of it was mentioned in school.

The farm's needs were constant. The cycles of responsibility were endless. Somehow, this spectacle of labor bore a bond between Trevor, Kami, and Darren that became the farm's strongest life-form. For a few short years, Timmy and I were gifted with being part of it. Whether carrying dairy crates or produce or leading herds of cattle across the fields, the three of them exemplified a seriousness beyond their years. They also found appropriate times for fun. Lowering bushels for an impromptu game or midfield dance off. When their work prevented these excursions, there was theater in the subtle intersection of their routines. An eye roll, secret word exchange, silly handshake. The secret codes of youth and friendship.

The Simonelli boys and Darren were almost inseparable. With Kami, they were a family. The boys could be swinging elbows and wrestling each other to the ground under the whistles of a dozen referees, but she could get them to stop within seconds. It was like she held an invisible joystick controlling them. Their relationships brought the most vibrant life to a farm already home to thousands of living creatures. But as with all living things, nature was in silent control.

Trevor's, Kami's, and Darren's senior year was the best year of my life. Our drives to school in the smelly market van were a daily court of hysterics. I often wished we'd drive all the way to the Canadian border. When I left them at the high school parking lot to walk across the field to the junior high, something was lost in my life every morning.

Kami wasn't pushy. She wasn't attention seeking. She was their sister, though to Darren, their relationship was budding into something more. She had their backs and they had hers. You could hear a needle drop on the barn floor in a storm when she told them what the girls they thought about were saying. They all performed well in school, but only Kami clearly explained to any of the adults what they were learning or how they were evaluated. She had what Dina called intuition, and I remember her face when she'd look at Kami standing beside these three large, sweaty boys, wondering how they'd get through a day without her. There was no shortage of extremely strong women where we lived, and years later I wondered if it also took the other men time to adjust to how differently women were treated elsewhere.

In their own ways, our parents made sure the farm wasn't our whole life, and while it never appeared to be fiscally thriving, the markets meant there was always cash. If Kami was with us, Dina was quick to give Trevor a twenty-dollar bill for a trip to town. If Kami wasn't, she most likely wouldn't ask where we were going or if the truck had a steering wheel.

Trevor, Darren, and Kami were the best of both worlds, country and cultural. We lived on a farm, but they all fit in with the rich kids whose parents owned the businesses around the ski resort outside Franklin. The boys and Kami knew how to talk to those kids, and it appeared they even had some genuine friendships among them. The five of us together beyond the farm was the best of times. When Kami wasn't there, it was some of the scariest.

While the farm made up half the population of Dalmaqua, the population of Franklin was several thousand. Concord was over an hour south and in between were hundreds of miles of lakes and mountains that defined a little bit of everyone, whether they were the reason people stayed or the obstacle preventing others from leaving.

Franklin's Snow Eagle Resort created a string of weekend traffic and a catalog of ski shops, restaurants, and motels that far exceeded the needs of its resident population. The town was our first real taste of life beyond the farm. We'd set up camp in the back row of the Sunrise Movie Theatre and hover around the plastic tables between Folly's Double Scoop, the best soft serve house on the strip, and Boller's Pizza House. Walking up and down Main Street, Trevor and Timmy took turns holding hands with Kami, playing the role of a farmer couple coming to town for the first time. The skits were endless, and after passing the shocked tourists, we'd fall over with laughter into the nearest alley or parking lot, dropping to the ground from the weight of silliness. When Kami laughed hard, her shoulders rolled inward and she snorted, causing Trevor to do the same, minus the shoulder roll. Darren laughed, but his emotions were balanced. Nothing went too far. No level of love, humor, or pain made him really budge. It took years to learn how wrong I was about that.

When Kami wasn't with us, the boys were different. Like when a domesticated animal strays from its trainer. The boys talked about trouble with other kids, and Darren and Trevor weren't foreign to trouble. Once when Kami was preparing for a cello recital, Trevor took a few dollars from the Farm Store cashbox for ice cream, which I believed he always returned. Dina trusted the boys and had a lot of reason to do so, but maybe too much at times.

One unseasonably warm summer night when the mountain air forgot we were so far north, several girls called Darren and Trevor as we walked with our ice cream cones. The evening's humidity required focused attention to the quickly melting ice cream, which Kami called *cone management skills*. She had names for everything.

It wasn't rare for girls to flirt with Darren and Trevor, but it was less common with their younger brothers around. I sat with Timmy while the three girls wearing different color tank tops approached our brothers. A thick girl with dirty blond hair wore a red shirt that squeezed her breasts into her chin. She hugged the older boys and then asked who I was. Darren told her, and having not hit the growth spurt that would eventually push my legs upward, she grabbed my shoulders and pushed my face into her firm chest. Her thigh pushed against my crotch as she rested her chin on my head, like holding the hand of a child afraid of the dark. I felt my middle move for the first time beyond the privacy of my own room.

Her fingers gripped my shoulders and then pushed my body backward. "Easy there, Farm Boy. Being Darren's brother gets you a hug, but that's it."

I slung the backpack from around my shoulder to cover my embarrassment and pushed the twelve empty cans of Coors Light I'd collected from beside the river into my crotch. At that moment, the sixty cents I hoped to retrieve for recycling felt less valuable. I then silently recited what I'd heard Timmy tell Darren a year earlier when he had a boner in class as the bell rang, and I thought of a cow giving birth.

The girls said goodbye to Trevor and Darren, by then all but ignoring Timmy and me. Without Kami around, Timmy and I immediately felt younger. Trevor and Darren were more on edge, and soon it became clear why. We walked to the outskirts of the parking lot where the farm kids or mountain boys, or whatever they called us, often sat, freeing the five round plastic tables for the resort kids.

There were four of them and some words were exchanged that I couldn't make out from where I stood some ten or so feet behind them. Darren and Trevor had a solid and trustworthy maturity. They were taught when to walk and when to fight. Hockey and Walter had taught them this. They were also strong as hell and partially fueled with testosterone and anger.

"C'mon, we're just gonna slowly walk away. If we can, this is best avoided." Trevor's calm voice was consistently and comfortably controlling.

Timmy, who was a goofball at heart, licked at the sides of his cone with an exaggerated frequency, as much in response to the evening's heat as to distract his older brother.

With his lips angrily pressed against themselves, Darren mouthed, "They've been wising off all summer, T. They deserve a taste of their own medicine."

"I know, but they're liquored up, and our brothers are here."

"Stop treating Timmy like that. He's as tough as you. Let's do this." My brother's fists clenched.

"Calm down, Darren." Trevor's voice was instantly older than his years. When things were serious, Darren knew when to follow his friend's lead.

A few steps farther, a beer exploded on the concrete behind us, spraying the backs of our legs and the surrounding pavement. We all stopped, initially amazed by the spectacle, then resumed our steps. Or at least I thought we all had. There was some laughter behind us.

"Next time I won't miss, you fucking farm boys. Where's your little pet? Ya know, the little nigger girl."

My ears stung. My heart stopped.

It was *that* word. The one I knew existed but had never heard spoken. Naively, I thought it was a term of historical context. But there it was, ripping through the stale mountain air loud enough for a few couples and other groups of kids to hear. Then I only noticed two other legs beside me, and they were Timmy's. When I turned around, our brothers were ten or so feet away.

As if rehearsed, Trevor threw his hands in the air, yelling, "What did you fucking say?" as Darren jolted horizontally and round-housed the largest of the boys, who I suspected had said the meanest remark I'd heard to that point in my life.

In the seconds before he fell to the ground, I saw him attempt to cover his face. That's when it became apparent how much he towered over my brother's tall but still undeveloped frame. Trevor charged another boy, pushing him into several metal trash cans. Before that one's body reached the ground, Trevor punched another boy in the face, knocking him straight down. It looked like the fourth boy ran away. I watched Darren's elbows cock up and down as he pummeled the body beneath him. In total shock, I watched Darren's attention shift between the other two boys, who were both starting to fight back with Trevor. Out of nowhere, I was knocked to the ground with what I later learned was a punch to the side of my head.

My only memory was watching my ice cream cone dance in the air. It was the bottom. My favorite part, and I had a formula for sucking the last drops of strawberry flavor from the cone's wafer crevices. The last thing I remembered was the splat of a pink liquid as my head did the same on the concrete. I woke up on our couch the following morning with a stunning headache. My parents, Darren, Kent, Dina, and their boys sat on the couch and surrounding chairs. It was the only time we were all ever in the same room, and the first words I heard were from Dina to Trevor, Timmy, and Darren who all sat beside each other. "To be clear, what prompted the fight doesn't reach our Zoya and

Kami." She paused, momentarily in deep thought, then restarted without using the term "our," which in some context felt inappropriate. Everyone knew it was from a place of endearment.

"What prompted the fight doesn't reach Zoya and Kami," Dina continued. "They've already overcome more racism than we'll ever be aware of. This would break their hearts."

Dina walked over to Darren and kissed him on the head. "I don't care what anyone else says, you did the right thing." She took a large step to reach Trevor and kissed him on the head as well, though his shorter hair didn't lend itself to a hair scratch. "I'm proud of you." She stepped back and quickly scanned the four of us. "The opportunity to spill blood for stupid reasons will be countless. What happened last night wasn't one of them. You did the right thing. JB, keep that ice pack on there will ya?" She looked at her watch and left the room.

Within seconds, everyone else followed but me.

For all of us, that year and every year thereafter ended several weeks later. Some moments in life you don't forget, like watching Kami walk over to me with Timmy and Trevor on their way to the river. Maybe it was her glow, a moving spark of life and love that everyone standing beside her always felt. Her kindness was contagious. Her presence was currency. The way she wore her red bandana with her flowy hair made you wish she'd never disappear from your view. And the grandest part of all, on top of everything, she saved her best for Darren. He did the same for her. But there was no kinder moment than on the late afternoon of my twelfth birthday, days before their prom.

One of the boys wished me a happy birthday, but I couldn't remember which one. Kami turned around, and with enthusiasm she rarely expressed beyond the private company of Darren, she yelled to Russ, who leaned against a post beside the Farm Store. "You promised to join us for summer's first swim. Now at it, Russ."

We were all surprised, having never heard her at such volume. We all smiled. She extended a big wave, and there was a grandness in her relationship with everyone on the farm, but especially the boys. She was family. Tough and tender. Their glue.

"Yeah, like that will happen," Trevor quipped.

We watched Russ contemplate in real time finally doing something fun, or something with people close to his age. We all felt something lift in him in front of our eyes. It may have been the first time in his life when he knew people were watching him, waiting to see what he'd do. One thing, but not the only thing, Russ and I had in common was that no one paid much attention to us. His first steps resembled more of a wobble. Then he straightened his posture and walked directly to the river, avoiding the detour to the bluff where we gathered.

Kami hopped the remaining steps to where I stood beside my mother and gave me a kiss on the top of my head. Though I didn't, I pretended to feel her lips on my skin.

"JB, the little brother of the sweetest guy in the world," she said. Her smile was two rows of teeth so straight and perfectly white that it resembled nothing else on the farm. She looked at Darren with an abbreviated frown, which we all knew was really an upside-down smile. She traced her lips downward with her fingers. Darren must have shared his promise to our mother that he'd stay for my birthday dinner and cake. "I'm talking about you, Prom Date," she continued, pointing at my older brother.

Mother smiled, though not as wide as Kami, and placed her hand on the shoulder of her older son, feeling a moment she wished to bottle and hold forever.

Every time Kami spoke, I was reminded of her impeccable pronunciation. Her large round eyes were like embers surrounded by a field of snow and her skin the color of chocolate flowing from a fountain under bright lights. Her hair was a sea of endless curls until the last strain rolled perfectly inward as if directed by a gravitational pull, making one wonder if her hair ever ended. She saw my brother's best, and we were all happy it was her, but also jealous that he didn't have enough love to go around. She was a ray of light for the whole farm, and a beacon of hope for our family. She gave us hope that one day the heart he extended to her could reach us as well.

In those long but brief years, Darren and Kami exemplified a type of relationship I had not seen before, and sadly, not since. There was warmth. There was trust. There was a drive to see each other's best before their own, and every conversation anyone heard between them made this explicitly clear. Their bond wasn't only solidified by the curiosity to explore, but by putting into action the values they developed on their own and together. Their relationship, I once heard the professor say, was one of the few examples of how Kent and Dina's vision for Mountainbrook Farm had been fulfilled.

Kami and the boys walked off to the river, and we never saw her again.

7

WHEN WE RETURN TO the gas station, the old man is standing in front of the glass door with his hands on his hips. A noticeably less aggressive posture than earlier. He nods to Malik and looks to the ground, but Malik's eyes are already there.

"I've seen people walk away from their trucks because they couldn't reach the gas station, but you're the first to walk away after filling up."

His words are spoken to the air around us instead of to Malik or me, and I get it. Sometimes it's easier to talk to air, and the energy only slightly lifts when he walks inside. Too much isn't adding up.

Was his nod an apology, I ask myself, not yet willing to ask if I'm trying to create a narrative or understand one. Maybe he saw something in Malik that he hadn't earlier. Maybe he saw something in himself. Maybe he felt what at times is an unavoidable confusion when race enters a situation. Maybe it was an acknowledgment of our own shortcomings. A unified frustration that our country is torn by disease, protest, and racism. Still racism. Or maybe the old man's nod was good riddance to a young man too high on the respect he thinks he deserves but continues to fall short in showing much of it to others. As we pull away from the pump, a small piece of paper flaps under the wiper blade. Malik reaches around the windshield and grabs the paper, scans it, and tosses it on the floor of the truck with a chuckle.

"Is that a receipt? Why was there a receipt on the window?"

Malik doesn't say anything, curving his back outward to stretch his spine. The truck's passenger seat springs are uneven. Another reason why Terri rides there only if she must.

"Huh," Malik says like I awoke him from a deep sleep.

"Huh? What do you mean, 'Huh?'" I retort. "C'mon. What happened back there?"

"I can tell you." His post-stretch body appears a few inches taller. "But I'll start by saying that the one and only Mr. Leroy Roberts would be proud."

"Who?"

"Who Who CaChoo. C'mon, Brown. Mr. Roberts! The, um, the dean? Was he the dean?"

I'm not sure if Malik has asked a question or made a declaration.

"He taught all the boys the ninth-grade Life Skills class."

"I sort of remember. No, I definitely remember Mr. Roberts. Biko's Director of Culture and Community." *It was my favorite title of a class at Biko,* I sarcastically say to myself. "What does this have to do with the store, Malik?"

"You think I did something stupid, don't ya, Brown?"

"No," I answer too quickly, offering no time to consider a question that Malik knows isn't about stupidity.

"It has everything to do with it." His straightened posture elevates his words. "I've seen that man's look on the faces of White men, and a few women, since I was like around eight years old and first entered a room with a cash register." Long seconds pass, possibly stuck like everything else. His voice, the touch of metal on a winter morning, shifts from serious to one possibly mimicking a game show host. "You may refer to these rooms as a store." Malik pushes his hands away like shooing a gnat hovering around his head, but I don't see anything worth swiping at, maybe other than me.

I nod my head, silently thinking about the man's confusing remarks when we returned to the gas station. Too much emotion. Too many judgments. Or is it that we've entered a place with too much truth and not enough room for the casual notions we incorporate to deter and soften its impact. It's all a big misunderstanding.

"I remember around five things from Mr. Roberts's class," Malik says. "The first was that no White people came to it. Mr. Roberts said it was because there was no testing, but he also once said that some people don't really think it's an important class. I didn't think much about that."

I vaguely remember in one of my first years when Mr. Roberts announced a new course he'd teach for every ninth-grade boy with the purpose of establishing positive relationships. That we should all visit and observe. I remember thinking that, much like the class itself, it was a comical suggestion. What could I learn from him? Over the years, I forgot about it.

Malik goes quiet, possibly in deep thought about his old teacher. Possibly realizing that leaving town with me may not have been a better route than what his yesterday otherwise had in store.

"You're sometimes terrible at telling a story, Malik. What in the darn world are they?"

"Oh, you's want to know," Malik says, matter-of-factly.

I shake my head from side to side, possibly closing my eyes for a few seconds.

"The second was the whole code switch, ya know, the talking between White people and Black people. You remember that? It was all the jaunt in middle school."

"Yeah, I remember the code switch phase, but I never thought it was to help kids understand how to talk and present themselves between White and Black people, Malik. I thought it was to help students transition between talking with their peers and talking with adults."

Theatrically, he lowers his chin and, using two fingers, he pushes his chin to face me. His eyebrows rise into his forehead. "At Biko, what's the difference?"

I want to push back, out of instinct, really, but what would I push back on? That his comment makes me feel uncomfortable? Up and down head movements. No predators. No prey. No victims. No antagonist. Everyone is safe. It's all one big misunderstanding.

Nodding my head now feels more like an instinctual device than a comforting notion, so I continue, thinking I've figured it out. The check engine light blinks several times and Malik and I slam the dash at the same time, our White and Black hands converging. Same moment. Same angle. Part of me wants to laugh, and maybe he wants to laugh, and maybe neither of us wants to laugh, and maybe there's absolutely nothing funny to laugh about. When I see the shades of our skin land together, I close my eyes for the slightest of seconds. A momentary lapse of reason. The predators are everywhere. Everyone is someone else's prey. There's always room for more victims. The antagonists are quietly, and then not so quietly, among us. None of us are safe. I retrieve my left arm from dangling out the window and push my thumb into my temples, trying to squeeze the new voice from my mind.

"Brown, I don't know if you's listening, or caring about this, but the third thing was to not sell drugs."

I can't believe he has to ask if I'm listening, though he has every right to. I think about all the years hearing about kids selling drugs. Quick money. Instant recognition. Immediate importance. The pull to have what others wanted, or worse, needed. Arguably one of the most chronic problems in the neighborhoods where my students live, and for the first time I realize how little

I know about it. *How can I focus so deeply on preparing my students for better opportunities with such a limited understanding of their risks?*

"Malik, what are the, the, the um," I say, or rather try to say, stumbling on genuine curiosity.

"Are you trying to ask what drugs are sold on the streets?"

"Yeah, that's what I was trying to ask."

"Just about all weed, shoot, which is now legal in DC."

"Weed," I repeat, as if I've never heard the word before.

"Mr. Roberts's brother was a police officer and he came in and spoke to the class. He told us about the drugs in the city and what bad shit they did to you. But honestly, in ninth grade we already been around tons of people smoking weed. They's mostly just chillin'. It was when the sippin' started that fightin' came. I remember Jamal telling Mr. Roberts's brother, the officer, that his cousin smoked weed to help him sleep to end another day in a place that he wished he wasn't. The whole class heard that before, like a bunch of old men in the barber shop. Mr. Roberts's brother said, in almost the same deep voice as our Mr. Roberts, that there's a lot of gray, but my job is to enforce the law. Everyone just being quiet, looking at the man. He was large. He was Black. He was in a uniform. That all not that common."

The energy behind his words fades with each syllable. Then Malik stops talking. He looks like he's seen a ghost. He turns his head a few times to both sides of his body, possibly looking for something, or to make sure what he's looking for isn't there. Another big exhale. His voice lowers, but more from what sounds like boredom than emphasis. He's not through a question he's committed to answering. He slams his hands on his thighs.

"I remember! The fourth was to not get a gun." He shakes his head a few times.

Instinctively, I prepare to ask if he's okay but resist, afraid of any chance that he'll be honest. *Wait. What if he was standing behind the truck yesterday because he's not okay?* I stiffen up but with far less grace than Malik's posture adjustments. A jolt of something runs through me, like the coffee my body craves but multiplied. It's not excitement. Not self-awareness. Not mindfulness. I shuffle through the emotions Terri uses to define her spiritual presence and intention. It's none of these. Self-consumption? It's not that either, though I'm getting close. Then it becomes clear. Like most things beyond a classroom, I realize how helpless I am.

Malik rattles off a list of reasons that kids get a gun and how he and his classmates had to raise their hands when they heard a reason they personally experienced or knew someone who had. "We all raised our hands, and over the next few minutes, the class was a silent sea of arms going up and down in the air. He told us about all the places we could go for help, but of all the real and at times even helpful points Mr. Roberts made, we all knew nothing was gonna protect any one of us more than having our own gun. Some, but not all of us, also knew we had no greater chance of getting shot than by having one, too."

Malik shakes his head, then nods, thinking to himself as looks out the window for a long moment.

"It's crazy what I remember from his class," he continues, "yours, too, considering I barely passed either. But Mr. Roberts shared this lesson about how creativity can sometimes be life-saving. When he worked in a corner store that was getting robbed, he'd scratch one ear for the owner in the back to call the police or the other ear to grab the gun. Roberts got all quiet when we hit him up with questions about grabbing the gun ear, or maybe that's when I stopped listening. But me, Jamal, and Lewis turned the silent ear scratch game into all kinds of messes in church and class." Malik pauses again and looks down. "I don't even know why I'm telling you this," he almost whispers before turning back to the window. Sadly, neither do I.

The crying wind and the hum of an abused engine form a siren that danger is approaching. The wind that transformed into gray noise hours ago has no more value now than silence. It appears that Malik has finished what's most likely the longest segment of anything he's shared. I shake my head. Part in agreement. Part in solidarity. Part consumed with the notion that his most expansive comments about anything so far have to do with weed and having a gun. Then it strikes me again. I'm not really listening.

This isn't about Malik yammering on about weed and guns. It's a young man reflecting on the important lessons of his teacher. We curve around another bend in the broken rural road as my mind navigates beyond the Biko parking lot, to the housing projects on 33rd Street. Jackie Robinson Park to the left, where under cooler weather, old men play dominoes and checkers while intermittently drinking from brown paper bags. The litter of fast-food packages surrounds their feet. Beyond that, another series of housing projects and then a nicer condo development where, rumor has it, a White couple has purchased.

Until now, I interpreted Mr. Roberts as the school's human mascot. A kind soul with many responsibilities and, to my understanding, no formal job. But he knew something far greater than most of us. That through fate, nature, and design, interwoven into the beauty of his students' communities were endless risks. His teaching was built around preparing our students to overcome them.

While Roberts possibly skipped the complicated, or maybe overly simplistic foundation of teaching pedagogy, he made up for it in practicality and relevance. He met students where they were. He knew the paths that became increasingly difficult to overcome without an education. He knew the considerations that young Black men would take to assume an upper hand, albeit one sometimes misguided by an exchange of short-term safety. Our kids, all kids, crave a sense of purpose. A sense of being something. Of being someone. To have meaning. My students' neighborhoods offered them both the shadow of these needs, and at times, these needs themselves. Roberts knew the false opportunities promising them value. He knew the tactics employed by racists to see young Black men as suspicious, as well as the unfortunate realities that sometimes justified such suspicion. Ultimately, he knew that maybe one more trusting voice giving warning of these dangers could save a few more young Black men from the pitfalls of racism.

The false comfort of distance now has us moving farther from home, where I need to go back to. Every mile offers new excuses. *Which tried and true excuse will I pull off the shelf next? What am I doing here?*

Terri needs space until her Covid goes away. Terri wants a family. I need to write letters, of course. All true. All cover. More masks. But there's something. And time is both the gift that keeps giving and the curse that keeps taking the people I love away. What must happen to heal? The blurriness between denial and acceptance. Why am I so reluctant to start a family with Terri? Why am I so scared of giving her a family that could so painfully break? How can I understand why Darren did what he did? How can I find my brother? A deep plunge awaits, where good people go to understand bad things.

I also need to get away from what feels like a daily dose of the antiracist doctrine Becker throws in our faces. One could think it's the only concept teachers should focus on. Maybe she needs us to. Maybe we need her to. Maybe kids like Malik need her to. It feels like it came out of nowhere. Thinking about how Becker seems less focused on what students learn and more that our instruction isn't what she calls racist. Her need to include the words "for our Black and Brown children" into every sentence and how it eliminates her from ever having a bad idea. How could someone offer another perspective after she says that everything is "for the wellbeing of our Black and Brown children?"

By talking about equity all the time, the topic has become more ceremonial than transformative, and that's where I'm lost. How many times could our teachers and staff say the key buzzwords in one meeting? Who could be more antiracist than the other? Does she feel that our teachers are racist? Does she think I'm racist because I don't continually use the language of an antiracist? *Am I?*

Malik picks a newspaper off the dash, and his face vanishes within its borders. The outside article, now a few inches from my face, has the headline "Winchester Church Refuses Mask Mandate." We're barely three months into the pandemic and there's already a sense of helplessness. Emotional fatigue and anger rarely play well together.

"Hey, Malik, that was four."

"Four what?"

"Four things you remembered. What was the fifth? You said you remember five things."

"Didn't know you was paying attention." The irritation of his calmness is reaching new heights. "Wait, ain't you listening? The fifth was to always get a receipt."

My mind awaits the class bell to ring, but there's no class bell here. No scurry for the door. No watching the slow crawl of the second hand on the clock sloth toward the forty-fifth minute past the hour. It's easy to frame Malik as an exceptional case in complicated dialogue, but I know the opposite is true. Malik, when he's needed to, thrived in communication. So profound at it in some ways, it diverted attention away from what he's maybe trying to hide.

"Wait, wait, wait," Malik says.

New energy, and the thought pops into my head that he'll turn to me and say something like, "Hey, Mr. Brown, I just remembered, everything is okay. Can we go home? Can you drop me back off at my apartment? We're good? It was all one big misunderstanding." I know better by now.

"I actually remember a sixth thing from Mr. Roberts's class."

I must admit that the clarity of Malik's memory surpasses that of any student I've ever met, though he's also the first to essentially install themself in my truck so I could find out.

"On the last day, Mr. Roberts asked us what he should do differently for the following year's students, and Jamal said that he should change the name of the class."

Then silence. Waiting. Not because Malik is trying to hang something beyond my reach. He thinks he's answered me fully.

"To what, Malik?" Again, too much energy. *Scale back the interest. What if he knew that I cared? That I needed to hear this? That I need him to help me?*

"Oh, now you want to know everything, Brown." And before I can blink he says, "Being Black."

"Huh?" I cringe. I know so many words. Why *huh*?

"Jamal thought the class should be called Being Black. Ya know, and when he said it, we all laughed." He inhales a sharp breath. "But after Jamal said that, I remember us looking around at each other. Like we also knew there was absolutely nothing funny about it. It was a pretty accurate title." He turns away, preventing me from seeing him.

I'm curious about what a person's face looks like when they admit such a poignant truth, but I return my attention to the road. Worn out median lines, sections of broken guardrails, and sadness. Lots of sadness.

Sad that at a time when kids on the other side of the city are choosing electives to elevate their understanding of the sciences, math, technology, and humanities, some Black kids need time on mandatory life skills to help them. To help them what? I stumble on words that should be easy to assemble.

I take a long breath, realizing… *What am I realizing? There it is.* Realizing that our Black students had to take a class to increase their chances of staying alive. *There, I said it, though not out loud of course.*

The following minutes pass trying to silently follow Jamal's lead, thinking of appropriate titles for a class I never attended or understood why our students needed to. Until this conversation, it was a class I hadn't remembered existed. I recall walking by the class once and seeing kids eating at their desks. I assumed the class lacked structure. Lacked a curriculum. Lacked metrics to show whether learning happened. Lacked a real teacher.

None of these assumptions were accurate. Malik's reflection on the influence of the class is beyond sufficient evidence. The class wasn't initially built into the schedule, and because appropriate changes weren't made when the class proved to be of value, its timing had to be carved from two of the only flexible areas in our student's day, lunch and recess. How criminal that *those* were the two flexible areas.

I scramble different phrases around in my head, wordsmithing course titles revolving around the theme of being Black when the rules are White. I stir on it, pull at it, make myself remember things I don't want to know are there but need to. I remember Mr. Roberts's brief announcement in one of my first orientations that he was starting the class. He spoke quickly and uncomfortably to the gymnasium full of teachers who fidgeted in the metal folding chairs like students received redirection for doing.

"Malik, I still don't get it. What does Mr. Roberts's class have to do with the store?"

"Aren't you listening? When I asked the old man back at the store for a receipt, he said that it wasn't necessary. I told him it was."

I'm void of energy to speak. I'm drained and unsure if it's more to do with the 95 degrees blowing in through the windows or the conversation. I'm sure it takes massive energy to continually explain the challenges of being Black as well, and maybe even more so to White people who've been in your community for fifteen years.

The clock light is too dim to read in the afternoon's brightness, and I have no sense of internal time. We left the station three-quarters full and we're between that and half now, though a leaky tank wouldn't be out of the question.

"We spent like a week on how we feel going into stores, knowing adults are looking at us like we're stealing. And ya know, we made some stupid lists of things to do to prevent some shit. I don't know. C'mon, man!" He scoops the crumpled receipt off the floor and tosses it on the dash.

We're constantly missing each other. When he's interested in his message being heard, I'm trying my hardest to tune him out. When he starts revealing something I want to hear, he retreats. His frustration is everything plus, and the plus, I admit to myself, might just be what I'm bringing to the conversation.

My receipt request is for an expedited return or exchange. Malik needs a receipt as evidence that he's not a thief.

Too many things are broken. Malik can't go in a store without a shop owner thinking he's a potential thief. The shop owner has watched countless kids that look like Malik steal off his shelves. Malik fears that a minor traffic violation can have him on the ground, or possibly shot. The officer knows enough kids that look like Malik carry guns and have to be on guard. It's almost impossible to rationalize reason, pouring fuel on society's ultimate polarity. We all see the same things differently.

"Hey, Brown, there are things that you just can't understand because you're Wh—"

Then I realize that he's not pausing. He's said enough. I think about Mr. Roberts telling Malik and his classmates they wouldn't have visitors. That it might be one of their few classroom experiences without White people, though I'm not completely confident Mr. Roberts really said that. I can't help but think of all the classes I observed to study different instructional techniques and classroom leadership models. I never thought, not once, to observe the one class that would help me understand my students' lives.

What he said isn't wrong. It also shouldn't be offensive, but I take it as such. *That.* That's where the work is. I dive deeper into this mental sphere spanning fifteen years with most of my waking life around young Black people who've given me, instilled in me, graced me, cursed me, captivated me, imprisoned me, and blessed me with lives that I may not have taken the steps to truly understand. Or is it because people who look like me wanted it that way?

The cocktail of heat, wind, dehydration, and truth spin my mind into a farmland decorated hallucination. Semi trucks in the shape of road spirit animals threaten to crush my truck of lies from the side. Hundreds…no, thousands of tiny Black fingers point at me in my mind. Behind them, the sound of laughter. So immersed in the moment's sad humor that some cover their faces with their hands. When one particular young boy removes his hands, I see that he's not laughing at all. He's crying. Crying. Crying because God placed another adult in his path who thought he knew what was best for him instead of really knowing.

With Malik looking out the window, I pick up the half-crumbled receipt and smooth it on the wheel. $2.10 for two cans of soda. A handwritten message bleeds through the computer ink on the other side: *Sorry for not having paper in the register reel. Next time please be more patient. I also lost my cool.*

8

"I'VE SEEN MR. ROBERTS a bunch of times since Biko. Well, not really a bunch, but a few," Malik says, startling me after an hour of silent southbound driving. Lost in our own thoughts along baking backroads.

"Where," I say too quickly, feeling like I'm making up for the past decade of dismissing my colleague as an old man nudging wisdom on tardy students, yet inefficient in tracking detention and permission slips. While other teachers analyzed the merits of their lesson plans, assessments, projects, and reports, Roberts was squishing dozens of students with their faded orange lunch trays into the extra room beside the counselor's office to teach them survival strategies.

"He's come into my uncle's shop."

"What kind of shop?" *Unnecessary eagerness. Too much curiosity. Over analysis. Stop. Keep the train moving. Control what you can control. Maintain focus. Follow directions. Get to simple.* "Were you able to fix Mr. Robert's car?"

Malik smirks.

I know that face. Now too well.

"Of course. We fix everyone's broken everything. Problem is getting peoples to pay for the repairs, so we got a few cars that ain't ours, but for some time they ain't really theirs either, ya know."

Was one of these cars the one he borrowed?

"I stopped working there a month or so ago. Just no business and people be stupid."

I want to correct his grammar *all the time*. Squeeze the flawed usage of plurality from his mouth. Then I realize exactly what I mean. I want him to sound less Black, and I silently curse evil words about myself for knowing that I'm more consumed with the language of Malik's communication than his content.

"So, you lost your job because of slow business?"

"Yeah, something like that." Malik then perks up in his seat. "Wait, did Jamal and Lew tell you something different?" He pauses again, taking a few seconds for mental calculating. "'Cause sometimes those two, and especially Jamal, be talking too much." Edge in his voice.

"They care about you." And as the words leave my lips, I realize this is probably not my winning message. Nonetheless, I follow up, "That's something."

"Yeah, maybe. But they also too proud or something."

"What's that mean? Too proud or something?" But I know what it means. Jamal is working toward being a teacher. Lewis has a job working at a digital gaming company. They're making something of themselves.

He turns away and looks out the window. "No, they cool." Malik bounces his legs a few times. Jitters maybe. Hard to decipher if he's speaking from a place of jealousy or friendship, and then it's clear. "I mean, who could be a better teacher than Jamal? He cares. And think about how dope new video games could be with Lewis's twisted mind." And then he stops again, caught between deep thought and intention. His mouth hangs open like someone took away a map to the next word. "Let me take that back," he says. His eyes never appear to leave the road straight ahead.

I vaguely remember years ago, kids calling Lewis *Twist* because kids are cruel and shameless, and because God made part of Lewis's body twisted. I assume because of this, Malik realizes another description is more appropriate.

"Yo, Brown, like for years we'd play these games and Lew would sit there saying things like, 'Oh, it'd be cool if the dragon could breathe fire instead of just stepping on people,' or 'I want to see my man talk shit after he runs fifty into the end zone,' and we'd be like, 'Yo, that would be cool.' But really, these games were more graphically advanced than anything we coulda imagined. Only Lew was thinking about how they could be better."

Malik gets quiet, and from the side of my eyes I can see a faint smile. We pass a series of trailers with a large Fuck Biden flag lofted by enough of a breeze to read every letter. It's the first time I've thought of the former vice president's candidacy in a few days.

"I remember Jamal and me looking at each other when we was all digging out on his grandmother's couch, playing games all day. Secretly laughing, ya know, like our inside joke, and Lew yelling and ripping into us, smack-talking like, 'I'm dominating you two boys' and then it be over and you'd have to wait like ten minutes for him to get on his coat and shoes. I remember thinking how, how, how it just ain't right that he had to, ya know, like bounce from a place where he was so strong and dominant and then in real life, if we was being chased and came across a small fence, everything could be over."

Malik has a pattern of saying these profound statements and stopping, creating endless frustration and if nothing else, a coarse listening experience. It's as if he's also talking to himself. I might be doing the same. But without Malik the only story here is mine, and that's one I'm looking for distance from.

"I'm proud of them two. And maybe one day they'll be…" Malik turns back out the window.

Why couldn't he finish that sentence?

"Maybe they're proud of you too," I say, having no idea if it's true. Maybe a slight sense that it's not.

"Shit, proud of me? You paying attention, Brown? Me, I'm sitting here in the middle of nowhere with you, because, because… Ah, forget it."

Wait, you've got to finish that. Because of what? Why can't I say this out loud? What's the worst thing he can say?

"Tell me about your uncle, Malik?" No, this isn't what I want to ask. Well, I mean it is, but not right now. We were so close.

Malik breathes deeply and leans back in the seat. "My Unca, he asked so many questions, it was like he was thinking out loud. I loved being around him." There's care in his voice and he starts to sound like a storyteller.

"Loved? Is he no longer with us?" Eyes straight into the road. *If he doesn't want to talk, that's fine. Was this who Jamal and Lewis spoke about?*

"No. Covid. Wiped him out last month. He was 54." Malik slides one hand's palm down over the other palm that's face up. It takes a moment, but I think it's a wiping signal. "He was good at showing people he understood them. I admired that. He had people trusting him, and, and heck, they should've. I think one of the intrestin'…"

And I tune out here, silently repeating what I heard. *"In-trest-en,"* and after several misused seconds I trail back to Malik's words.

"…parts about my Unca was watching him when people rolled in. They'd be all hot and up about this and that. Fuming. He'd take the rag out his back pocket. He had this smooth way of wiping his hands real slow. Around each finger, up and down, like he was trying to slow everything down. Like he was hypnotizing a brotha. Fold that rag right back up and slide it into his back pocket. Smooth as it came out. Then look up at ya, like he made you watch him do that. In those twenty seconds or so, every angry brotha got some calmer too. Man, it's crazy that we also talking about Mr. Roberts, because my uncle was like that. He'd calm 'em down. His last words to everyone when they all mad was, 'We gonna fix it.'" Malik interlocks his fingers and moves them from his lap to behind his head. His arms guard his head like a railing and he spreads his elbows outward.

The only action I know to show my support is nodding my head, and this must be getting old for Malik by now. I don't have answers, or at least good ones for him. He found the wrong person to escape with, though I'm not even sure that's what's happening. Or have I found someone to escape with? Either way, I should stop saying, "But what do I know?" It's evident.

"Darn it," and I pop my hands off the wheel in what probably looks like the most pathetic finger explosion. Sadly, the gesture neither reinforces my message or my confidence to expand on it. I quickly return my hands to the wheel. "Like maybe, when you're in a store, you already got emotions flowing, senses spiking, what not, you know what I mean? If you know you're not doing anything wrong, you gotta project that, right? Let anyone's racist or thieving thoughts stay in their head and don't put that burden on yourself."

Malik stares at me for a moment, his expression inscrutable. He drapes his hoodie over the searing metal of the window's frame, then leans out with armpits on the hoodie. Elbows slicing the wind. Chin resting on his hands. I silently repeat back what I said, and I'm sure a few teachers at Biko would say this suggestion is racist, or racially insensitive, or ultimately reflective of how culturally blind I am.

And in the following seconds, I ponder how many stores Malik should have to navigate before we're satisfied his mental skin has thickened with immunity to people's judgment? *Nice, JB. Malik and everyone like him should ignore racism. Yeah, I get it, it's that they're sensitive. It's on them.* No, I argue to no one in particular. *That's not what I meant. It's not what I meant. JB, it's what you said. Yes, it is what you meant.* And this silent and private conversation dies an invisible death, or does it?

I debate the legitimacy of criticism from people not here, who haven't said these things, and others who just aren't real. But I also see it. That's how Becker's morning meetings went. Cooper would say what felt to me like a benign comment, like our male students should pull up their pants when they enter the school. Another teacher would say that's racially insensitive because some families cannot afford a belt.

When Cooper asked about our response to students wearing their pants low and singing offensive lyrics to popular songs in the hallways, another teacher branded his comment racist. "The music reflects our students' daily struggles and fears," she said. Cooper threw his hands up in the air and walked out of the room. At the doorway, he turned around and said, "Fine, then we shouldn't have a rule that offensive language isn't allowed at school. And while we're at it, we should also get rid of the rule about how pants should be worn because maybe that's also racist. C'mon." Cooper walked back in the room and grabbed a donut out of the box. "Is this racist too?" he said, holding the donut up and then ripping a bite off with his teeth before exiting for good. As his footsteps faded down the hallway, I thought about how our students' learning journey was continually advanced because of Cooper's teaching, but at what cost for being in a constant state of not winning adults over.

Around the bend of the mountain road, I mouth the topics we've taken into yet another valley: Receipt. Uncle. Jamal and Lewis. Blinking truck light. Malik is Black. Darren. The farm. I need to write letters to graduates. Covid has killed almost 200,000 in this country alone. I'm White. Kami. Tomorrow's meeting with Becker. Social justice protests consume the streets of American cities. We're in the middle of nowhere and don't know where we're going. A slight tension releases. It's all on the table, or is it?

I'm still not sure if the shooting yesterday morning had anything to do with him. He's still on his connection between Mr. Roberts and his uncle. Too nervous to ask, but the feeling isn't nervousness. *How the hell did I become a teacher?* I calculate what to ask. *What can I know? What did Jamal and Lewis tell me?*

"I'm sorry about your uncle, Malik. He sounded like a unique man." *Unique. What does that mean? Another bad word selection.* "Wait, if it's your uncle's shop, why did you stop working there?"

Malik slowly slides himself back inside the window before responding. "This other guy, Antwon. He really owned the shop. My uncle and Antwon were in the Navy together. For supposedly two best friends, they didn't talk much in the shop. The whole place was covered in Desert Storm posters. At around 5:00 p.m., their friends would come over and they'd sit behind the shop and laugh and talk about their tours, politics, kids, what not. Like I mentioned before, I swept the garage slowly just so I could listen. It was like they never heard a sound from the four-lane highway some fifty feet away."

I run through his story to see if he answered my question. No, I think. His ability to offer just enough in his responses has satisfied people questioning him since middle school. Responding thoughtfully but without direct answers has kept Malik's ideas, decisions, and intent at bay for many, and now me, again.

He taps his legs, which he's done a few times before he starts talking. "Yeah, well, ya see what happened was, Antwon thought I was doing some shit that I wasn't, but I couldn't tell him. The ways I tried to tell him didn't work either. Another chapter of me trying to do the right thing backfiring." He makes a gun figure with his hands and turns his pointer finger to his forehead and dramatically blows himself backward, limping his arms to this side. His teeth glisten from the side of my eye, but

I'm frozen in my thoughts, realizing how little control I have over the situation.

"You shouldn't joke like that, and I mean it."

It's as angry as Malik has heard me, or maybe anyone has heard me, in a long time. Maybe years. Definitely years. His signature smirk flattens across his face. Safe to say that I still struggle with kids who always joke. Always trying to get teachers off their game. I loathed the disruptions.

Malik, Asia, William, Jeremiah. Stop. This list could literally scroll down the valley, but I've never thought to group these students, the constant jokers. Always pushing. Routinely distracting. All with above average intelligence and academic ability when it served them. Dumb as cardboard or appearing to be so when it didn't.

Despite graduating, they all struggled along the way. And we pushed. We pushed. We pushed and we pushed. The extra help. The reading tutors. The blond-haired graduate student math assistants. The this and the that and everything to help them graduate while not addressing the real reasons for their behaviors. Never the root cause. No big push for counseling or therapy. Students acting out because the structure we established for them wasn't working. They didn't need us to tell them in new ways to conform to our help. They needed us to adapt to their needs. They hadn't developed the skills to communicate that they were in trouble. Nor had the people beside them been trained to truly listen. And now, trying to understand Malik enough to grasp why he's in trouble, I'm clueless.

"So, Antwon fired you from the shop?" All I can do is shake my head and then I see my mistake. Malik must interpret my shaking head as dissatisfaction with the story instead of my real intent, to clearly understand it. I abruptly retreat. "Wait, I'm getting this together. Why did he fire you?"

"Now's not the time, Mr. Brown."

I pause, searching anywhere my eyes and mind will take me for a North Star, but I only see a blank map, and all I can think to say is, "Call me, JB. I don't want to be Mr. anything right now. I'm not your teacher."

A slight intensity releases. The rush to force pieces together evaporates. Malik's calmness deflates another situation that he doesn't want, and for the first time, I willingly join him here.

"I was at UDC for what my uncle called a hot minute, but it was really a semester and a half. Ms. Robinson said it was the right move for me."

An overtold tale. Ms. Robinson directed everyone to the city's community college who wasn't ready for a four-year program, or would never be, or who never were. I wonder what would be different if her job was to guide students to the best place to advance their lives instead of only to college. Sure, the city's community college was a pathway to higher education for the academically reluctant, but did every Biko student denied access everywhere else need to go there? Even students who explicitly preferred careers in a trade and would have instantly benefited from a program aligned to their interests were discouraged from pursuing paths suited to their goals. Biko had a story to tell, and come hell or high water, 100 percent college attendance was at its core. But she embraced genuine care for our students every day and our students knew it.

"What happened there?"

"Does it matter?"

Don't I have the right to ask? He said he was there for a hot minute. It's clear that it didn't work out. Do I need his grades or attendance records?

"Mr. Roberts," I say softly, repeating his name again and again for no other reason than to pass the time.

"Put it this way, of all the risks Mr. Roberts tried to prepare us for, I chose confirmation the hard way. I'm just lucky to…

Hey, what you gonna do about this flashing light? You cool with this, Brown?"

Stupid light. Just as he's about to tell me what led him here or led him to where he was before he was here, or before that, he stops. There's no sense in trying to make these connections. Another flashing light. Mechanics throughout the capital region wiped their brows, baffled by it. Other than a few trips to New Hampshire, I rarely traveled. Over time, the check engine light evolved into something more than a light. Something bigger than a visual alarm that one of the metal devices, hoses, or plugs under the dented hood required attention. It became a signal that despite the masks I hid behind that whispered I'm okay, the dashboard light reminded me that I wasn't.

No matter how many times I looked away from the danger, this little light reminded me that it was still there. Always close. He's not really gone. He can still get you. At the last shop in southern Maryland, the mechanic celebrated his discovery. It wasn't a mechanical issue, but faulty wiring. So amused in his diagnosis that he called in the shophand to announce his finding. The light wasn't a true indicator of engine malfunction, and as he was about to pull the wiring to the dash warning codes I surprised him, and myself, and told him to leave it. Malik's hand moves toward the stereo power button.

"You mind?"

I tell him I don't care, trying to remember the last time I heard anything from the speakers. A few seconds later, the beautiful sounds of bluegrass instruments fill the air and Malik starts bobbing his head, though I'm not sure if he's mocking the music's rhythm or enjoying it.

The music is Terri's, the album she was given at the bluegrass festival we attended every autumn. She'd volunteer in the health tent for a few hours each morning, tending to minor bruises, twisted ankles, and the occasional bad acid trip. When the music started, it was like it flowed through her arms, legs, and hips. I loved watching her swirl and spin in colorful sundresses that matched the surrounding foliage. Even as scheduled sex around Terri's ovulation pushed me to find her anything but sexy, I never lost the feeling I had when I watched her dance. Terri spoke about the excitement of live instruments playing in sync. The energy of being in motion beside total strangers. How a life naturally and perfectly absent of perfection now had something close. Her words were poetry.

At first, I was envious Terri had found a place where she could be what and who she wanted, but after a few hours of the music, I wanted to grab my sneakers and run far away. Once, I went for a long run during the set of the Infamous Stringdusters, her favorite band playing now. When I'd finally returned, she asked if I wanted to be here with her. That she'd been waiting for me. I didn't respond.

For Terri, the music had a message and drowned the truck's unpleasurable sounds and discomfort. I could fix the popped springs in her chair. I could fix the A/C. I could clean it. I could paint it. But then I'd erase the only thing that connected me to my family.

The music moves through solos of different instruments that had I not seen them performed live, I wouldn't believe were possible on a guitar, mandolin, standup bass, dobro, and fiddle. I return my gaze to the road and the music takes over the truck, the landscape, our minds. Alongside each song's exceptionally crafted instrumentals, lyrics tell the sad tales of hope, love, and second chances.

When the old CD starts to excessively skip, Malik throw's a "c'mon" into the air before it stops altogether, and again the only sound is of the rushing, static, overbearing heat wind. I find Terri's streaming channel on my phone, and "Charleston Girl" by Tyler Childers barely plays before Malik joins the beat, moving his hands in sync. The lyrics about relationships subdued by hard Appalachia living feel like a soundtrack to the string of trailer park homes we pass. Each verse fills the void of our not listening to each other with someone else's despair and loss.

Malik yells over the wind and music. "Ya know, Black folks be rappin' about all this stuff."

Buffalo Springfield's "For What It's Worth" comes on next. Within the first guitar string pluck of the song's intro, Malik says he may have heard this before, but he's not sure. The song's poetic description of revolutionary hopefulness in the late sixties feels oddly relevant. A tempestuous gust of wind blows the newspaper off the dash, but Malik captures and comically tries to tame it, and although his effort is a brutal attempt at entertainment, the frustration deepens. After several seconds, he yells, "Fuck this!" and slams the crumpled mess onto his lap. The page facing upward is littered with stories about the pandemic and protests.

Two John Prine songs play in sequence as the Shenandoah Mountains hug the road. The professor played this music from a cassette radio no bigger than a cereal box outside his trailer for years. To me, it sounded like the songs were more talking than singing, and I figure Malik is hearing them for the first time, but I can't be sure. It's been more than twenty years since the words to "Hello in There" punched my heart for the first time, and when the song is over, Malik nods his head and whispers to himself, "I guess it doesn't matter." Sometimes the last thing you want to be is a timeless song.

While the music offers a small respite from ourselves, it's not enough. Malik gives the newspaper another go, and I remind myself that folding a large newspaper with the wind blowing is ten times more cumbersome than at the kitchen counter, but he brings little of his own grace to the exercise. After several seconds of paper wrestling, he tosses the crumpled mess on the dash. The unevenness of the folds makes me anxious, and I contemplate pulling over to realign the crease.

Malik cups his fingers under the glove box latch, but I notice his venture too late. As his arm retreats, a rambunctious pile of maps, old parking tickets, truck repair receipts, and sticky notes erupt from the space. Even if double the size, one would think the glove box incapable of holding such an onslaught. It's where papers go to die.

He gives me a sideways look. Part smirk. The mess is on the level of a practical joke, and I knew this would happen. Ironically, of all the things happening, this is the only one I could have prevented had he asked. I never open the glove box.

"Oooookaaay," he entertainingly over pronounces. "Little head's up that you stored aisle five of Staples in the glove box would've helped here, Brown." He takes it in, possibly wondering what to pick up first. It's the first thing to lighten the mood, or maybe my mood. After some shuffling, his white tennis shoes emerge from the rubble. He picks up the *Appalachian Trail Through-Hikers Guidebook* and thumbs through a few of the well-worn pages. "Isn't this the trail we were on yesterday in Harpers Ferry?"

I don't answer. Multiple signs clearly marked it as such. He knows this.

"What is this book? Oh wait, I get it. I think." He flips through several more pages, possibly reading words on each page, or no words at all. "For such a long walk in the woods, it looks like you can't as much piss without knowing where you are. I thought people did this to, ya know, not really get lost but to be away. Kind of hard to feel like you're entering the great unknown with this, huh?"

I thought that book was long gone. I could have sworn I intentionally left it somewhere. Anywhere.

I reply, "You're right, the guidebook helps hikers know where the trail goes, and—"

He interrupts, "Doesn't that dumb patch of dirt in the middle of the trees do that?"

I bail on calling him a wiseass and instead explain that the path is interconnected by thousands of other trails. As the Appalachian Trail, and the interest to complete it grew in popularity, there arose a need to help hikers find water or plan food stops in towns or at rural gas stations like the ones we've come across. For a lot of through-hikers, the detailed maps offer ideas for mailing packages ahead and information where the next cabins are to sleep. It's hard to take on a challenge like that without this information.

Malik flips through the book at a pace for which I assume comprehending anything is as unlikely as hiking the trail without the book. He calls out the names of different cabins, notable rivers, towns, and lookouts. "What was that like? Did you find crazy people? Where did you sleep? This ain't the kind of thing Black people do, Brown. Who does this? Nah, really?"

"You being serious?"

"Yeah, I really am. Who wants to do this?"

"I don't know." I just want the conversation to go away. Or maybe it's the people having it, but I know what I really want to go away. The fact that the question stumps me. *Who wants to do this?* My mind swirls, recognizing it may be the most straightforward question anyone can ask about almost anything, and how far away my mind has ever been from considering it. "People looking for adventure, I guess. Others, I don't know. Maybe they're looking to be in nature."

Malik looks at me like I'm making this up.

"Some are at a transition in their lives. I don't know. I'm spitballing' here. Ya know."

"Why'd you do it? Which was it? Adventure, nature, transition, spitballing? Everyone's looking for something, huh, Brown?"

To the degree I felt stumped seconds earlier, it's multiplied. Maybe if I handled the more general questions better he'd never get to the more personal ones. Maybe I'll tell him he's not being serious. *What do I say?* It's not worth throwing into the pot that my list was incomplete. Sure, I'd hear stories of hikers' quests of triumph, conquering nature, and certainly the overdose of those looking to be at one with it. The graduates, the tree huggers, the divorcées, the Jesus seekers, and trust funders, only to name a few. Sure, some stories came out early and often within and beside the cabins and tent sites of northern Georgia. Beside fires surrounded by fresh legs, clarity, and optimism. In the first few hundred miles, hiking stories of grandeur were as commonplace as blisters.

But not everyone had a "Eureka!" moment, and as the trail climbed north, I learned it was the stories not shared that would often frighten you the most. The trail gave everyone a place to hide. A place so untamed and unconventional that anyone could feel they fit in. A place that touches, tugs, and at times pounds your body and mind with the simplicity of an earlier time, yet never far from the information now pouring from modern accessories like phones, watches, and tablets. It used to only be about the next water source and food stop. Back then, that was the value of the book.

What I found was that some weren't looking for a place at all. They were searching for themselves. But Malik's right, or mostly so. We're all looking for something. For me, the Appalachian Trail was more than a winding path some twenty-five hundred miles through the heart of the hemisphere's eastern wilderness. It was a place where those in search could find and, those like me who were running away, could hide.

"Ya know, Brown, the truck offers some competition for which is worse, but this book smells like shit." He moves it from his lap to his face several times to confirm, or maybe just to make stupid faces as his nose barely touches the ripped and stained book cover. "And if there's such a thing as a book chiropractor, this one needs it. Terrible literary posture."

He can't stop, I tell myself. Malik looks through the pages at a slower speed. As he does, I remember the book more and more. The planning. The maps. The notepad where I counted miles and anticipated footsteps from Springer Mountain in Georgia northward. Every night my arms and head stretched beyond my sleeping bag, my headlamp shining into its pages, exploring the next day's terrain. Keeping distant the thoughts that the next day would cast within me. Falling asleep to the same question. *Is the trail bringing me closer to or farther away from where I wanted to go?*

A streak of nervousness runs over me like a Smokey Mountain stream after rainfall. Malik is flipping back and forth between two pages. *What is he doing? Worse. What is he thinking? What is he concluding? He can't possibly connect these pieces. There are not enough clues in his hand. I'm almost certain of that.* Then he runs his thumb along the smoothness of both pages. *Maybe there are.* Everything tightens. *I need to get that book away from him.*

"So, Brown, all the pages are well worn until this section." He flips between the pages, now slower. Looking for something, his pointer finger tracing letters from the page's valley to its summit. "Ah, got it. It feels like the book wasn't even opened after this point. The pages weren't even bent. Did you end in Damascus?"

I'm certain what page he's talking about. The moment seems overwhelmingly clear, like needing to go to the bridge, and it's striking to feel something with conviction. Outside the classroom, purpose was not in my DNA. Beyond the presence of rows of desks and their surrounding boundaries, intention was often an illusion.

Having studied the map back at the station, I knew the east–west routes through the mountains. The north–south corridors were memorized. I turn off the route heading to Skyline Drive for the second time and onto Route 340 to Waynesboro. Then Interstate 81 South.

Malik is right. The things I don't say are what others sometimes hear the loudest. *Everything ended in Damascus.*

9

WHILE THE SIGNAL IS good enough to stream music in the rural valleys of southwestern Virginia, its strength was far weaker for the millions of kids, and mostly poor Black ones, who needed to rely on it when their education went virtual several months ago. At 6:30 a.m. on Monday, March 9th, like thousands of mornings before, I reached my fingers under the truck's door handle and suddenly stopped. School closed yesterday.

I sat with my shoes on at the stool in our kitchen despite promising Terri I'd remove them at the door. Becker's last email at approximately 9:15 the previous evening instructed Biko's staff to stay home and await further instructions. By the time I saw it around midnight, nearly forty teachers had replied to her PS question at the bottom, which I only noticed when trying to piece together the responses. The first was from Tonia Howard. Who else would it be? She asked us to pray for our students and families. After that, teachers from every grade level responded with notes like "absolutely," "sure thing," and "say when and where." Only then did I scroll to the bottom of Becker's note. Underneath her initials, she asked for volunteers to hand out the few dozen laptops we had, and more as they arrived. School was going virtual for at least the next week.

I estimated several dozen people handing out several dozen computers was enough so I was surprised by her email that morning asking me personally if I saw her request for volunteers. Sometimes the pace of our largely Teach for America trained workforce moved at exceptional speeds. Becker and many of the other young women spoke quickly and with undeniable conviction. At times, I envied the efficiency of their communication. Other times it felt like professional theater. I refreshed my inbox several times, catching Becker's follow-up email to me around 9:00 a.m. and then another to the entire staff. Gillespie, a middle school math teacher was first this time, thanking Becker for her leadership and plan. It felt like a game of who could respond fastest. Who could prove they were the most aware and responsive. Or maybe that's what leadership was. It had almost become an insult within our teacher community to say that you'd think something over.

Becker's latest note instructed teachers to prepare packets for the next week and requested volunteers to distribute bagged lunches as so many of our kids relied on the school for the day's first two meals. I did not know what to do. I had no packets. I didn't teach with packets.

Terri worked every day that week and when she came home, it was like she had seen twelve hours of ghosts. On one of those first nights, Terri sat on the stool next to me in the kitchen and asked, "Are your students okay, JB? What about their families?"

I turned my head but didn't answer her, realizing I hadn't thought of them, or specifically, that I wasn't thinking of them that moment. My only thought was how the disruption affected me, but I was fairly certain she couldn't deduce this from the silence. She could have asked me anything, and she chose the most appropriate question possible. Minutes passed, and I still didn't know.

"We're seeing so many people from Southeast. I've been thinking about your students' families all day. I remember a dozen or so years ago when I joined you for the school hikes. I knew some of your students then. I can't believe the racial disparity of the virus's victims and severity. Have you heard anything, JB?"

In my prolonged silence, I realized I didn't even have the courage to pretend. To say something profound, albeit untrue. When things got tough. Were essential. Moments when action was required. That's when I froze. The opposite of the people I was raised beside, now lived beside, and worked beside. It wasn't a feeling of comfort, but something close to a relief that I believed my life of inaction never resulted in the suffering of another person. That lie I held close.

On Sunday, Rolando wrote directly to every teacher, though most of the message may have been a cut-and-paste, to share a link for a new virtual platform, Zoom, that we'd use for teaching. Per Becker's next email, the expectation was that we were to "replicate a high quality in-person instructional experience through it." Like many teachers, I had never used my computer for anything beyond email, PowerPoints, and the internet.

I took my laptop and sat on the couch beside Terri, the outsides of our thighs almost touching, and I recited what I understood. Biko teachers were being asked to transfer all our lessons and instructional plans and student work areas to a virtual platform, to hand out meals, and to distribute laptops. A new email from Howard then popped up on the screen.

> Dear Biko Family,
> I know many of you truly understand the horror
> facing our children and their families right now.
> To those of you who do not see this devastation
> up close, thank you for continuing to serve.
> I debated writing this because I'm sure my
> colleagues understand the severity of what's
> happening. But, if any of you feel that Principal
> Becker's request for assistance handing out
> meals, distributing computers, going 100
> percent remote with school, and other things

we're doing is too much, PLEASE question if this
is the right work for you. As teachers, we may
not have been born leaders, but the Lord has
made us so. This is the time to lead.
T. Howard

I read the email several times. Free of spelling and grammatical errors, which I often overlooked in correspondence from math teachers. Why an email like this? Then I realized. It could have been written to me.

New nervousness ran through me. Not only for my students and their families who were being found by this new disease quickly and without reservation, but for the weak bond between my comfort and routine. The only bright spot was in the last line of Becker's midnight all-staff email stating if any teacher needed anything from their classrooms, they would be allowed to access the building on Monday between 8:00 and noon. I was in the parking lot at 6:50 that morning, as I always was.

Walking up to the building, I saw only a few cars in the gravel lot. Gillespie's Prius, Rolando's minivan, and Becker's black SUV. I placed my hand above my eyes and spotted LaVar through the window of the locked door.

He pulled down the black bandana covering his mouth and screamed through the glass, "Sorry, JB, the whole school's getting professionally cleaned and I can't open the doors until the cleaning crews leave at eight."

When I walked back to my truck, I heard, "Mr. Brown. Mr. Brown." I saw a child but was unsure if that's who called me, so I kept walking. The boy called again, and I changed course. Within a few feet of the ten-foot-tall, black-painted iron bars, I deciphered the voice as Jaden Holmes, one of my forty-five eighth graders. Few kids offered a two-in-one smile and look of confusion. For a kid believing he has all the answers, his innocence whispered through the metal bars.

"What's happening, Mr. Brown? Why isn't school open? Will the cafeteria be open?"

I contemplated pushing my head against the bars like he was, at first to possibly make Jaden feel comforted, though unsure how that would. Then, because I felt the same way. Helpless and uninformed, though based on his question, more informed than he was.

How was Jaden here, not knowing what's happening? Then I wondered how was I, knowing what's happening? Where was his mask? Did he also need something to connect himself to what he knew? His routine? The pattern of habit that his fourteen years of life depended on? Was there not someone at home following the news? The emails and texts? Was it someone he knew but didn't trust? Did he need confirmation? Did he need someone else to say it's true? That everything is changing, at least temporarily, or maybe indefinitely?

I stared at his eyes as they bounced around the building, roof, left side wall, right side wall, back to the roof, font door, back to me. Jaden's eyes worked like this in class, pushing the adults around him to determine he was off task. At times, I was one of them. Holding the cold bars, I wondered how many of us asked him what he was thinking. What he was feeling. Was he using his eyes to guide himself somewhere, or to something? Was he learning?

What happens to the kids whose families don't check email? How could he take his backpack and walk his normal path, not second-guessing his actions when no one in his neighborhood was doing the same? Jaden looked up as a flock of geese flew over our heads toward the Anacostia River. In class I rarely understood what Jaden was thinking. But here. Now. Finally, our minds found familiar ground.

Where are they going?

"What are we gonna do?"

A few seconds after his question, I looked back at the sky. The flock adopted a migratory pattern with two arms shaped like an arrow, one side longer than the other. I hoped that Jaden would again look there too. That he'd find his answer there. Afraid to tell him that I didn't know. That I'm asking the same question. Instead of squeezing my temples through the bars like he did, I put my other hand on the cold metal. In all these years, it was the first time I truly recognized the tall gate.

Stepping backward, possibly for the first time, I noticed how the bars wrapped completely around the entire school property. It felt like one of us was behind bars. Then I realized we were. But which one? What was the purpose? To keep us safe from them or them safe from us? Thinking about our kids' reference to Biko as a prison. Limited choices and bad food. Jaden continued to lean his head through the gap. The skin on the sides of his face pushed back with an ounce of comic relief.

"Mr. Brown, my grandmother told me to go to school today, but I don't think there is school. Today? Right?"

How could his grandmother not know this? The whole world knows this. As the seconds passed, I thought about how there's never been such an abundance of information and such overwhelming distrust of it. It took years after I started teaching History to learn why the Black community would have valid reasons for being tragically concerned about a new virus, and even more so when a vaccine would be presented to cure it.

"I don't know what's gonna happen, Jaden. I know that you have to be safe and be careful."

I looked past Jaden, wondering what that meant to him, though unable to look into his eyes to possibly find out. He turned his head upward, but not necessarily at me. His eyes said, "What do you know about me being safe?" Nonverbal communication from teenage boys was sometimes the most legible. I contemplated leaving but stayed, gripping the bars, thinking about Jaden in the first week of class this year.

He was out of his seat and pacing the back of the class. His seventh-grade teachers shared this practice with the request that if he wasn't disrupting other students, his new teachers accept or at least tolerate him continuing the strategy. Another poorly worded student accommodation by a caring adult. His classmates were used to Jaden's pacing. It had taken me many unfortunate years to understand not only the validity of the request but its necessity. Jaden started this practice in the school year's first weeks, and oddly I was comforted by his movement in the back of the room as he stood in front of maps and posters on the back wall. While his behavior would cause disruption while seated, he was practically invisible to his classmates as he silently paced the floor behind their backs.

On one occasion when the other students were exiting the room, I watched him slowly spinning a globe on the radiator in the back corner. His wide eyes revealed the sight of something new, possibly something profound. When I walked to the back, he stood there as if he hadn't heard the bell ring, appearing oblivious to the transition and sound of two hundred moving desks and footsteps on the floor above.

"You okay, Jaden?"

He extended his hands over the globe, feeling the raised contour of Asia's Ural Mountains under his fingertips. "This is it, Mr. Brown," he softly said, his voice a blend of sincerity and innocence. Sadly, also a hint of embarrassment. "Ya know, us?"

I thought of how years ago I would've told Jaden to put down the globe and carry on. To assure him, while knowing it might be untrue, that he already knew the answer to his question. That reflection was evidence enough that I wasn't prepared to teach. Now I could only admit that I knew more, albeit not much, and while on most days it wasn't enough, I'd like to think that on that day it was. He may have never seen a globe before, or maybe one not so close with maps beside him to compare. He held it in his hands, his fingertips gripping the earth like a mythical giant, as many young boys felt the first time they held a globe in their hands.

"This is really us?" he repeated. "All of us?"

Our eyes locked in an intense moment of silence until a distraction in the hallway urged me to redirect my attention.

"Man, I thought it'd be different." His words were distinct, quiet, and trailing with what I thought was amazement, but then maybe disappointment.

I was about to ask him why, or to request he tell me more, but the footsteps of new students arriving reminded me of my responsibility to greet them at the door. I told Jaden he needed to get to his next class, and I patted him on the shoulder before I turned around. A few steps away, I heard him again but louder.

"Wait, Mr. Brown. From out there, this is what they see?" His eyes alternated between the sky beyond the window, me, and the globe in his hands. Even more quietly than before. "Everything we do happens here?"

And while I'm sure it was intended as a question, I made my mind hear it as a statement and turned around to catch up to the flow of students entering the room, a necessary step to confirm my knowledge of a new roster of student names. But there it was. The moment. The connection. Whether it was insight or a greater level of confusion, I may never know. But it was these small and subtle moments of wonder and discovery that made the work fascinating. I walked away from Jaden as he stood on the other side of the gate, and I thought about that conversation.

Yeah, everything we do happens here.

With the eighth graders, I started the course with three dice on each table. Eighteen numbers were written on the board.

Though it changed every year, next to each number was a brief description.

1. A girl in rural India
2. A boy in a wealthy family in Chicago
3. Born with a rare but treatable illness in England
4. Born with a rare but treatable illness in Bangladesh
5. From a religious minority group in Saudi Arabia

A student at each table rolled the dice and connected their number to the number on the board. I'd ask them to briefly share what they thought their life would be like if they lived with this identity. It was an opportunity to hear their voices, understand the intellectual currency they're arriving with. Their level of curiosity.

There were no rules, correct or incorrect answers, or second chances. It was more important to get them talking academically in the first class than to set classroom expectations or seating arrangements. A rare opportunity to pay as much attention to redirecting students interrupting as those interrupted. To see how their minds worked and listen to what they know about our world. Few knew much.

Regrettably, or maybe strategically, I never listed the options of being born a Black child in Southeast Washington, DC or a White one on the other end of the city. Even when the oversight crossed my mind, I told myself the activity could become too personal. Why create any chance of shame or embarrassment, I thought, though I was mistaken as to whose feelings I aimed to protect.

Sometimes the activity built the energy I sought in fifteen minutes. Other times it took almost the full class period. Once or twice, not at all. As learners, the World Geography content was perfect for eighth graders. They were attentive and had seen enough of life to think they understood it. Biko's seventh-grade teachers made sure that every year their students' understanding of the branches of government and early American experience were sharper than the year before. Beyond that, not so much.

I tried to capture several themes in that first class. Our world is an overwhelming place, and we'll learn about the smallest amount of what one can learn in a course like this. If we did it right, you'll enter high school with more questions than answers. I was never certain if any of those themes had been apparent, but on day one I knew the most important message was clear. On this big and evolving planet, the circumstances and conditions you were born into are all too often the most critical factors deciding your fate. So much depended on our initial circumstances, and though not my own words, I told my students that those circumstances were often a cosmic role of the dice.

When LaVar finally let me into the building, I hop-skipped past the office and up the steps. Room 217, my safe place. I flipped the light switch and immediately the desk phone rang. Not an optimal sign for someone in search of hiding. It was Rolando, and after some banter about our families but mostly his two sons, he assured me that all the eighth graders and then he corrected himself, the ones who picked them up, had computers and were ready for remote learning. That I needed to be as well.

"They should know how to log on and access the school's virtual platform," he confirmed, though it wasn't confirmation I sought. It didn't dawn on me to ask how many students had picked up laptops. "Talk soon, JB," were his last words.

I wondered how many calls to teachers he had already completed and how many he still needed to make.

At home the next day, I logged onto the first class at 8:25 a.m., a full twenty minutes before its start. I followed Rolando's cheat sheet and nervously rechecked my appearance in the tiny box I occupied on the screen. Thirty minutes later, I received his text:

> You have 7 students
> to be let into your class.
> Everything cool, JB?

Then the phone rang. "How is that possible? I'm here," I assured Rolando.

He told me I had to "let them in."

I clicked frantically, finally finding the screen's "admit participants" icon, and new square-inch boxes popped onto my screen and shrunk to smaller boxes. I exhaled with relief. I was with my students again. I couldn't have known how much I missed them until seeing their faces, or at least the faces of a few of them. Some students I had never seen up close. Then I looked closer, and the pictures weren't of them. One picture was a dragon, one a cash sign, three cars, a basketball player, several boxes with the default illustration of a student, and finally, a few live visuals. The pictures of large Black men with no shirts wearing sideways hats startled me. I quickly called Rolando back.

"JB, what's up?"

"The pics of cars and athletes. What is that?"

"Students' screenshots."

I didn't need Rolando. I needed a remote teaching tutorial for dummies. A third of the students' screen names were their first and last, while another third straddled the bizarre with the infuriating. Pooping, Soul Sista, Dopeness, DunkOnYou, Lazer, Suga Momma, Dragon Butt Cheese. The final third of my class wasn't even there.

I quickly redialed. "How do I take attendance if they don't have their names and I can't identify them with their screenshot?"

"We're working on it, JB." More than a hint of irritation in his voice. "Anything else? My inbox is blowing up with similar questions." Then, after my confounded pause, "You're just gonna have to figure it out," he concluded.

Trying to sound calm, I addressed my class for the first time online. "Hi, I mean, hey…I mean, can you hear me?"

I repeated this several times while turning up the volume.

Then a message from Sierra Cartel appeared in the chat box. "Mr. Brown your muted."

I squeezed my teeth, wanting to respond to her grammar, but the moment called for more practical action. *How do I unmute myself?*

One week. Then it was two weeks. Three weeks. Then spring break came and went. When I next returned to the Biko campus in April, the perennials had sprouted in the front garden. More and more weeks of confusion followed. I resorted to lengthening the United States unit because it was the only thing I could think of. Yes, my students had laptops, or most of them anyway, but they needed content I could manage. For the first time in years, I considered distributing the pile of brand new textbooks, still wondering why they continued to be purchased despite annual threats of looming budget cuts.

Reminders about the volume, mute controls, and the school mandate to have their full names represented on screen became a daily management routine. The orchestration to limit the group sound for questions to be heard and then again for answers to be shared was constant. I was routinely looking up, then down, back up, figuring out who was talking, then down, then up to listen. At some point in that first week, a student called out the text picture they'd sent around. Only then did it become evident that while I was teaching, they were also in the separate worlds of their phones, texts, and other social media chats.

Staff emails were overwhelmingly about our students being on live camera instead of having a screen picture. Both sides were animated and valid. Naturally, nobody asked me, nor did I volunteer my position in the event I had one. I asked students about the mandate in each class after the spring break, and their responses exposed how wide the gap was between my knowledge of students' lives in my class and beyond it.

Tonia Dosket kept the camera off because the electrical outlet was beside the kitchen table where people constantly walked by. Anaya Aspen to preserve a weak internet signal also used by her brother and sisters. Raven Winters sat on the bathtub rim, in front of the shower curtain, her laptop balanced on the toilet cover because the best signal was in the family bathroom. "It's the only quiet place in our home," she whispered. Raven tried to use her apartment's laundry room where the signal was its sharpest, but some high school kids doing the same thing told her to leave. Alonso Ashwin was in the car with his mother in a library parking lot in Prince George's County, just outside the city.

I was experiencing almost none of the challenges my students were. It was like I was living in a different world than them. Then it hit me. Maybe I always have been. When I looked back up at the screen, more than half the boxes were gone. Within seconds, the few remaining flashed into absence and only when the last student disappeared did I realize class ended minutes earlier. Seven of my twenty-three students for the next class were waiting for me in another virtual classroom.

Considering the circumstances, in the weeks that followed I was amazed at what my colleagues were accomplishing. There was a boldness in their work. In their discussion. In my listening to their discussion. It started with leadership.

Becker requested an afternoon teacher debrief from 3:00-3:30 daily, and the stories were bleak. A teacher shared how one of her students kept having smoke blown in his face by someone off-camera. Another teacher spoke about insistent background yelling. This seemed more prevalent with the younger students, who were more likely to have siblings and adults closer to them. Cooper sent me a text about an overweight half-naked woman walking back and forth behind one of his students. I didn't respond, thinking how he might not be the model I sought, but that afternoon I was surprised when Becker shared that Cooper had the highest online attendance rate in the school.

Only then did it dawn on me that our leadership, and rightfully so, were tracking attendance. The technology was also there to observe classes. And then the biggest shocker. If nearly all the teachers were experiencing only around sixty to seventy percent attendance, where were the other students?

Parallel mountain ranges, the Blue Ridge to the east and the Allegheny to the west, squeeze in as we head farther south through the Shenandoah Valley. A heady combination of heat and bluegrass has lulled Malik to sleep, so he misses the sign for Charlottesville along Route 64 East and the pit in my gut returns. The sign defines not only where we are but where I wasn't with my tenth graders. Unlike my experience with the eighth graders, my challenges with the older students didn't start with the pandemic—they started in the first class.

We were barely into double-digit minutes when Jasmine Fulton raised her hand. "Mr. Brown, at the end of eighth grade, I thought we's, ya know, us as a country was moving all post-racial. You even said it yourself. Obama was a great president. We all felt like things were changing, really changing. And, um, just two weeks ago we got the Ku Klux Klan back marching. This time without their robes, through Charlottesville. That's just some hundred miles from here, right?"

This wasn't a question. Jasmine's reference to events from a week before were still as fresh as the scent of the Anacostia River that drifted through the open window. The Unite the Right gathering was the largest and most violent public assembly of White supremacy in decades. Spurred, they claimed, to protest the removal of a Confederate statue from a park. First it was carrying tiki torches and spewing racist chants. It turned deadly the following day when clashes between civil rights groups and White supremacists ended tragically for one young woman when a driver rammed his car into a crowd of counter-protesters. My students were following all of it.

I knew these students. I was looking forward to class with them again. For better or worse, they knew me, and I'd like to think their last impression of the eighth grade was positive. But that was gone. They arrived having fully executed the core lesson from two years earlier. Be aware of what's happening in the world around you. I wasn't ready for it. And I certainly wasn't prepared for the wave of emotion that accompanied it.

It took some processing to infer if Jasmine's comment was directed at the disgust at what's happening, or that my teaching led them to believe events like that wouldn't happen again.

Nia Lodge was the first student to back Jasmine up. "Hell yeah, preach it, sista."

Keera Townson spread her arms with her palms down, flapping her hands downward with the intention to quiet her peers. It worked. "I thought you said groups like the Klan were essentially dead. That they were essentially in hiding. That they had numbers so low, they were practically a frat for old racists."

A couple of quieter but affirming "yeahs" and "awhaws" followed. I felt a distinct and orderly relief when I saw an arm raised neatly to my side, then joy that it belonged to Marian Taner. I told Keera I liked how she spread her wings to quiet the class, and she nodded her head, unsure if it was an act worthy of praise.

"How did we leave your class feeling like we making it somewhere, that we really becoming more equal, but you didn't tell us straight on this stuff?" Marian said, not completely sure if her remark was a question.

The truth was I didn't know. How could I tell them I had no insight or clue that a widespread community of scattered White supremacist pockets was sprouting around the country? That those quietly present groups were being rejuvenated by often cryptic, though sometimes quite clear messages from the president. Klan protests in the past few decades had received news coverage with barely enough members to fill the screen. What our students and everyone in the country was seeing now was different. According to my current and former students, my teaching had led them to believe that it wouldn't be.

I encouraged every remark. I thanked students for caring deeply. I responded to the others with equally affirming gestures and responses. In between, I interjected comments of agreement. I felt like I was swimming upstream to ensure the conversation was one of agreement, but it didn't feel that way. I would have called my demeanor one of solidarity, but I couldn't say that my students collectively shared this assessment.

Even recognizing the validity of their points, everything happening was everything I should have hoped for as an educator. My students were engaged. Intellectually present. Caring and using their skills to appropriately connect critical thinking and emotion to their understanding. They were aware of enough on which they spoke to speak knowledgeably. What more could they possibly do to show their teacher that they'd showed up to learn? Then Cedric Warner raised his hand, and in hindsight, my several years of experience should have warned me that what he'd say may not align with the general consensus, but there we were.

"How is what they're doing different from when Black folk say they'll only shop in Black owned stores and eat at Black owned restaurants? If we can be pro-Black, why are they racist if they're pro-White?"

In the milliseconds before what followed, I thought about meeting Cedric when he was in seventh grade. Exceptional posture for a short kid with a belly that would grow wider than his height rose over the years to follow. Glasses that rarely held their position on his face. I liked him, as I did most of the kids who were bullied and teased. The socially awkward. I didn't understand him well, nor his home life. Gwen called him an Uncle Tom, but many of their classmates didn't understand the reference. Cedric did, but just shrugged his shoulders. Possibly another missed teaching opportunity. Though he sometimes interjected provocative comments to what should be the recognized safe intellectual boundaries of our class, he avoided conflict of all shapes and sizes beyond it. Maybe that's what bonded us.

I lowered my head, reconsidering that a deeper representation of multiple perspectives was what this class needed. While Cedric's comment held fragments of truth, it also felt disconnected, and his sentiment was met with instant rage.

Cedric turned sideways in his chair, expecting a degree of respect that even the most offensive could expect on the first day of school. For several minutes, I redirected the classmates who were now yelling at him.

When things seemed to calm down, he stoked the fire he lit, and one he should have been allowed to, when he calmly raised his voice. "No, really, someone explain to me the difference. I'll listen."

There was a dash of quietness, which turned into a welcomed silence.

I then extended my arms outward at a ninety-degree angle, palms upward, and titled my head. "Can someone respectfully answer Cedric's question?"

Janice Copeland, who everyone knew would just say what she wanted to say if she felt like it, leaned back with her arms fully raised into the air. Her large gold hoop earrings leaned against the outside of her shoulder. "Mr. Brown. What don't you see? Them marching in robes when their ancestors who did the same burned crosses and hung Black people from trees. That's threatening to me. To Black people. It's hurtful. It's prejudice. I can't see that and feel like we're moving forward as a country in the right direction. Can you?"

The frustration toward Cedric was predictable. The storm of frustration directed toward me was not. Wasn't my responsibility to protect Cedric's right to an independent thought? Not everyone felt so. In hindsight, that was when I realized my failure to distinguish between an independent thought that was not racist from one that was.

A strange and even rarer silence for this group of students followed her question.

In hindsight, it may have been the moment where they needed their teacher most. The one they trusted to explain the complexities of this chaotic situation with grace, compassion, and clarity. Instead, I doubled down on their silence and struggled to get through the lesson plan. I stumbled on my words while distributing the syllabus and particularly when I asked what words we thought of in response to the term, *American History*. Sure, most of the kids slowly went along with the lesson, but not to the standards I set, and I never rebounded from that first class.

Whether real or imagined or evident or solely within my own mind, this was when the shift started. It wasn't the type of silence where people talk about pins dropping. It was the type of silence where you could hear a lot if you were truly listening. There was a shift in the way students saw me after that first class. A shift in the way they thought of me. A shift on whether I was possibly one of the White people they'd been warned about.

I spent the nights of those first days of the school year retelling myself every twist and turn of that particular class. Asking myself if I was teaching my students about the America

I wanted them and me to live in instead of the one we really did. It was the first time I felt my students did not see me as someone explaining history, but rather as someone who all too often was defending it.

10

WE EXIT ONTO JEB Stuart Highway, ironically named after the Confederate general who was for a brief time one of John Brown's captors. We pass the Dixie Petro gas station on our left with flashing signs for lotto tickets and 24-hour service, and I wonder about who would possibly come here in the middle of the night.

After several turns around the mountains, a yellow-then-red traffic light welcomes us to the downtown strip of stores. A bank and feed shop mirror each other behind their own relatively small parking lots. Then a strip of two-story buildings for several blocks behind an overly wide sidewalk. The usual economic residents of a rural Appalachia town. Café, liquor store, general store, medical clinic, and a post office operate between scattered vacated windows. Across from the Holston General Store, a few people sit and stroll unmasked in the town square. Several benches, unoccupied picnic tables, and informative signs line the park's perimeter. Almost nothing is recognizable. Malik appears fully awake, looking from side to side with a calm uneasiness.

For a place I've thought about so much, all of my immediate impressions feel foreign. Everything about being here feels wrong. We enter the Damascus Regional Campground and pass the Large Group and Boy Scout sections, then a sign that directs campers to choose a spot and return to the self-registration kiosk to submit an envelope with the fee, site number, and vehicle information. Despite every site being empty, I circle the loop twice before pulling into a spot.

"You sure this spot gonna work for you?" Malik asks sarcastically. He surveys the several-acre plot devoid of humans. "'Cause we can find another spot if you want." His smile transforms into frustration. He opens the creaky door and something in the engine jumps, making a sound like a short burst of air releasing before settling. It's a new sound. Malik walks up to the hood, places his hand on it and immediately pulls back. "Running hot!"

Suddenly, all I can think about is Terri. I shouldn't be so far away from her after telling her that I'd be within a few hours of home—easily seven hours away at this point. I did this to myself. My soaking wet shirt gives my skin a momentary chill.

Malik kicks a pinecone into the air, and I walk aimlessly around the site eager to kick something as well, but there's nothing. We stand some fifteen feet apart. Not close enough to look each other in the eyes. Not far enough away to miss the subtlety of our expressions. For the first time, it's increasingly clear neither of us is sure why we're here, yet feeling, somehow, it's also no accident. That we're both running from something, and even more strangely, that we may need each other to find out what it is.

Nonsense, I tell myself. *Nonsense. This is simply an accident. The culmination of a series of miscalculated judgments.* I whisper "fuck" several times, realizing how foreign it is to hear a cuss word from my mouth. Maybe the frustration is pouring through. With a full tank of gas and credit card, I could continue to hide.

"Why are we here, JB?" Malik's voice is calm and direct, and it's the first time he's called me by my name, and in the slightest of metrics, I'm relieved by it. He sits on a large tree trunk beside the truck. A ray of late afternoon sunlight reaches the ground through the trees. I pop the tailgate and slide onto its well-worn grooves. After he realizes I've not answered, nor appear to have one to share, he breaks a branch and flicks small twigs like a lunch table field goal. Neither of us have a script for what's next.

"I never knew my father, Mr. Brown, I mean, JB." He makes a sound between a chuckle and choking, then quickly gathers his composure.

I realize again he's moving us forward when I'm stuck.

"For the most part, I grew up with my grandmother and uncle. My mother, well…" He pauses, possibly considering how to explain what happened next, or whether he should. "She, she, um… Well, from everything I heard, my mother was amazing. Smart, and I mean Doreena Deans-level smart, Mr. Brown."

I'm caught off guard, jogged by a familiar name. Then I remember Dory, one of the brightest scholars in Malik's grade. Dory was quiet, a persuasive writer, and an avid reader. She excelled in class but limited herself beyond it. She was one of the students you could pair a struggling peer with effortlessly, and I probably grouped her with Malik several times. I imagine a tall Dory with her glasses and neatly flattened hair sitting next to a short Malik with his wide smile and attention span of a gerbil. A thirteen-year-old boy.

My attention has swayed from Malik at the least opportune time, again. Hoping my body hasn't sent an unintended message.

Malik faces the ground, but he positions his eyes to the uppermost parts of their sockets, possibly gauging whether I'm listening. He digs his elbows into his knees and rests his head on his hands. "She was one of the first Black women in Howard Medical School." He straightens his back. "My mom was beautiful, and she was going to be a Black doctor." A smile whips across his face between the words *beautiful* and *Black*. "She'd just finished medical school over the summer and was ready to start her, her ah, I'm not sure what you call it, but it's when you become a practice doctor or something." He extends his hands to different places on the log, realizing that he cannot lean back. *Continually amazed at the frequency of his movement.*

"I'm not sure if I remember this with my eyes or I've recreated it after hearing the story so many times from my uncle, but even before med school, she'd take me to daycare and then lift the mattress she slept on in our room and lean it against the wall. She'd pull a square fold out table from under my crib and study all day. Barely getting up to pee." He shakes his head. "Can you imagine." Malik's voice trails, offering no clue whether his story is taking off or landing.

Above us, the pine needles start to move, followed by the first breeze in days. At maybe the same moment, we both notice a small doe in the next camp spot some fifty feet away. She sizes us up, rotates her ears in every direction, lifts and lowers her front leg, and returns to graze.

"My mother lost everything, or should I say, had everything taken away. Her doctor job, her relationships."

I use his pause to assess the list. *Everything.*

"But worst of all, they took her spirit. Everything changed. It's like I can't move on. Every time I fail at something, I realize how a little is taken away. Then I think of her and how almost everything was taken away, and she didn't even fail like I am."

I think about how the log Malik sits atop is uncomfortable and he shifts his sitting bones forward and backward to find the right spot. What can he be talking about? This isn't what I expected. I was waiting for what felt like more standard fare. *I got into it with the wrong group of guys,* or *at first, I was moving a little bit,* or *he insisted that I had as much time as I needed to repay.* Not this. I'm not sure where to direct my attention. The doe is gone, and nowhere on the several-acre lot offers clues as to where she is.

"I've never really accomplished anything, right," Malik continues. "I've never really failed at anything because I've never really tried, ya know. Maybe part of me is afraid of having things taken away. Like she did."

His ability to find calmness amid the pain is extraordinary, and after several days of looking at each other, for the first time I stare right into Malik. Caringly, but still distant. Caught between feeling grateful and burdened that he's sharing more about his life.

What's holding him back? What's holding me back?

Albeit a shallow journey, my extended life experience suddenly offers me a level of insight. The more we share we need help, the greater chance we'll be let down by each other. Suddenly, this becomes my mission. Position neither of us to share or need more so we're not let down by the other. I breathe deeply, confusing this illusion for clarity. The feeling lasts several seconds before I see the mirror. Again. Then the masks.

Malik lifts his feet off the ground, trying to balance himself on the log. Balance. What Terri talks about, and within the cloud of Malik's trauma that needs me to be present, I can't stop my mind from wandering to her. To our first and last argument several years ago.

It was days before I paid the invoice for our second round of fertility treatments. I stared shockingly into the treatment brochure. Emotionally numb by the process, I walked through our 700 square feet of home, stopping short of reaching Terri sitting on the couch. I wanted to look at her. Tell her that we'd be okay. That I could be her family, but I did neither. Somehow, unintentionally or otherwise, we did not speak for several nights. Then she stood in the doorway as I attempted to move between the apartment's two rooms. In hindsight, it was one of the most powerful moments of our life together.

She lifted her hand. "JB, I'd say that we need to talk, but actually, I need you to listen." She was gentle in her assertiveness.

I took a few steps back, and though I knew the landscape of our apartment well, I briefly turned to assess my options.

Before lowering her hand, Terri bent in her fingers as if forming a fist, but then it looked like something more frightening. Like the shape of a flower bulb wilting in the hot sun, unable to grow without its essential needs.

I stared into her face, marveling at how she used to bend her cheeks when thinking deeply and it never caused a wrinkle. Now, the lines under her eyes and beside her nose were prominent. Strangely, even more beautiful.

"I love you," she said, then she moved her head from side to side. "I love you, JB, but you've turned yourself off. Maybe not everywhere, and from what I can tell, certainly not in your work. Ya know, your teaching, but with me. You've turned the most powerful element we've each ever been given, off."

I stood silent and motionless, with my mouth open like a confused child. Spiritually stunted. Wondering, yet overly clear, what she was talking about. Terri walked a few feet and then stopped, and I thought of how I always made noise when I moved but her movements were silent like an owl in flight. When she turned back toward me, she held a hand over her heart and placed her other hand on top of the fingers upon her chest. She pushed her lower lip into her top lip. I followed every movement on her face.

"Your heart, JB. Your heart."

I wanted to bring my hand to my heart, but nothing moved, not even inside me. I wondered how scared I've become of losing something I love so much again.

She leaned lightly against the wall. "Life isn't about figuring out how to avoid. It's about how to safely engage. And dare I say it, JB, to even engage to help someone when it's not safe. Not to wonder what I'm feeling, but to ask. To help the person who needs it most when they need it. To feel something powerful in being there for someone. To know you made a difference."

As gracefully as she'd arrived in the doorway, she spun on the heels of her socks and walked out of the room.

We did not speak until several days later, when we were driving home from the annual bluegrass festival. Two medical volunteers called out at the last minute, and Terri accepted one and a half of the extra shifts. The week before, she'd spent her two days off volunteering at the children's nonprofit medical clinic not far from Biko. Instead of listening to the music while she worked, I took two long runs.

On the drive back home through the mountains, I heard Terri humming. Her eyes were closed but not sleeping closed. I figured after two days in the medical tent and the rest of the time dancing, she'd prefer silence. She'd be tired.

Her humming lasted awhile until she seemed startled, as if snapping out of a trance. "Oh, we're still in the mountains. So beautiful. Can you find a spot to pull over, JB?"

I pulled into an overlook. Endless fields of lush life under the slowly setting sun to the west. Her head swiveled several times, and I felt like she absorbed more of the area's beauty in seconds than I could in days.

"I was momentarily overcome with sadness that I'd awake to the highway, or worse, be close to home. How do you feel, JB?"

It was a beautiful sentiment, though I insecurely wondered if it held tones of insult. Her question was full of an unwelcome brightness. I may have not answered, or possibly I'd grunted the sound one makes when they piece together "I don't know" into one short, barely recognizable phrase. Her vibrant smile faded, but it wasn't gone, and I appreciated her ability to not fully let go, as possibly I had.

After a few minutes I asked what she was humming and Terri shared it was an old hymn her father sang when she was a child. Unable to remember the actual words, she repeated the simple line that soon felt like a hypnotic prayer. Again and again, she sang,

> Life is people.
> Life is people.

Terri turned to me with a feeling of peace and harmony, and something else. Something, possibly more profound. "JB, remember several years ago we went to the Kennedy Center for the free symphonic concert? Remember when the cellos transitioned from their solos and created their long, trance-like sound? Thundering through space. Vibrant and thick, yet gentle like a small wave breaking before a mountain lake's shore."

Her words added immeasurable life to the scene she depicted. Yet, when those cellists played, I was transported to Kami playing on the bluff between our home and the farm.

Seeing me speechless, or maybe in thought, she asked again. "Do you remember, JB?"

I told her I did. Never had I heard her speak with such vivid and graphic description. I nodded my head and our eyes locked as they had throughout the concert. Terri extended her hand and I placed mine inside hers. I gripped her bony knuckles, feeling radiant life.

She placed our hands on my chest, offered a subtle smile, and whispered to me through her blinking eyes, "Yeah, you. Flawed, scarred, and scared, I'll take on this mystery with you."

Long seconds of eternity passed. With it love and forgiveness and the thought that like she'd said, in my stained world of masks, I could still find myself. Be something.

"Find that sound, JB. You got it? Now, together, just this once."

Life is people.
Life is people.

Malik is looking around the campsite in almost the same way the deer did minutes earlier. Eyes in search of what's needed to live and the threats that risk it. But unlike the doe, his eyes say something else. How did we get here? Why are we here? What do we need to do to leave? If this inclination is accurate, then for the first time, we're almost definitely on the same page.

"What happened, Malik? Where is your mother?"

He lowers his head in a way that casts doubt as to what will follow. An answer, or maybe he'll walk away. If I were him, I'd choose the latter. It looks like his eyes are scanning the ground. Possibly searching for the same pinecone we've alternated kicking. Both of us wondering how we're in a forest with only one pinecone to kick.

"She had everything." And Malik pauses, possibly considering where he's going or to whom he's talking. "Well, almost everything. All the work. All the perseverance. Overcoming all the racism, and here she was." He looks to both sides, arms bent and hands on his hips. "Here," he whispers, or at least I think that's what he says, but he doesn't make sense. Malik shakes his head, "And then so quickly taken away."

I wish there was something to distract us from this moment. But whoever's above has intentionally moved every obstacle, making it clear this is the conversation I need to be part of.

"Here I am, Mr. Brown, a total mess up. Almost twenty-three. Already been in jail. No job. Something in me burns. To understand. To get to the bottom of what took her away. The lies. If I could just go back to the moment where her life was stolen, and, and, and, I don't know. Do it all differently for her, even if I couldn't change the past. Do it again for her. I don't know. Then maybe…."

I say nothing. Do nothing. Intermittently stare at him for a few seconds and look away in search of something to say. To show him that I care, while wondering how true that is.

"The truth is, I'm not a fighter, but I want something. I'm not thinking it's revenge. I don't even know what that means. Actually, it means nothing 'cause I see it almost every day, and you did too. Those fools yesterday morning, shootin' at each other every few days. All they do is revenge, and our asses almost got caught in the middle of it. I just didn't have my radar on enough to know that the wrong people and the wrong cars were together in the wrong place." Malik haphazardly swings at the air off to the side of his body, followed by a more serious right hook into the invisible space where things we can't change still hurt.

Then I realize it may not be invisible.

What Malik doesn't know is that the man in front of him is someone else who's a total mess. Almost 41, married, and unable to give his wife a family. Unable to remember why he loved the woman who's done nothing but extend everything to him. *Burning,* that's the word he used. Burning. Burning to understand why my brother caused us so much pain. Why he tore into our father. Why he kept our mother awake, sleepless and distraught. Why he brutalized the very relationships trying to keep us together. Burning to understand why that river took away what we loved most. Burning to understand how I can convince my wife I am something worth holding onto, even if I don't know why she should. Burning to convince my principal I can be the antiracist teacher she and our students need me and all their teachers to be, even if I just don't know how to do it.

At least Malik is willing to seek these answers. To swing his fists at the demons holding him back. To know what he needs to do, or at least be willing to declare a truth in not knowing. I want to ball my fingers into a fist and, possibly for the first time in my life, swing violently into the air like him. To feel the sensation of aggression. To feel like I can be someone's fight. To let someone know I care enough to risk taking the blows, knowing every fist thrown can bring a greater one returned.

Malik releases his fists and stretches his fingers, then calmly turns back to me. "Here, look at this." Surprisingly, he pulls a wallet out of his back pocket and takes out what appears to be a small paper square. He gently unfolds it, looks at it with squinting eyes, tightens his lips, and turns it around before handing the photo to me.

For a second, our fingers grip different sides of an old glossy photo. The faded white crease borders a young woman kneeling next to a small boy whose smile definitely belongs to the man beside me.

"I was four," he whispers. "She was twenty-six."

Malik's beautiful mother is in a lush green dress, a holiday contrast from the soft red glow of her lipstick. The sleeves reach between her shoulder and elbow. Her knees are perfect round brown balls. She grips Malik's shoulder with her left hand and a diploma in her right. Malik's shorts end between his knees and pudgy calves and a blue T-shirt with the face of Mickey Mouse tightly hugs his small body. Her wide eyes jump from the photo, stealing my attention from her son's adorable smile.

The peculiar angle of the photograph shows an interesting landscape. On Malik's other side is an old brick post at the start of a red metal railing that runs along the extensive arch of the footbridge behind them. Such a profound curve for a bridge covering a low level of water. Tree branches overhang the water's edge. The slow-moving creek behind them reminds me of the Dalmaqua in early fall when the mountain runoff's been tapped.

I slide my fingers along the back of the picture, feeling the flaky edges of the delicate crease before handing it back to Malik. I take a deep breath, partly to show him his gesture means something to me, but mostly because it has. I don't know many twenty-three-year-olds who keep a picture like that in their wallets. I think about how looking at it makes him feel. How hurt he must be.

"What happened?"

As quick as the air settles with my question, Malik responds. "Don't worry about it," sounds like one long word. As he takes another look at the picture, I examine his face now as emotionless as the ground beside us. He folds it back into his wallet and rear pocket.

"We should go."

"Where?" Malik asks.

"I want to show you something, but we'll have to climb."

"A'ight. Funny, 'cause I was looking in that book and reading about the trails around here," he says with a new lightness.

"But first, we need to settle up." I hand Malik a twenty-dollar bill and ask him to walk back to the park entrance to complete the registration ticket and pay for a site. He slowly, and maybe too slowly, takes the bill and walks away.

We can use a break from each other. I walk over to the bushes beyond the campsite, pick up the lone pinecone and toss it back onto our site, and then walk over to kick it, watching it travel half the distance of Malik's kick. Absurdity.

I yell out to Malik, who is some fifty feet away and I think what crosses my face is something resembling a smile. "No need for a receipt."

He spins around. After taking a few steps backward, he tightens his lips and I want to think there's a smile in there, but there might not be. He flips me the middle finger, spins back around, and walks away.

11

DAMASCUS. NOW WHAT? WHAT was I expecting to happen? Alone in the campsite, a spiral of smoke rises in the near distant sky. An intentional burn, I presume, and the small cloud hovers like it did above the candles of my twelfth birthday cake.

Before I could replace the air in my lungs, we heard the first screams. Darren was immediately out the door. Then our mother and father. I walked to the window to look outside and saw Kent, Dina, and the Hungarian doctor, Imre, running over the bluff toward Timmy, who frantically waved his hands. For all the things that went wrong on the farm, screaming about them was uncommon. When I reached the river, it felt like half the farm was there. Timmy high-stepped out of the shallow water, onto the bank.

"Kami went under! She got caught in the current!"

Trevor, Timmy, and Darren were swimming wildly, popping up for air before diving down under again. Within seconds, Walter and the professor hopped into the still frigid waters and did the same. The men wrestled the current, and they soon exited the river on the other side toward an area of downed trees. Beside me on the shore was one other person.

Russell was all but a frozen statue until Kent squeezed his hands into the younger man's shoulders and yelled, "What happened?"

Mass confusion and screaming ensued in all directions. Dina, Imre, and my father entered the water, but my father only after removing his shoes. More yelling, now from both sides of the river while everyone jetted in different directions. I stood still, frozen by the apparent need to act.

Long seconds turned to minutes and then a sound I never heard at the farm pierced the screaming—sirens. They grew louder and multiplied with a slightly different tone, albeit unnecessary as there was no traffic to alert.

Yael, a steady summer farmhand, emerged from the trail. "Dina, help. The sirens are freaking out the cows during milking. Two of them ripped the transfer tubes from the refinery tank. They ran out, knocking the line gate electrical breaker."

Another first. Fear in Dina's face. Caught between her livelihood and the girl she loved, cared for, and promised to keep safe when she convinced Zoya to bring her young daughter to her farm to live, work, and thrive. The cows were now out in the road, scrambling erratically as the rescue vehicles blasted sirens.

"The cows are blocking the ambulance and rescue truck," someone shouted through a megaphone from the other side of the trees.

Zoya pushed through the last blades of the trail's tall grass before it ceded to the river's sandy shore. She was holding my mother's arm. "Kami, Konjo Kami, Kami, my Konjo," she yelled into the sky for anyone to hear. Maybe God.

Years before, Zoya had asked the boys where her Konjo was and Darren said that Kami was his Konjo and Zoya walked over and pinched his cheeks. "I know, my boy," she said. When she walked away, Darren told the boys the term meant "beauty."

Dina called for my father to meet the police and navigate them into our lot as Zoya charged the river. Our mother tried to hold her back, but she squirmed and twisted her small body from my mother's grip. The boys' bodies violently popped up for air and flipped over until their feet disappeared under the river's brown water again and again.

"C'mon, JB," Kent said, pushing me away from the river to follow him as two officers with long poles rushed through the tall grass.

"Which way?" one of the officers yelled to the women.

Dina pointed south in the obvious direction of the current, and the officers ran directly into the river. Within several seconds, Kent and I were blinded by dozens of rotating, flashing lights. Then a new face that would one day be familiar. Kent's older brother, Dale Simonelli.

"Cut the darn sirens and lights for crying out loud, Dale. We have a missing girl in the river, not a fucking circus. It's scaring the animals."

"Your livestock already cost minutes, Kent," Dale barked as he gave a signal to cut the sirens.

"Your sirens cost us those minutes, Dale."

Within the span of seconds and eternity, I peeked at my mother. Her arms were wrapped around the woman whose life would never be the same. Darren emerged from behind the debris of fallen trees on the other side of the river. Kami's arms dangled beneath her shoulders as she was gently held by the person who loved her more than anything in this world. The moment's piercing silence gripped the valley until interrupted by a sound equally as devastating.

"Kami Konjo. Noooooo!" Zoya yelled, falling to her knees. Her brown hands erected into the clear blue sky, occupying the space between our bodies and where no one knows what happens. "Noooooo! No! Noooo!" she cried, each burst more extreme than the one before.

My body, like the hearts beside me, was frozen. Mother and Dina knelt by Zoya's side as she screamed helplessly to the valley.

"Noooooo! Kami. Konjo, come here. Come to your momma." Her arms waved erratically into the unknown picture-perfect blue above us. "Come here now, Konjo. Come here now. Noooooooo."

Trevor and Timmy walked beside Darren as he held Kami's limp body. Timmy uncontrollably sobbed while his brother's face froze in shock. There were no words that day to describe Darren's face. Nearly a dozen hearts of my extended farm family held in the balance between certainty, hope, prayer and nature. Between our past and future. As Zoya implored the heavens, we hung our hearts on the small ripples chaotically dancing along water that was ordinarily still and life-giving. Watching, wondering, already knowing, fearing, waiting. Slowly dying beside and within ourselves with every passing second.

As the scrambling medics approached, Darren slowly lowered Kami's body gently to the ground, using his fingers to tenderly move the wet hair from her face. The medics alternated chest compressions and mouth-to-mouth resuscitation, trying to breathe life into her cold body. Trevor laid on his side next to her, rubbing her icy hands and arms. Timmy ripped off his wet shirt to wipe the mud and soil off the bottom of Kami's calves. Darren gently scooped Kami's black hair out of the dirt beneath her body, cupping her curly strands with two hands like he was handling the most delicate piece of life to ever live. To him, he was.

Additional paramedics crossed the Dalmaqua at its shallowest depth some hundred feet downriver. Trevor and Darren held their arms outward as Kami's long black hair swung back and forth beneath the stretcher. Dina, our mother, and the professor were forced to strengthen their grasp on their friend, their sister, their anchor. Zoya's keening shattered the blue sky. The sun slowly faded away from the farm.

The medics carried the stretcher along the trail path that ended at the No Trespassing sign at the end of the road. A small group of uniformed people crowded around and behind the stretcher, with Darren following, his mouth open like he couldn't breathe. Like this moment wasn't real. Over long and succinct seconds, the stretcher loaded into an ambulance and medics scurried to jump in the small space with Kami. It pulled away and the sirens again filled the air. The professor, Dina, and Zoya drove off behind it in Dina's van. Those who remained watched every light bend around the first and only curve leading away from Mountainbrook Farm, each of us standing in different places within this new valley of evil.

An odd silence fell upon the farm, cleaved by a booming accusation leveled by the last person anyone would expect to hear from other than me. Timmy had his finger pointed across a group of people standing in equal shock. That finger pointed at Russell Burke.

"You just let her drift by you, barely extending a hand to grab her!"

Like those around him, Timmy's body was soaked with brokenness. River water dripped into puddles at everyone's feet. But Timmy also shook with rage. He repeated his claim louder, and I watched Trevor's fist clench. Burke looked confused, and I knew what maybe no one else did. Russell didn't know how to swim.

Then Darren flew through the air and crashed into Burke, sending both bodies to the ground. My brother straddled Russell and unleashed a fury of punches. Blood spurt into the surrounding air as Darren yelled, "Why didn't you save her?"

Dale and Kent got there first to pull Darren off Burke, taking both men hooking their arms under his shoulders to finally do so. Burke raised his body onto one elbow, covering his bloody face with his hands. On the other side of the lot, Kent, Walter, and Trevor continued to hold Darren, and his manic craziness challenged the efforts of the three larger men. Trevor was the only one of us who had seen this side of him. More animal than man. Over time, the rest of us would too.

Two new officers exited a Jeep, and my father greeted the men who identified themselves as county investigators. Shocked, overwhelmed, and scared by my brother, I walked around the other side of my home to watch from a distance. The investigators spoke with Trevor and Timmy as Kent and my father stood by their side. Darren sat at one of the picnic tables as another medic held a bandage to his face. He'd suffered deep cuts as he'd maneuvered through the branches and logs that captured and subsequently drowned Kami.

Around midnight, the final two investigation trucks turned off their mobile industrial light trailers that had lit up the valley since sunset. When the last truck climbed up Herb Ross Road, I made my way to the window and sat atop the same flipped milk crate as the first night in our new home. The valley was completely dark except for the red light on the meat cooler, and I thought back to what Kent had said the day we moved beside the Mountainbrook Farm, when Mother and I first noticed this same red light on the thermostat door outside the cooler. "Ah, I guess something ain't right," were his exact words, and in that moment, there was nothing in the whole world that I wished were less true.

On the kitchen counter, my birthday cake sat untouched. The candles stood in the frosting for weeks until one day it disappeared with no mention about who removed it or where it went. The next morning, between the short amount of time when the young sunrise erases the darkness but hasn't lit the valley, I wandered outside and over the bluff when I realized that everyone else on the farm was also awake. Some sitting on flipped milk crates. Others standing in small groups. The stench of death was everywhere. The valley was an amazing host of colors as the morning approached, and I've never seen such rich violets and blues and oranges in the dusk sky anywhere since. Brief moments when the sky belonged to the day and the chill in the air still belonged to the night. With the right combination of sun, season, and perspective, you could see the dew drops on the eastern sides of the tall grass beside the bluff. With an uncanny sense of concentration, on that morning I stood and watched as the grass gently straightened.

A small flock of birds rocketed from the nearby bushes and I turned, curious about what triggered their abrupt departure. The shrubs moved with greater sway until a body emerged. Darren. He was wearing the same clothes and his legs had horizontal streaks of blood, which I figured were from the endless thorn bushes around the river. He parted the last tall blades of waist-high grass with a biblical, palm-down hand motion. His mouth opened, reminding me of how he looked on the first night in our new home, when we'd stood in front of Mother's painting of the child running. Away.

I said Darren's name into the air, looking at his frozen eyes. I wished I had placed a greeting in front. I wanted to say something else, but I didn't. I repeated his name, a whisper this time, hoping he'd hear and look at me. He was broken.

"Where are you coming from?" I asked. A bold question considering my communication limitations. I looked into his eyes, and for the briefest of seconds, he did the same. I wanted to hug him. I wanted to say I was sorry. I wanted to tell him that being twelve was the worst thing that had ever happened to me. That I wanted to be eleven again. That I hated Mom for making him be at my birthday dinner, even though he didn't want to. If he had been at the river, none of this would have happened. How could he not hate me?

But none of this happened. Instead, we stayed where our feet positioned us. A tractor's engine backfired several fields away, startling the remaining birds in the bushes behind him into flight. Appearing to sprout directly from his body. My eyes followed the last and slowest bird into the sky. When I turned around, Darren was walking away toward the river and nothing in that moment of sad evil could have prepared me for the person Darren would become.

Then another unmistakable sound filled the valley. Dina's van returning down our road. Its distinct low-frequency moan became louder the slower the vehicle moved. They pulled into the lot, and I ran to the bluff to look while remaining unseen. Zoya, Dina, and the professor exited. The professor walked to his trailer where the door had been left open. Dina held Zoya's hand as they took small steps toward Dina's apartment. They stopped partway, and Zoya turned around, followed by her friend. Her sister. Zoya looked toward the river and the pathway where her daughter had taken her final steps.

I watched their bodies rival my motionless state, but that was a false observation. Our states couldn't have been more different. I was hiding from everything with hopes of watching the world pass by and here were two women who took complete control of everything that was capable of being tamed. I squinted to see Zoya's eyes, who a little more than twelve hours earlier was the mother of a thriving, beautiful, smart, and near-perfect human being who was excited for the prom with her neighbor and best friend the following evening. Who was months away from attending college up the road at Dartmouth on an academic scholarship.

Eighteen years of motherhood. Starting within a widespread famine in a homeland she'd found the resources and willpower to leave. A family, culture, and community left behind for the glimmer of hope and safety for her young daughter, then only an infant. A month in a motel room in Concord until she met Dina, and then a fresh life on her new friend's farm. A journey that now left her childless.

For the first time I thought about what it meant to be a parent. To create. To foster. To give. To sacrifice. And then to lose without warning. I thought of my own mother standing there, lost in her friend's grief, not knowing that she'd soon feel the despair of losing her son, albeit slowly and to the disease of anger, violence, and drugs. An unwelcome gulp of air forced its way down my throat. Half of my face felt locked from clenching my teeth, and I intuitively pushed my thumbs into the side of my jaw until it released and several droplets of blood dripped off my chin to the top of my bare foot.

When I looked up, Zoya was exactly where my gaze last held her, but in the moment's distraction, she'd stopped holding her friend's hand. Her hands were by her side. Her mouth, just as I'd seen on my brother's minutes earlier, open and unavailable. A farm harboring constant and dependable sounds now only harvested silence. One of Zoya's knees slightly jolted inward and her body briefly kinked before she collapsed to the ground in a puddle of soft brown arms and legs.

Within seconds, Trevor ran to her side as did Imre, who had just finished repairing the electrical fence alongside the road. They slowly lifted Zoya to her feet as Dina gently wiped the fresh dust from her body. They held her fragile arms and guided her into the Simonelli's apartment where she remained for several weeks.

Summer's heat arrived early over the next few days. The remainder of June and July felt more like the scorching afternoons of August. On a farm, every month has its own narrative, its own identity. The months their own character in the valley's story. I thought of every place with shade as I'm sure others did, but there was no hiding from the heat. No hiding from the shock. The pain. And slowly there was no hiding from what the shock morphed into. Sadness.

The most beautiful and shady place of all was under the large oak on top of the bluff where the metal foldout chair still sat. Where Kami had played her cello for what felt like hours of bliss on warm days under the valley sky. Her music always started softly, playing to the landscape that immediately surrounded us. Soft, low notes reflected the river's slow and deceiving flow. Fuller sounds followed, rising with the hills to the east, building like the mountains above them until her bow cast sounds like the patient roar of a large animal protecting its loved ones. Her cello narrated the light moving through the sky between the towering peaks as its deepest notes hugged the clouds, momentarily preventing sunlight from reaching our fields. I've only heard music like that once since, at a Kennedy Center concert with Terri.

The year before I took my binoculars to the bluff and after spying the farm's animals and license plates of the trucks belonging to its staff, I focused on Kami in her chair. A soft wind elevated the last curls of her hair that hung beyond the chair's back. The slow push and pull of the bow across the large, vibrant strings. I moved the binoculars up her body, for a moment stopping at her bare brown shoulder that gently rotated beside the strap of a dark blue tank top. I watched for long minutes as her face appeared to pray with the music in an invisible motion worthy of stillness, because nothing was still on the farm. Her eyes were locked closed in deep concentration, and I was mesmerized. Her music was a gift to the valley.

Darren became a new person. My brother was returning home at all hours of the night. Rumors reached our parents that their older son was earning an unfavorable reputation in the neighboring towns. Searching out every kid he thought or knew had racist thoughts toward Kami, starting fights with them. Driven by a blind nobility and visible rage, nearly all these fights were unprovoked. Slowly, the rumors of Darren's drug use entered conversations around the farm. Mother cried when he didn't call or return home for days. When he did, his clothes stank of alcohol. His bloodshot eyes held the absence of hope. Our father also retreated, knowing that Darren would no longer listen to him.

One evening, I hid behind the couch when Darren returned after three days as our mother sat with him, tending to his bruised body but unable to offer the same care for the bruises within it. Soon, every time he came home physically damaged, I presumed there was at least one other person in a similar state. Rage never injures just one.

She cried into his shoulder. "I don't want to lose you, Darren," I thought I heard her say in between sobs.

Verbally absent, he extended several deep breaths. Possibly feeling the power of her words. Possibly filling his lungs with fresh farm air after several days awake and high.

That winter, we again encountered Dale Simonelli, who at times would bring Darren home. The following spring, newly promoted Sergeant Simonelli sat our parents down and explained the types of trouble Darren was getting into throughout the county, and most likely, beyond it. Kent's brother called it a courtesy visit, knowing how Kent spoke about Darren and the hardship the family had endured the year before. He told our parents he'd do what he could without bringing the law into it, but that would soon be difficult.

When he left, it was the first and only time I heard our mother curse. "Do something, goddammit!"

Maybe it was to her husband. Maybe it was to everyone else who couldn't hear her except him. I sat on the top steps, unable to see their faces but imagining their words spoken through the crinkles where skin bonds the deepest of hurt and love. I wondered what my father was doing when he heard my mother's plea. What was he thinking? What was he feeling? I thought of Zoya losing her daughter in an instant. Then of my parents, losing their son with a cruel slowness.

"What? What can I do?" I finally heard him say, his voice sullen with regret. With inability. With love. With fear. With cluelessness. Sadly, without hope.

"He's going to hurt someone, or worse, himself," Mother said before crashing backward onto the couch.

Father tried to talk to Darren. In the few attempts I heard, there was more compassion in his voice than at any time I'd heard him speak before. For a man who held his head high on endless fields and farms across the region, he hung his gaze on the ground during those months. There was no insurance policy for this.

The fear our mother nested in her heart spread to my body. When I heard an unfamiliar sound in the house, I felt jittery and wondered if he'd returned. I had seen his violence. I had seen what he could do to another person. I had seen what he did to himself. I wasn't certain he wouldn't hurt me. With every minute of the day I fed this uncertainty, and it grew.

Darren was destroying us bit by bit. When the phone rang, Mother froze at the high possibility of it being the call every parent dreads. My parents rarely spoke. They no longer had anything in common except helping their eldest son. I had become all of an afterthought. The only conversations between them were about Darren or about people trying to help him. More stories about Walter and the professor started to surface. How they were driving up north to retrieve Darren from the county jail where he was routinely retained but never arrested, but Kent's patience was thinning.

My tenth-grade year was the first time Darren was gone for long chunks of time. Timmy learned Darren was living with a group we knew was into trouble and drugs. That spring, my mother asked me to speak in the front room. The last few years had been hell for her. She looked older. Her hair significantly grayer. With open eyes and a slowly closing heart, she was watching her son slowly kill himself, and she felt that nothing she could do would stop it.

"JB, I need to leave." My mother bit her bottom lip. Her eyes were again swollen red.

I didn't know what she meant. I didn't know if she was done talking. Was it a question? A statement? I looked down and thought I saw her hands move outward, but if what I saw was accurate, they retreated just as quickly.

"I'm going to Montreal, and I'm not coming back." Her lips started to shake in rapid snaps. She inverted her hand to slide her thumb under her eye, sending a tear to the rug. My mother then took a step forward and kissed the top of my head, which by that time required her to rise on her toes.

Standing inside the open door of Tessa's truck, my mother slowly turned her head across the landscape of her home, then to the river and back again. I stayed inside with my hands on the wood bar in the middle of the screen door. The faint light of dawn in the sky. She raised her arm from her elbow, smiled, and climbed in. Tessa hit the gas before my mother had even slammed the door. I watched the lights follow the road's bend and I cried, frozen in place for what felt like hours, or a lifetime. My mother was gone.

The spring melt was early. Green grass covered parts of the valley that would normally be buried in snow. Trevor returned to the farm between his Marines boot camp and deployment. It was a warm April morning when a rundown old sedan pulled into the dirty lot and Darren exited the car. I heard Zoya yell his name as she carried mason jars between the Dairy House and Farm Store. Someone, and I never understood who, was still communicating with Darren. I'm not sure how else he would have known Trevor was home. Zoya set down the jars and ran her small legs across the lot. She gripped Darren's frail and upright body in her arms.

Darren's hands shifted as if to complete the hug, but he didn't. His body was mobile but little beyond that, though he found it in himself to lower his head on Zoya's shoulder for a moment. His long, messy hair covered her shoulders. He had grown taller, and as he gently pushed away from her grip, he handed her an envelope. Then he gently wiggled the rest of his body from her grasp and walked toward the car before stopping when he saw Trevor.

"Hey, friend," Trevor quickly pronounced.

Darren nodded, his round cheek bones rising into his eyes.

"Who are they?" Trevor asked, taking a few neutral steps toward Darren.

From inside the car, I heard two of the kids loudly whisper, "Yo, that's Trevor, right?" and "He's a Marine now."

Darren cupped his lips and turned back toward his friend, unable or not sober enough to answer, and he raised his shoulders.

Trevor walked past Darren, stopping about ten feet from the car as quick words and shuffling bodies sounded from within.

"Get on outta here, boys. There's nothing here for you." Trevor's green T-shirt was tucked into his pants, his hands bent on his hips.

The driver's side window lowered and an elbow casually slid out and rested on the sill. "Hey, Trevor. I remember you. We're good if you're good," the thin face said. "We were cool. Nothing's changed, right?" The boy's rotting teeth showed under large lips.

"Na, I got big problems with you being here, and you're gonna leave," Trevor yelled.

There was a pause, and Trevor looked over at the lot as Darren's legs required several steps to fully turn around. I stood beside Timmy and Zoya, and from the corner of my eye, I noticed Walter in front of the Dairy House garage door. Then Kent. I hadn't seen all these people standing in the same place since that day.

Suddenly, the back car door swung open and a body emerged, yelling, "Who the fuck you think you're talking to?" as he slammed the door closed. "There's four of us and one of you, punk-ass bitch."

Before the *tch* sound spewed from the boy's mouth, Trevor whipped forward and pushed the boy backward, and his body snapped around the curve of the vehicle. Trevor slammed his fist into the car's hood, and within seconds, the engine started as another kid dragged his friend into the back seat.

"Tell them to leave, Darren," his old friend demanded.

We all knew Trevor could have told them himself, but he was forcing Darren to make a choice.

The silence was briefly interrupted by one of the ratty-faced kids urging Darren to "forget this War Machine." Darren's feet were locked, torn between the drugs ravaging his life and the man who'd been his gravity and friend since he set foot on Mountainbrook Farm. Before Trevor had left for the Marines and Darren took off, they'd looked similarly matched. Now, Trevor had training and conditioning on his side. Darren had madness.

Darren charged across the dirt toward his friend. I thought Trevor would move, and I later thought maybe he'd let Darren tackle him on purpose. Both men's bodies went flying to the ground, igniting a dust cloud. They rolled over each other a few times, and as they made their way to their feet, they separated and squared off. Kent, Timmy, and the rest of us watched from the side. Not interfering, knowing, or presuming how this would end. Hoping.

Darren rushed forward again and threw a roundhouse fist, but Trevor dodged it. Darren's own momentum pushed him to the ground. My brother repeated this move several times. Suddenly, the car's engine sparked, and the vehicle peeled out of the lot. Darren charged Trevor once more, but instead of dodging, Trevor moved slightly to his side and cut a hook into

Darren's body. My brother spiraled to the ground and laid there for several seconds, hunched over in pain, gasping for breath. No one needed to rescue my brother. Trevor was already doing that.

Darren gathered himself and stood. He put up his fists toward Trevor, wobbled, and lowered them. He swiped his wild hair from his eyes and raised and lowered his chin toward Trevor several times. The Marine stood some twenty feet away with his hands on his hips, able to continue but making it clear that this decision was Darren's.

My brother turned his back to all of us and put his hands on his knees. It may have been a surrender, but it wasn't the small battle Trevor cared about. After a long moment, Darren stood upright and slowly walked up the bluff to Kami's metal chair. The first time I'd seen anyone approach it. He gently glided his hand along its back and then lowered his body to the ground, sitting cross legged beside it. Just as he'd sat when Kami played the cello. My brother lowered his head into his hands. Several minutes later, Trevor crossed the lot with what appeared to be a wet towel and two cans of beer. He sat down a few feet from his friend and remained there for hours. That night, just after Father left for the store, there was a knock on the screen door. With words absent of expression or care, Darren asked to talk with me.

Why did he want to talk to me?

"Let's meet down by the river, JB."

His eyes looked watery as he walked off. Was that from the fight with Trevor hours earlier? Scars crossed his face that looked older and skinnier. I wondered if he was on drugs. Why couldn't we talk in the house or outside? Why meet him several hundred feet away? Fear sprinted through my body. I knew something bad was about to happen. Something bad *was* happening. I didn't move. Couldn't move.

In a few minutes, he was back. "I thought you'd be at the river." No warmth. An edge in his voice. Fear turned to terror. Every part of me sensed it.

"I was a, a, a, afraid to go down there, Darren," I tried to say, or thought I said, or planned to say, though I'm not sure what he heard. On our front porch, we stood several feet from each other.

"You still afraid of ghosts?"

Anger leaked from his eyes. Whatever he'd planned, I think he saw it cast away. He just looked at me. The skin around his eyes started to cave into his face. His brows formed a hard crater in his forehead. His lips rolled inward, and I thought about whether I should run. I thought about whether I was going to be hurt. I thought about whether I was going to die. My eyes darted between his hands and face until I could no longer bear to look at either. I closed my eyes and heard a gasp for air. The kind of quick breath someone makes within a bout of crying, but I didn't want to believe that was true.

"I'm just sick of it all," I heard his powerful and broken voice say. "Everyone I love. I just slam them up against the wall. It doesn't matter that I hate myself for this." His tone softened with each word.

I opened my eyes to find his red and watery eyes locked on my own. "I'm scared, Darren," I found the nerve to say. But I'd meant to say, "I'm scared for you, Darren."

He looked at me with rage, but rage weakened by something. Maybe it was doubt. Maybe it was sadness. I wanted to believe it was love.

"You're scared of the dark, scared of ghosts," he said in a softer voice. He turned to both sides as if looking for something, then placed his hands on his hips and hung his head. "JB, I'm the ghost you should fear the most." He looked down, again, searching. Contemplating.

About what, I wondered.

Suddenly, surprisingly, Darren wrapped his arms around my whole body, gently pushing his bony chin down on top of my curly hair. "Things will be better if I'm not here."

Say it, say it, someone, please say it. Someone please say, "I love you."

He took a step backward. I did the same and closed my eyes. Helpless, or was it hopeless? Helpless to anything that happened next. Helpless to protect myself. Helpless to protect my brother. Hopeless to reverse us ever getting off the exit at Herb Ross Road on that first day. Despite all the love, all the joy, all the friendship, somehow this was the price for all of that, I thought.

Then, on a night without cloud or storm, a deafening thunder ripped through the still sky. When I opened my eyes, Darren was no longer standing in front of me.

12

SOME TWENTY YEARS OF trying to drown these memories and it appears that some of them have learned to swim. When I opened my eyes, Darren was beneath me on his knees, having crashed through the porch's old wood, unfazed that parts of his legs filled a crater lined with piercing splinters.

He slammed his hands into his head and clutched his long hair in his fists. With a thunder that lacked volume, his hopeless words reached the mountaintops. "I want her back," he said softly. "I want her back." Softer. "I want her back," said barely enough to hear.

Then silence.

My legs and everything they held froze. The crossroads of wanting to return the hug he'd given and run away. At first incapable of either. Then a balance shifted toward yearning, wanting to pour love through my grip. To show him that although I didn't know what it meant, I was his brother and that had to mean something.

Darren pulled himself up from the wreckage and took a few steps toward me. Fear replaced the love that seconds before had ripped through my body. I had no reason to trust him, and we both knew this. Confusion soared. He pushed the hair away from his face and extended his hand. The crevice in his forehead showed compassion, or so I wanted to believe. He gripped my shoulder, and I pushed my body toward him, refusing to miss the opportunity again. Squeezing my life into him. His hard biceps pushed into the sides of my cheeks. I felt his chin resting in the same place Kami kissed me a year before. In the back of my mind, or was it my heart, I wondered if I'd ever see him again.

For several years after that night, sightings of Darren were rare. Stories and rumors circulated about him sneaking back in the middle of the night when he knew the professor would be awake after late drives from upstate New York. Midnight visitors to the farm were uncommon and usually cars turned around at our dead end. With my room facing away from the river, every night my eyes followed headlights across my bedroom wall as travelers trundled our valley road toward the river, but on a late fall evening when I was seventeen, a pair of headlights disappeared in the middle of my wall. Someone's lights cut around a half-mile up the road, and I knew it was him.

I rushed my jacket halfway over my body and crept through the shallow early season snow to the southern tip of the knoll in time to hear faint knocks on the professor's door. The light in his trailer was already on. I tried to make out my brother's face in the dim glow from the trailer's windows. Darren's hair had gotten long. His shoulders were wide, but his body looked skinny. Or was it frail?

Each footstep broke the thin line between ice and powder, and I feared I'd be heard. I wondered what Darren would do if he saw me. Would he walk toward me? Hug me? Or would he lower his head in shame and retreat? Darren leaned against the trailer with one foot and placed his head in his hands. The professor wore shorts and an old winter coat. I covered my ears to break the sting of the November night breeze. I couldn't hear their initial discussion, but Professor Farace had a voice that carried.

"Darren, we have choices. Our lives are a collection of decisions."

My brother pushed his body off the wall, and I finally saw his face. He'd heard this before. His high cheek bones were more pronounced, confirming a diminishing health.

Leaning against the large maple, my twitching foot slipped, cracking a twig frozen in the ground. The professor and Darren looked in my direction. *Come out and say something, JB. Be a man. Be someone. Be anyone. Anything. Just stop being so afraid.* As well as anyone, they both knew the farm's countless sounds and those beyond the ordinary. I never asked and I certainly could have many times, but I think the professor knew I was there.

Darren cupped his hands around his eyes and looked toward our home, a peculiar move considering the minimal light in the darkness. But I believed it was his way of saying, "I see you, JB. Thank you for caring about me, JB. Thank you for not forgetting about me, JB. Thank you for thinking of me as the person you and I wish I could be, JB."

"These wounds. These wounds you speak of, Darren," the professor continued as he pushed the door to his trailer fully closed, "if we look hard enough, we can find what we need in them. They're where you'll find the maps and keys. To show you the way. Only you can decide what you find in your wounds."

My brother shook his head, sending his shoulder-length brown hair into a frenzy as the night's second breeze whipped in from the highland.

My body became numb, a response to temperature and emotion. The professor had always referred to my brother as his most challenging student.

Fresh gusts of freezing wind blocked any chance to hear what they said next. After a long hug with Farace, he walked away from the circle of light and pulled what looked like a letter from his back pocket.

I expected to see Darren cross under the light above the Farm Store entrance as I crouched on my knees, studying the landscape. The sound I thought I heard, the distinct whisp of the Dairy House door, was confirmed several days later when I saw Zoya in the field adjacent to her apartment. She flipped pages over each other by the minute as she read, only to toss each page into the endless gusts of the new winter's early wind. The papers danced in the shallow sky until they disappeared over the crest leading down to the Dalmaqua. For a few days, I searched for any sign of them before giving up, thinking that anything written with so much heart may just as well deserve a mountain breeze than a reader.

The light from the professor's trailer flipped off, leaving me in essential darkness except for the faint light from my bedroom lamp, a marker in the low sky. Several minutes later, an engine started and headlights pierced the darkness about a half-mile up the road. I inadvertently lowered my running sneakers into the same footprints I'd created earlier going in the opposite direction as I headed back to my bedroom, wondering why the professor talked in such grand terms. Why instead of spouting stupid phrases like maps and keys, he didn't just say the truth and tell Darren that his wounds are where he could find the power to, to, to… But I also couldn't find those words. Those right words. The night's strongest gust blew off my hood and momentarily I thought I realized what the professor was doing. His reference to maps and keys. *They're…* But the thought was carried off by another blast of early winter wind.

***

"Yo, Brown. Yo, Brown. Mr. Brown."

I think I heard him. I'm not sure if I heard him. Then I heard him for sure.

"You seen a ghost or something." An ironic choice of words on Malik's part. How long had he been gone?

"Maybe worse. Ghosts aren't real," I whisper, unsure if Malik hears me.

The need to leave is overwhelming, but I've already driven too much today to muscle another seven hours. *We'll leave early in the morning,* I tell myself, but I can't tell why Malik is looking at me. The last few days have essentially assured him that I'm not hiding answers. *Coming here was a mistake.*

"Malik, we need to go."

"Back to DC, really? Then why'd we just pay for this here campsite?" He holds up the registration ticket.

His response throws me, and I'm not sure if it's surprise or remorse in his voice. I still can't read him. Maybe we can end this mistake and push through the night back home, but that option seems less desirable when I look up at the trees, which rock back and forth from a wind barely felt on the ground. With a few hours of daylight left, I consider that there may be a purpose in being here, even if it's not a clear one.

"C'mon, I want to show you the Appalachian Trail that cuts through these mountains. It's just some quarter mile down the road." I can't keep up with my own redirections, but Malik takes it in stride.

"Oh, alright, good. 'Cause, like I said, I read about one of the trails around here in your book. I think it was called Freedom Lodge."

I don't confirm his comment and walk past him, somewhat shocked the campground is empty. Local schools must have not ended the week before like us. Summer is only a week away but who knows what summer means in this new age of Covid. To our right is the parking lot and the trailhead heading south goes to the Freedom Lodge. Across the street is a small sign with letters carved into the wood board:

Appalachian Trail North
Greenbush Cabin – 3 Miles

"So, I was reading about this cabin, or is it called a lodge? The one I just been talking about. We should go there. How about that?"

I'm thrown off that Malik has a preference. That he remembered the names of these places. Of any place.

"C'mon, JB. Let's go this way," Malik says with a dose of unnecessary joy.

Where is that coming from?

He waves me into the parking lot with his head, but there's nothing he can ever do to make me go there again. There's nothing anyone can ever do to make me go there again.

"Listen, I really want to go across the street and this way," I say, pointing beyond the road to the trail heading north. *How do I get out of this?* I think about how to make this pointless discussion even more pointless. One beyond debate, but he's insistent. "You're right. Freedom Lodge is amazing, and if you ever come back, you need to go there."

Malik's eyebrows rise in confirmation of the comment's absurdity. "I'm sorry, Brown," he responds and then pauses. He's gone back to humor, which I can't fathom why is where he recedes. "Did you just say *the next time I'm here?*"

I nod my head, possibly raising an eyebrow, and I don't know how to tell him that the last place in the whole world I'll ever go is Freedom Lodge. And of all the fake purposes and revelations I thought coming to Damascus would bring, still, none of them involved going there.

"Yeah, I get it. It's beautiful and although unlikely, if there ever is an opportunity, you should definitely go there. It's really one of the more special places on the trail. But for now, for today, let's go north. There's something I want to show you." It's as truthful and straightforward as I can dishonestly be.

Malik's eyes remain in a comedic role. Or maybe he's not in a comedic role. Maybe it's his way of processing the situation.

One absent of sense. One not much clearer to me, but at least I know why we're here. Or I think I do.

"Okay, okay, okay," he says, and even seconds after advising myself to not interpret his joking negatively, I recognize that I can't. Malik raises one of his arms into the air, pointer finger facing up. Even considering the story he told me not an hour earlier, his theatrics are on high. His other hand on his hip. "Hear ye, hear ye! I declare that the next time I am in—wait, where the fuck are we?"

I don't answer him.

"I declare that I will head south to Freedom Lodge." Malik lowers his hand and almost instantly the smile fades from his face like a shadow meeting new light. His eyes make it all clear. He's not joking on our situation. He's joking on me, that I'm hiding things from him. That I'm hiding things from myself. Things I still can't figure out.

"C'mon, Brown. Like my ass ever gonna be here again." We take a few steps across the road and both stop in the middle. "But for real, if I ever do come back, you heard it here first, Mr. Brown. I'm going south to Freedom Cabin." He forces somewhat of a smile.

While it probably doesn't reach the outside world, I try to do the same. "Noted, Mr. Drummond!"

Malik forces himself to follow me along the trail, and we reach the first of several long switchbacks. The air is thick, and we don't stop hiking upward for close to thirty minutes. The view from the crest of the mountain ridge is profound. I remember that. Despite thousands of miles, few views are consistently above the tree line until hikers reach New Hampshire. We stand several feet apart, looking into different corners of the western sky, our hearts heavy with different emotions. Different demons.

"Mr. Brown, I mean, yeah, JB. You remember 9/11, right?"

What's going on? What's he doing? What could I have said?

"My family was out here on a big church retreat. My momma had just finished medical school, which I told you about earlier, when we took that photo."

I remembered. I think to tell him that I remember, that I'm hearing him. So he can know that maybe, although not in the most glorious way, his story means something to someone else. To me, I think. But I don't.

"I was only three or so, but I've heard enough stories from family members, though not everyone." His last three words trail into another untold story. "What happened was, I mean, from what I heard was that my mother left this retreat somewhere"—he looks around as if our view from 1,500 feet above the valley will confirm his assumption—"somewhere out here, maybe, at some campground. She left to go to the store. Nothing to it. She then went to the gas station and police showed up, accused her of stealing from the food store she'd been in. Straight up crazy, right?"

The sun starts to set over the western sky, yet still a full ball of star above the horizon and we descend to avoid hiking in the dark. Why is Malik still on this story? Could it be possible that behind all the joking and theatrics is a trauma so devastating that for once he didn't have the words to describe it, so he spent most of his life engaged in distractions?

"What happened next, Malik?"

He seems relieved, if an exhale of air can infer this. Then he looks surprised.

I haven't asked many questions, which I now realize may be exactly what he needs.

"She didn't do it, of course," he retorts, acting exactly the opposite as to what I thought he sought seconds earlier. Like I was accusing him. Like so many adults in his life. Like I don't believe him.

I lower my head, taking a step back from the cliff. I'm not good with heights, and worse with conversations like these. Up, down, present, distant. Years circling around the truth, and now we're both struggling to find a release.

"As anyone falsely accused, and I mean straight up absurd levels of falsivity, my moms, she was defiant. She resisted." His words, and even the appropriately made up one, fade as if they've been spoken countless times but to no one. Like there's just not enough care left to give. "She told the officers there was no way she did that. Yes, she was in that store, or whatever store, and that the lady was rude to her. But there's no way in the Lord's name that she stole any food. She actually left with a bag of paid for food. C'mon, man."

Malik breathes heavily and closes his eyes, apparently not appreciating my new attention on him. The top of his body briefly topples, and upon realizing how close to the cliff's edge he stands, he takes a half step back like I had. He turns to face me, and I don't know what he sees, but he's looking into me. Asking or telling me something in a tempered silence.

"And then I guess the racist police had the evidence to place her at the scene of the crime when whatever made-up crime happened. She swiped at an officer who grabbed her arm. Mind you, this ain't that long ago, but no one had a phone camera then, I think. It was all their word against hers."

I think of how terrible of a story this is. I want him to know I feel this way, but all I say is that I'm sorry. *Sorry for what?* A tear rolls down his cheek, trailed by a second tear, and an unbounded self-anger consumes me because it's only the tears of a grown man who probably hasn't cried since he's a kid are the evidence I need to know he's speaking his truth.

"What did this have to do with 9/11, Malik? You asked me if I remember then. Of course I do."

"The retreat was the week of the attack, but my mom only planned to stay two days with her new job starting Wednesday. I stayed with my Unca and Auntie, and when we returned home, she wasn't there. She was arrested *that* Tuesday on her way home, at a gas station. When she apparently, or so they claimed, smacked an officer who tried to take her purse. She was kept overnight in jail—*my mom*, the nicest lady in the world. Only some folks in my family had cell phones, but no coverage where they were, somewhere out here." Malik looks around as if the *here* he's referring to is really right here. "Then the whole world was in confusion. The next morning, the judge and officers didn't show up. Court was canceled. She spent three days in the county jail before they let her out. She missed the first days in her new job, then lost it permanently. Downhill from there." Malik's hands are balled fists.

I've seen that before.

He breathes deeply, releasing an unspeakable pain that I now know follows him everywhere. Chains him. So, that's how it happens. He unravels his hands and turns away from the cliff, easing the tension in his chest with steps closer to safety.

"I can't believe she had that experience. That you had that experience."

"Changed her whole life. She was never the same. None of us were."

I look down at my shoes, remembering how common the view was nearly twenty years earlier. How much of the trail I missed because I was always looking down. On what others called a defining pilgrimage, I spent most of it hiding within the natural world, hoping that it could do the healing for me. Yet then and still now, unaware of how healing really works. We reach the pavement and both of us keep walking, crossing the road into the empty parking lot.

Nothing could have prepared me for what life felt like when I was last on this trail, at this spot. And it hits me quickly. The world around and within me. The world around and within Malik. The wounds around and within Malik. The wounds around and within me. It all changed here. This is where hope died.

I walk several steps away and, in the diminishing twilight, I remember to call Terri. I repeatedly hit her name atop my speed dial list, twisting and turning my body in every configuration, but it's not a signal I'm lacking. It's an answer. Unsure if I feel stunted, dejected, or relieved, I return to the site and sit on the log beside the fire, feeling a new sense of heat but aware of little beyond that. Terri needs me, and I don't know what to do.

"JB. Yo, JB. Mr. Brown. You acting all weird on me. You's alright? I know you ain't the most talkative, but you gone mute on me, staring into the fire. You canceling me, bro?"

"No, I mean, yes. No. Sorry." I fill my lungs with bitter air, unaware of the transformation from dawn to darkness, or Malik building the impressive fire before us. My mind's moving too fast. Too many directions. "You made this?"

"Did you? See anyone else here?"

"Nice fire," I respond, less sarcastically than him.

The tent is set up a few feet away, and my blue ground pad is spread across the truck bed, curling at the ends from being rolled most of the year. I contemplate telling him it's his night to sleep in the back of the truck, but it isn't worth it. No one else deserves that.

"Your eyes were open. Was you sleeping, Brown?"

I look around the perimeter of where the fire lights the ground, making it look like something more profound than the trampled dirt of a commercial campsite. A gentle but brisk breeze blows in. A welcome opposite of the scorching wind that's felt like an endless cycle over two days. The top flames bend over the steel pit ring as Malik rubs his arms up and down.

"I got an extra shirt in the bag, Malik. Help yourself."

He passes in front of the fire and his body transforms from fully lit to darkness, then I hear the zipper of my old high school track bag. The movement in the bag feels like it exceeds the necessary navigation of the bag's few contents, making me feel uneasy.

Wearing the headlamp, Malik holds up my bag, poking his fingers through several holes and rips in its thinning fabric. "How in the Lawd's name does this actually hold anything, JB?"

"Do you want a shirt or not?"

"Just jonesing on ya, and a bit on your bag, that's all." He pulls out an old long-sleeved red flannel. One I would've liked to wear had I remembered it was there. He holds up my old blue Expos hat, a gift from my father when he took Darren and me to a game in Montreal decades ago. "Cool, JB?"

I'm about to tell him it is, but my voice fails when I notice the fire's light illuminating the front of his body. Instead I nod and he rolls up the sleeves and buttons the shirt to just above the round crest of his white tank top. The headlamp light shifts, and I hear the unmistakable sound of full cans smashing into the side walls of the old Coleman cooler.

"Who knew we was driving every bent road on the planet with a twelve pack. You waiting for the last ice cube to melt before you drink these, JB?" He has an odd way of asking questions. Nothing is straightforward.

"Yeah, that's what I'm waiting for." For the first time I want to call him an idiot. Maybe it would lighten things up.

"They're still cold," he says, more seriously. "Want one?"

Malik returns to the log where he'd shown me the picture of his mother. Two pressurized cans pop open in unison and the cheap beer flows down my throat, slowly erasing the dehydration. Less slowly, the sadness. Two more tilts and the bottom-shelf brand nectar disappears. I grab two more as Malik squeezes his can into art, erasing my curiosity if he wanted another. The second beer goes down slightly slower.

We repeat this cycle. Saying and hearing only "thanks" when receiving and handing off the cold aluminum. The low-level alcohol adds to the numbness we offer it, occasionally looking up to glance at each other's face in the firelight. Malik transfers another log from the pile beneath the picnic table to the flames.

If his mind is moving like my own, he's wondering about where things went wrong. How we got here? What could have been different? How we change the past? Better yet, erase it. The fire casts bursts of light onto our bodies and the dirty white truck a few feet beyond us. I'm certain this is what he's thinking. We both lost everything that weekend. But I'm not ready to tell Malik this.

"What ya thinking about, Malik?" I finally say.

The immediate response is predictable. Nothing. Then resentment. At him, for being the only one to talk to. Then me. For expecting an hour of silence beside the fire to seamlessly morph into conversation.

"How to move forward," he says just above a whisper.

The fire crackles, sending embers into the sky. Several float to the ground and sizzle before fading to nothing. Despite the low volume, the power of his words carry beyond the tops of the flames. They stir in the smoke before becoming darkness. I clear my throat as if I'll speak, but I don't.

"I've seen what's gonna happen if I can't get my life on track. They're all around me."

I sit with his words, certain that he's stuck in the past like me. Still licking his wounds. Trying to break the chains. Then in a streak of orange light cast from the flame and slight breeze, I see his face and it looks different. It is different. He's focused on how to move forward. How to evolve. I nod my head, sensing that he may think I'm affirming what he's shared, but I'm not. I'm wondering how I'm not focused on the same.

"Thanks for the shirt." A serious voice, then he makes a popping sound with his finger in his cheek each time he pushes a finger into one of the holes in the arm area.

"It's old, what can I tell you."

"Is this the shirt you wear to church, JB, 'cause it sure is holy."

I can't help but laugh a little, and he seems surprised.

"Thought you'd like an old White-guy joke." He points to the tent with his chin before looking back at me. "Cool if I use the tent and Terri's sleeping bag again?"

I nod. "Sure."

The tent zipper lowers and then rises. The official sound of camping.

Now alone, I think about 9/11. What it meant. How it transformed a country. A world. How it relates to Malik's family, and I circle the fire several times, wondering if my body is settling or stirring. Wondering if Malik is sleeping. Wondering what he meant when he spoke about moving forward. Wondering if instead of waiting for him to seek my guidance, he might be the one providing it.

After peeing for two solid minutes, I slide into the truck bed and lean against the window. I hear the zipper lower, followed by another two-minute beer drain on the other side of the tent. The fire is fading, and I grab one of the remaining cans of beer and pull the student roster from the bag. With my teeth, I remove the pen cap and carry on with one of the few calming activities.

Hours later, I wake to the familiar feeling of vertical metal in my back. I must have slid off the ground pad. It takes a few seconds to feel the moisture of the morning dew through the old sleeping bag, at which point it cannot be ignored. I snake myself back onto the thin, blue rubber pad as four empty beer cans fall off the bed's guardrail, onto the thin, dented metal beneath it, casting a deafening sound in an otherwise silent campground.

The sun must have risen more than an hour ago, but it still holds behind the trees and I realize it's not as silent as I first thought. Birds are singing. Several branches sway from the movement of small animals. My stirring knocks the small collection of empty beer cans off the truck bed's sidewall and it sounds like the back of a small car driving newlyweds away from their church wedding beside a sea of well-wishers. This is more than I remember drinking, explaining the headache. At the other end of the truck, the two letters I wrote last night sit on the wet metal grooves. The papers have absorbed the moisture, blotching the black ink of every word. I lower my head, remembering these were good letters. I think. Malik's shuffling around in the tent is a welcome sound. It would be good to leave as early as we can.

Returning from the latrine, I notice a necessary and unwelcome sight. Malik is bent over with his head under the hood. In almost twenty years with this truck, the hood being open and quick departures have rarely been inclusive.

"Morning?"

"Hey, Brown," Malik says, not lifting his head or turning around. "You got a flashlight in one of those boxes? I mean, if you ain't got a flashlight in those two big Going Camping boxes, then I might have to revoke your Boy Scout badge."

"I wasn't a Boy Scout, Wise Ass."

The familiar smirk. "Wise Ass. A'ight. I like that," he says, his eyes still focused on the engine.

How can he feel happy this early in the morning? I hand him the light, all but ignoring his theatrics, and follow his eyes as they scan a particular area close to the front bumper.

His pupils jump around the mechanical landscape, strangely in sync with the bird's morning chirps. "I was thinking about that weird sound in my sleep, Brown. I think I know what it is."

His seriousness isn't something I want to lose, and I stand beside him with the light.

He directs where he wants the light with a stick, poking it into the engine's belly. "Ah ha. Looks like that belt is loose. Hop in and start the engine," he says, followed by the sound of disheartened and deprived mechanical horses.

"Cut it, cut it," his demand echoes from under the hood. "I got this, JB. I think we can get this going soon. If not, I got another way to get that light off."

The first and second parts of his declaration don't add up. "What's that?"

Malik squeezes the stick under his armpit and turns off the flashlight. He then wipes his brow. The humidity is already thick. "This old guy in the shop named Buddy taught me one of the best ways to get rid of an alert light."

"What's that?" *Why does everything have to be a story?*

"We'll cover the dashboard display with some duct tape. You'll never see it again." Pause. "You didn't find that funny?"

"No, not really. I just want to get out of here. We need to get back."

"Well, let me look over the rest of this junk box to see what else may need attention, but I think I got it." Malik returns to under the hood where he's deep in concentration.

"Hey, Malik," I yell, standing on a log, trying to balance myself. "Why did Antwon fire you?" I extend my arms like wings of a plane, testing whether it will elevate my balance or unravel it.

His fingers grip the outside of the hood and then he slides his body, wrapping his head around the hood to get a good look at me. "Really?" His voice is matter-of-fact and calm. He then steps away from the truck, slowly wiping his fingers individually with a rag. "Couple of guys were running parts out the back door." Another pause, but this one feels different. "Side hustle. They knew Antwon kept a shallow eye on the books. I started to figure it out when this one guy, who Antwon placed a lot of trust in, started assigning me trash duty. That usually got pinned on the new guy." He stops talking and uses the flashlight to scan the surface of the engine shaded by the hood and low sun.

"What's taking out the trash got to do with it?"

He fixates on the truck, scanning up and down for indicators of what's preventing us from leaving, which I interpret as a sign that our mechanical issues are close to being resolved.

"I noticed the trash was heavy and being placed behind the dumpster instead of inside it. When I looked inside, there were new motor parts. I figured out what was happening. Worse was, these other guys figured out I did too. I didn't want in on it. Antwon been good to me." Malik again pokes into the crevasses of a dark, dirty, and uninspiring engine.

A few seconds pass and I try to think of questions, but nothing comes to mind.

"Yo, Brown, grab me a longer stick that's straight, a'ight?"

His request temporarily curbs my curiosity, and walking back, I feel the repetitive vibration in my pocket and notice several missed calls from Terri. I hurl the stick toward the truck and it lands beside Malik's feet.

"I'll be back in a minute. I need to call Terri," I shout.

He yells back something from under the hood, but I don't hear what he says.

At the road, my signal returns and Terri answers before I hear the first ring.

"Where are you? Are you okay, JB?" Her words are rapid and careful, but something is lingering close by.

"I'm fine," I whisper, then realizing there's no need to do so. I repeat myself at a louder volume and it sounds less caring.

A series of deep coughs follow, and I move the phone away from my ear for a moment.

"JB, are you there? I feel terrible. I'm short of breath. You didn't call or text last night. That scared me. Are you okay?"

I don't know what to say. I can ask how she's feeling again, but she answered this. "Should I come home?" The offer settles into the thick humidity.

"Please, JB. As soon as you can. I think I should go to the hospital. I'm not breathing right. I've seen this, and now I'm feeling it. Can you come now?"

I open the mental road atlas in my mind. I know those ripped and creased pages well. "Of course. It's about ten, and I can be home by five, okay?"

"By five?" Terri instantly retorts.

There was concern in her voice too, and I start to absorb this new emotion. Fear. She's not one to ask unless the need is overdue. I sense it. I know it. This is serious.

"I thought you were only a couple hours away in the mountains. Why can't you be home sooner, JB? I need you."

"I know. I know." *What can I do?* "I'll be home as soon as I can. Please. Please, rest. I'll have my phone on me the whole time. I'm leaving in a few minutes. Okay. Terri, okay?"

"Please, JB. I need you home sooner. Please. Why will it take so long?"

"Look. I mean, I'm sorry. We got farther away than I planned. I'm so sorry for missing my call last night. I tried, but I was out of the signal's area. My fault. Again, I'm sorry."

"What do you mean *we*, JB?"

My signal drops before I can answer, and I make several futile attempts to reconnect before shoving the phone back in my pocket.

I walk away from the road, crossing an overly rounded foot bridge that leads to town, but that's not where I'm going. I don't know where I'm going. Mentally mapping time backward while running out of time to map. Where can I be for the noon call with Becker? Rest stops along Interstate 81 must have Wi-Fi signals. Even less confidently, I tell myself that despite our differences, Becker is reasonable. I'll start off with an apology. I'll tell her about Terri. Honestly, why wouldn't I, or more to the point, why *haven't* I? The thought to tell her I'm with one of our former students doesn't cross my mind.

This isn't going to be simple. Becker wants something and I'm not it. I get it. I think of the last meeting with her. How was I able to navigate that? None of that's clear now. I pick up my pace, only now recognizing how indirect the route I chose is.

Maybe I should quickly read the last article Becker shared. Why aren't I thinking about Terri as much as this? Who sends an article to the entire staff in the first week of June? Predictably, the same teachers responded to the whole community the next day, thanking Becker for the article's distribution. Her vision. Her steadfast focus on antiracism. Why aren't we talking about the kids who are failing? Where are the emails about summer school? Where are the conversations about the nearly one-third of our seniors who haven't completed their graduation requirements? Could I create the time to read Becker's emails if I knew she was as focused on the work we need for students to graduate?

I step off the road because my detour has cost minutes I don't have. I pass a picnic area with tables and grills under a pavilion and enter the next tent loop as a gap in the trees throws sun on my face, blinding me, and I'm forced to stop. I spin away from the sky and lower my hands to my knees, shaking my head, hoping the blindness is temporary. My hands canopy my eyes as I slowly raise my head, cautious to not repeat what's blinded me and marveling at this small circle of radiant sunlight piercing the surrounding trees.

The light transforms from around me to within and somehow becomes a light of awareness. An awareness of healing. Of Darren. The only person I've ever heard described as the devil and angel, and now he consumes every part of me. I push myself beyond the horror and brokenness, into a world I never knew but heard existed. Darren's recovery. In her last letter to me, Mother called it her miracle. After nearly seven years apart, of Darren living among the drug infested quarters of Montreal and beyond, he had also found a light. The light of sobriety. Through letters from Trevor and emails from the professor, I learned of my brother's challenging and definitive choice to reinvent. To repair. To find something new. To secure his light.

Darren entered rehab when he was twenty-three. His life became one of daily AA meetings. He struggled fiercely, but to my knowledge, he never touched alcohol or drugs again. He became strong again. First in his mind. Then his body. No one really knew whether that strength reached where it mattered most. His heart. The professor wrote about the books Darren was reading. About his fitness routines. He'd started taking classes at the community college and became certified as an EMT. The professor said Darren possessed a need to save.

A letter from Trevor shared that he'd visited Darren in Montreal. That he'd joined him for one of his meetings, the second of three he'd attend that day. "He paces the apartment scanning the paper for meetings to attend, tagging me on the shoulder to run around the city to occupy the hours in between. If it weren't Darren," Trevor wrote, "I'd think this routine was impossible to sustain." Ultimately, my brother decided that if something was going to rule his life, it should be AA and not the drugs that drove him there.

The following spring, the professor emailed that he'd seen Darren and my father talking on the back porch. True to form, there were parts of his writing I didn't understand. In one run-on sentence he mentioned that Darren's pathway and conviction had become so powerful he was starting the long and compli- cated path of reconciliation, a concept that only became clear years later when I learned about the steps to recovery. A few days before my college graduation, a voicemail landed on the communal phone in the dorm suite.

Your brother Darren called. He wants to talk, read the note from my suite mate. Beneath that, *Didn't know you had a brother.*

I read it a dozen times. Separately, every word made sense. Linked together, they were a foreign language. What did this mean?

The call was followed by emails from a New Hampshire community college address asking me to write him back. I did not. More followed. I had nothing to say. This wasn't happening. I'd spent years building a mask over the memories of him, sometimes telling myself that I was an only child. What good could come from this?

As my parents cordially sat beside each other at my graduation, all I could think of was that neither was around when I thought their oldest son was going to kill me on the porch. I slid the diploma sideways into my backpack to leave the Keene apartment for the last time. When the phone rang I was sure it was the RA to confirm my departure.

"Hi, JB. It's Darren."

His voice familiar and alien, six syllables were enough to rewrite the world's story and instantly the fear of fresh memories accelerated. Then excitement. My ears expanded, wanting to hear more. To pick up every subtlety. The muscles around my chest tightened with energy. With risk.

"Congrats on the graduation."

I think I said "thanks," but I don't remember hearing anything, so I may not have responded. Darren made it seem that way when he spoke again.

"So, JB, I'm relieved to have you on the phone. Really. A lot has happened. Not sure you've heard. I'm getting healthy. I've been in AA for around two years, and I'm starting to feel good about what I need to do. One of the steps I need to take is to repair the relationships I damaged."

Then I definitely spoke. "Okay." Unsurprisingly, I paused for a few seconds, unsure how to continue. I'd never heard of a relationship being repaired. It made sense, but the vocabulary was unfamiliar, and I appreciated Darren not speaking with pauses as I did.

"I'm getting a lot of help. I got a lot to live for. People to live for."

These were new messages to me. I looked around the empty living quarters, thinking how I now had a four-year college degree yet no understanding of what it means to hear a person discuss the rehabilitation of their soul. The processing of every new concept infused more silence into the phone.

"Listen, JB. Can I try to make things up to you? Can I see you?"

I thought the lack of response may convey that my answer was no, but I couldn't find any way to say it. This was all moving too fast.

"I can't change what happened." His voice was softer.

It was real, or I continued to whisper to myself that everything happening was real. The question was, could I?

"Father said that later in the summer you're taking a bus down to Georgia to hike the AT. So cool. Guess passing all the hikers in town rubbed off on ya."

My brother's voice filled with a new energy, and I wondered where he stored it. But that wasn't it. No one really rubbed off on me. I wanted to be away from everything. Maybe my silence was affirming, but he was persistent. Then I remembered that he always was.

"Hey, I know this is a lot, but can I join you on the trail for a few weeks?"

Silence. Maybe this time he'd gone too far. Too many emotions were being pulled back. Too many masks were being stripped. I had to make this stop, and at the same time it was everything I ever wanted. Needed.

"Can we talk next week?" he said, offering me a lifeline.

"Sure. Okay."

"I'll have a map in front of me. Start to think of a meeting spot. See ya, JB."

That afternoon, I headed back to the one constant I'd known since I was eight years old. I didn't want to return to the farm. Darren had made it so I didn't want to be at home. It was a broken place where broken people still lived, and I didn't want to be anywhere near there. But I needed money, and the morning following graduation, Dina had me in the fields pulling early season rhubarb and asparagus beside the professor. In the afternoon, I cleaned the Dairy House near Zoya. The same tasks that needed to be done years earlier all needed to be done now. The farm felt different, or maybe I was different. It felt like a slow-moving operation, or perhaps it was the people who were now slower.

That was it. There were no kids running around. Other than the mainstays who had been there since the day I arrived, it felt like everyone else was relatively new. It didn't feel like a community. It was an operating dairy farm where people were trying harder than anything to make a living. Like always, their efforts only bore questionable results. But Dina was happy to have me there, and I spent more time with Walter that summer than I had in all the years before. He was noticeably older and slower, and I wondered how long his body could manage the physical labor his responsibilities required. Kent's physical decline was more apparent than his friend's.

Every minute back at Mountainbrook only elevated the need to retreat, to be alone, and I thought of canceling the hike because even there felt like too many people. Then I remembered Darren was planning to meet me. In my mind, this relatively straight line of over 2,000 forested miles became interjected with lava pools and quicksand. I needed to leave the farm, for good.

A week in, I was eating a sandwich at the kitchen table when Father got on the phone. It was a longer conversation than I remember him having in years and it sounded like what it might be like if Father had friends. He then lowered the receiver to his waist and said Darren wanted to talk to me. It hadn't entered my mind that it might be my brother on the other end.

"Hey, JB, pretty cool that Father and I are talking, huh?"

I didn't think it was cool. Father was by then a near broken man. His wife was gone. For years until his resurrection, his oldest son had lived among the soon-to-be-dead. The old man's deflated soul was everywhere to see and I had nothing to bring the remaining life out of him. But as Darren embraced life, he was also slowly giving some of it back to our father, a remedy I could not have foreseen. In hindsight, I should have extended Darren more support, but it would be too late before I learned how much he needed it.

"Sure. I guess so."

Darren again asked about the trail. He was serious, and so was I when this time I instantly agreed. If there wasn't reluctance in my voice, there should have been.

"I have a map open in front of me. Do you?" he asked in a hushed tone.

I did. I'd been carrying one around since the last conversation. I asked Darren why he was whispering and what he said almost blew my mind.

A friend from AA had set him up with a job at an insurance company in New York City. "You wouldn't believe the size of the building I'm working in, JB."

But it wasn't his words I heard. It was my beating heart. Darren shared that he'd used his first half-year's paychecks to pay Father back for the lawyer. Then he'd bought him a new white pickup, which was now old, dented, and chronically plagued with a persistent check engine light.

"I've saved enough for a flight and a bus to the trail. Call me when you're a month out. That will give me time for a two-week notice and time to check on Dad."

It all felt too new, too perfect. Like everything I'd hoped for, had I known there was hope. Our plan was to meet at the trail's halfway point in Harpers Ferry. Like it was set in stone. We'd meet at ten, on the tenth day of the tenth month, at the bridge.

I would leave for Georgia on the first of August, far later than anyone expecting to reach the end before winter. But that wasn't my goal, though I wasn't sure what was. It would take me around a month to get to Damascus, some 450 miles from Springer Mountain. Then I'd call Darren, as it was a solid month's walk from there to Harpers Ferry.

"Our plan is fail-proof," he said. "From there, we'll hike together. Plus, I have big news to share."

"You sure?" I asked.

Then Darren infused the only pause of our conversation. It felt interminable. "I owe it to you," he said.

In those words I built a pyramid of doubt. Dug a cave of uncertainty. I wasn't sure about the hike, but I was certain our phone conversations had been the happiest moments in my young adult life.

Several months later and barely accustomed to the heavy backpack I'd been carrying for approximately sixty days, I practically skipped down the trail from Freedom Cabin and when I entered the parking lot, a young couple was leaning against their car smacking hiking boots together. Chunks of muddy earth erupted into the space around them.

"Have you heard?" the woman asked.

"Heard what," I may have said.

"Two planes struck the Twin Towers in New York City this morning."

At first I didn't understand her meaning. Without seeing it, how could anyone fathom the reality associated with these words? My bottom lip dropped from shock, but mostly confusion. Slowly, I realized what this meant. I remembered more of what Darren had shared about where he was working. The second building.

I called home that afternoon from the payphone beside the police station in town. No answer. I called the Dairy House. No answer.

After several calls to the farm office, Dina picked up and immediately asked where I was. "Darren was in the building. We're pretty sure of it, JB. We're almost certain. Are you there? JB? JB?"

Dina's voice had been that anxious and scared only once before, and as I lowered the phone handle, it missed the receiver. I craved being back in the woods where what was already dead remained so. Where there was no news, and the only terror was what you brought with you, and I was already packing plenty. The metal cord whipped the black phone into a frenzy of chaotic circles as a patrol car with its siren blasting entered the parking lot and parked beside me. The sirens silenced as I walked away, but not before hearing the definitive sound of a woman screaming from behind the tinted rear window.

I want to tell Malik about what 9/11 did to me. That maybe we can use this as a way to, to, to…but I then admit that I can't find the destination I hoped for. Terrorism and racism. A national story of the trauma we created among our own and the horrible blow struck from borders beyond, and I had the privilege of only suffering from one.

I'll tell him. I declare it to myself as I cross the campground field dotted with deer pellets. I'll tell Malik everything. Even if he won't tell me anything more. *That's it. I'll let it all out to essentially a stranger who I'll never see again. Then we can drive home with that mountain lifted off my shoulders and it will be enough. It will be forever behind me.*

I'll take the call with Becker. I'll apologize, though I don't know what for, and I'll make it home in time to get Terri soup and medicine. My steps feel freeing. The girl in Mother's painting is running across the field and I'm running beside her. Her blue dress skips over the golden tall grass and I yell to her, "I can help! I think I can help!" and she digs her heels into the soft ground.

"No, JB, help someone who needs it." A sign. Something. I can do something. I'll tell Malik that he just has to tell me, if he wants to, and I can help him. Then we'll hop in the truck and leave.

But I can't, and it finally has nothing to do with being too scared of the truth. There's an empty void above the ground. Malik and the truck are gone.

13

SHORT CIRCLES IN THE dirt beneath my feet confirm what I know. Malik and the truck are gone. In every direction there's no evidence to suggest the contrary, and the solitude conjures soothing and fearful memories. Its epicenter, here in Damascus almost twenty years ago when it all broke. A voice says to let it in, but it's the same one that misguided me before. I sought out the Appalachian Trail to be alone. To occupy time. To process. To finally comprehend the realities of losing Kami to the river and my brother to the depths of addiction and violence.

When Darren called, everything I set out on the trail to secure was replaced with hope, then confusion. With every step, I wondered which was worse. The process to heal or reversing what you had to heal from? Every morning I told myself that I'd think about these things on the next mountain. Hundreds of miles passed. When I was on the mountaintops, I kept the memories in the valley only to anchor them to the summits as I descended. Occasionally asking myself what life meant. What caring meant. What being there for someone meant. What not being able to answer any of these questions meant.

The concept of meaning momentarily pauses itself as a large hawk flies low over the campground field. Navigating a sky of unanswered questions, I pace the campsite searching for yesterday's pinecone to kick. Searching for a plan. Where would he go? Why would he do this? Should I call the police? Do I report a stolen vehicle?

I notice the camping gear box on the ground beside the log. How thoughtful. Malik left my backpack and chair before he took off with the truck. There's a towel spread along the log where Malik placed the letters I wrote last night. A truly caring endeavor, if I can just get past him stealing my truck and leaving me alone in a campsite. And left with few options, I open the list of graduates to finally start my letters, instantly stumped at the first name on the list, Payson Adams.

While watching Payson grow and being part of three years of his education, he is one of the few graduates I still don't know well. I'm unsure who does. No solid group of friends. No sports or clubs. No relative ever attended a back-to-school night or teacher meeting. But when a member of Payson's family replied to an email weeks after I'd sent it, the notes were well written, apologetic, and attentive to my message. Those responses gave me hope.

Payson never exceeded expectations, never sank too far beneath them, and avoided trouble. That trifecta with a quiet demeanor will pass most boys and young men under many radars, and there's something troubling in this. It's these kids you read about years later, and often that news isn't good.

Payson didn't ask much of others, and I'm wondering why it feels odd that the adults in his life probably didn't ask much of him either. It was challenging to get him to engage because engagement meant waiting. First it was his eyes. Then he had to sit up. Each action generated a short delay within a longer wait. He moved at the slowest rate at which one could move without crossing the line of being too slow. Subsequently, you couldn't call on him in class, and maybe that was part of his play. Doing so was a momentum liability and in teaching middle school, momentum is everything. When the flow is negative or distracting, you have to break it. When it's working, you must do everything to sustain it. Payson, albeit likable in other ways, though none easily come to mind, was a momentum thorn.

The most meaningful bonding I had with Payson was toward the end of his eighth-grade year. After a week of spring-like temperatures, when jackets were shed for T-shirts, winter returned with a burst of frigid air. The truck was in the shop again, and I spotted Payson entering the campus as I pulled into the lot with Moira Elliot, Biko's librarian and the only teacher who lived in my neighborhood. A staff member since the school's opening day, she was a quietly phenomenal part of our community. Unfortunately, she was plagued by chronic illness that forced her to miss an abundance of time, but she turned reluctant readers into kids who could not put down their books, and that superpower was worth all the credit in the building.

Despite all the years together, as two introverts, Moira and I rarely spoke to each other. The first time I asked her for a ride, her only response was, "Both ways?" At her request, we met on the corner, though I repeatedly offered to meet in front of her apartment or directly at her car parked on the street. I appreciated opening a squeaky door other than my own. The intense volume of NPR revealed that she was either hard of hearing or soft to the idea of morning conversation.

As we pulled into the school lot, I saw Payson in front of the school wearing a thin T-shirt. He was tossing a football in the air. Catching his own throws. Crossing in front of the green light, he followed his catch with dancing feet to elude an invisible defender and I called Payson to toss me the ball from across the field.

"Over the cars, Mr. Brown?"

"If you're a good throw, you'll clear 'em."

Payson threw a perfect spiral into my chest. Faster movements than I've ever seen him do anything. I slid off my backpack and tossed him back the ball that, despite being poorly thrown, he caught effortlessly. I waved and walked to my bag, but he just as quickly tossed the ball back with a smile I hadn't seen before or since. I tossed the ball one last time before he returned to standing alone beside the small teacher parking lot, again tossing the ball to himself.

That afternoon, Payson was the first kid in his seat with his work on the desk. He raised his hand several times, more than in any class before. By the end of our long block period, which I also thought felt endless at times, Payson was again alone in his own world far from the class. He had done everything he could to thank me for noticing him, but the class was too long.

I learned that middle school students were like parking meters. The teacher has only small coins that must be consistently placed in their meters. Every ten minutes you have to place in another coin and your coins are compliments, encouragement, and recognition. Like a lot of boys his age, Payson's meter had a very short-term parking limit.

I'm a few sentences into his letter and reach for a new piece of paper because I don't like the way "Dear Payson" looks on the page, and I consider starting with his name and a comma, or his name followed by a dash. The morning's sun strikes through the trees as I finish my first letter, followed by another to our class valedictorian, Brittany Bannard, which was typically an easy letter because I'd write about their remarks at graduation, but that formula was out the window now. Then the loneliness amplifies when I see the next name on my list—Neville Brantley. I mean, Nevy. The new name he, now she, requested of classmates and teachers. The embarrassment of my confusion when I first heard of gender fluid. It felt like everyone had been using the term for years. The compounded embarrassment when I entered the phrase into a search engine. I didn't know Nora Simon was looking over my shoulder after having grabbed a pen from my desk.

"Why you looking up *gender fluid*, Mr. Brown?" she announced to the whole tenth-grade class.

"Please sit down, Nora," I said, hiding my frustration but worse, missing an opportunity to allow honesty to be our guide to learning.

"Ain't that what you been talking about, Nevilla?" she asked, walking back to her desk past a now mortified Nevy.

I watched his, I mean *her* head lower, but not before Nevy's eyes struck me from her desk. I felt terrible. Why did I have to do anything to bring attention to Nevy that way? I only wanted to understand. I should have simply responded that I was interested in learning more. That I wanted to better understand the community in which I worked. But I stumbled. Then I stuttered. My affect momentarily took on the notion of the assumption that I was looking at something I shouldn't have been in class. I asked Nevy to stay for a moment after the bell. I wanted to apologize for the insensitive experience that occurred.

"No, thank you, Mr. Brown. I'd rather just leave."

I couldn't blame Nevy for not talking to me after that.

Dear Nevy,

It's a few days after graduation, and I'm thinking of you as I sit by myself in a campsite a few hundred miles from DC. One of our Sociology classes, either from October or November comes to mind. We were reviewing key terms, like functional integration, social structures, and power, and I asked how these systems help us to understand our society. You looked up from your desk, appearing agitated. You said, "They all make me feel like I'm alone." I feel like that sometimes too, Nevy. I think we all do.

Recognizing this wasn't the answer I sought, I called on another student. I reflected on that class and then thought about your high school experience. I figured that you weren't maybe answering the question I asked, but that you were answering honestly.

Thinking about you now, Nevy, the one term that comes to mind is courage. The courage to understand yourself. To ask questions. To make changes that allow you to be your best self. The courage to love yourself! Even as you persevered through genuine questions from classmates and, sadly, a heavy dose of inappropriate comments.

I'll never forget your presentation on Italy in the 8th grade. Despite the magnitude of research you did, you chose to open your remarks with, "Well, if I lived in the country that I'm about to tell you about, I'd be a lot heavier than I am today." It never hurts to grab your audience with a laugh!

As my student in two classes, I enjoyed teaching and learning with you, Nevy. Like every other teacher at Biko, I liked you just the way you are. Wherever you were as a person, to me, it was you! As you continue to explore the world around you, I hope you will seek out trusting and caring hearts. No matter who you are, we all need someone to listen to us. Thank you, Nevy.

Jerry Brown
June 2020

A pit sinks in my gut when I look at Nevy's address—the Southeast Calvary Family Shelter. Another letter that won't reach a student, and I see my disappointment at having written the letter in the first place overshadowing any disgust that Nevy has lived there for the last two years. An outcome of sharing with his family that he was gay and then transitioning into a woman. I'd pay for that pinecone to kick.

I tell myself that I cared about Nevy, but long after other adults normalized Nevy's pronouns, I was still being corrected in emails. Instead of training my brain to correctly identify her, I complained about why our woke world is making everything so complicated. Why we're embracing every possible change for a few as a behavior change for all? Why every series of changes came with its own vocabulary. I'm sounding like Cooper. It's so hard, I tell myself, and then I think of Nevy sitting on a bunk in a room with other kids who've been kicked out of their homes.

The pronouns are so hard to remember.

I write three more letters before assessing the two Malik kindly set on the old towel are unreadable. I'll have to write to Antoine and Darrell again later, but it's what I didn't write to Darrell that consumes my mind—his comments in tenth grade that set off another class discussion I wasn't ready to have.

It was early in the year after some Biko students were jumped in the neighborhood around the school. A conversation about what several students saw ensued, but what these conversations always lacked was from those who knew the most. Like so many adults in the neighborhoods where our students lived, minding one's business was community code.

"Quiet mouths live to talk another day," a student once said.

I leaned on a desk in the front row to embrace what I thought was a mature conversation, but mostly hoping my presence would redirect their attention. Not surprisingly, neither part worked. The conversation evolved from what was happening in their neighborhood to other areas they felt unsafe traveling to in the city.

That's when Darrell said, "I feel safer walking by four White guys in Georgetown than I do four Black guys in Anacostia. I mean, think about it, really?" Those were his exact words.

On cue, my muscles tightened at the discussion of White people and Black people. Maybe I sensed his comment would escalate as Bernard's had. The initial response was quiet. Some students sat back in their chairs, possibly picturing Darrell's scenario, but that wasn't necessary. These situations were all too familiar. They lived them. One's surroundings are never far from the focus of Black kids in Biko's neighborhoods. I thought the conversation had sizzled. That we were all better for it. When the silence lasted beyond ten seconds, I rethought my comfort, then the reason for it.

Then Jamila's voice launched into the air. Not really a yell, but she was daring to be unheard. "Yo, Darrell. What you just said. That's racist as any and all how."

Darrell, who sat on the side aisle against the window and spent most of his time looking outside, shifted to face his peers in a posture that felt far from confrontational. "Yeah, how so?"

Jamila, a row back on the other side of the classroom, lowered her jaw into her chest. Her brows shot toward the ceiling. Neither were ones I'd peg for a public display of aggression, and knowing this, something felt safe. She waved her hands inward like she was herding cattle. "C'mon, people," she said, and I'm still not sure what anyone understood this to mean.

Lucinda, who everyone called Lucy, sat in front of Jamila. I admired how she rotated the top of her skinny body to its side while keeping her feet and essentially everything from the waist down neatly under her desk facing forward. Her earrings swayed from the abrupt movement. "Let's be honest, Darrell. You talking about walking down by the mall with all the stores where you shopping nice things and comparing that to walking down MLK Boulevard to get from the bus stop to home. I get you. You's just like that, but that ain't how I feel," she said.

Amira sat in the middle of the class, and I liked having her as a student. She had impeccable handwriting, and I could gauge the effectiveness of my lesson by her note-taking. Her hair was short like a crew cut, and she'd been tall for her age since entering the school as a seventh grader. When Amira raised her hand, Jamila told her to put it down and that the floor was now hers, like Jamila was a game show host. I couldn't help being embarrassingly impressed. Amira turned to her left and then to her right, trying to decide which side of the room she'd speak to. A conundrum of her position in the room's epicenter.

"I had this friend from volleyball camp, Alexis." She paused as the hood of her sweatshirt slid off her head. "My friend said she liked having me as her friend. She said, 'I think every White person should have a Black friend.'"

A few "ughs" and "ohs" circulated the room.

"I don't think Alexis meant it that way, or maybe she didn't mean to be, what's the word, um, so revealing."

I thought how White people sometimes say the stupidest comments, and then again I thought about how little of my students' lives I understood beyond my class. At times like this, I wondered how much I knew of them within it. Amira lowered her eyes after saying she didn't care about it. But if she didn't care, we wouldn't be hearing about it. That much I knew.

"At the time," she continued, "I thought about that comment all night. It was my first night away from home, so that kept me up, but anyway…" She did a little something with her hands, like several small circles, to reinforce to the class that she was moving back to her story. "What I realized she was saying was that it was good to have a Black person as a friend, though not necessarily me as the person to be her friend, or at least that's what I thought."

It was as if Amira was only really understanding the meaning of her synopsis right there, and all of us, even Darrell, felt the sting of this realization together, though it felt stubbornly disconnected from the topic, or so I thought.

"That's deep," Jamila said.

"Also true, and you know this," said another female student.

I thought it was Dana, but I couldn't be sure. Maybe it was the whip of attitude at the end. These conversations always made me feel like I needed to do more. I told myself to focus on two things: Let the conversation happen and then learn from it. I missed a lot along the way.

I crumple up the two unreadable letters. With Nevy's letter having almost as good a chance of reaching her, I toss them all in the fire pit. I need to move. I've been sitting too long. I try another balancing maneuver on the log, but the muscles on the outside of my leg tighten and I slip, slamming my feet to the ground. Just then I hear the familiar sound of an unhealthy truck through the thick air. The rumble transitions into a familiar sight as it bends around the campsite loop at double the speed limit.

Malik's arm rests on the windowsill. He's wearing my blue Expos hat backward and brakes the wheels at the exact same imprint on the dirt from where he left. To form, several seconds after turning off the key, the engine has a predictable cough, though more mild than before. He nods his head with half his upper body practically hanging out the window frame.

"What are you thinking? I mean really. You practically stole my truck, Malik."

Instantly, the just-under-the-surface smirk disappears. "What's wrong with you? What planet you living on, Brown?" He angrily rips his body from the cab and slams the door. He tosses me the keys, which fly just beyond the extension of my outward facing palm.

I take the first two steps backward before turning to bend down and retrieve them from the dirt.

"By the way, the motor's running great. I think it's good to go, though I'm not sure exactly where."

"What are *you* talking about?"

"I told you I had to test drive the truck to see if the belt was tight enough."

"Bullshit you did."

"Bullshit I didn't. Just as you were leaving with your phone, I yelled that out to ya."

I shake my head, clueless as to what he's talking about. Speechless about how to respond.

Malik rolls up the sleeves on the flannel shirt he's still wearing despite the morning heat. "Plus, I'm happy to kick those keys back at ya. My DWB radar was off the chart. The park ranger alone shot something into me through them thick-ass glasses."

"What are you talking about, someone shot something into you?" Despite the potential for collaborative healing that sparked new life into me less than an hour before, the returned frustration mounts. The feeling to be done with him returns, and I'd wish he felt the same.

"You just don't take someone's truck without asking. Or car or car parts or whatever."

Malik's eyes launch toward the sky where the blue has been replaced by a sheet of gray. He knows what I now know. Throwing in the car piece was inappropriate. Counterproductive. Fortunately, he lets it slide, again. Reminding me that to some degree, it might be his maturity that we're leaning on.

"First, like I said, I think your near broken-down-for-good, stupid-ass truck is running well now, though I should wrap that up with a big fat *maybe*."

"Maybe," I mumble under my breath loud enough for us both to hear.

"The belt had too much slack and needed tightening. Slightly less critical, but preventable, were the loose bearings. I tightened those too. Engines like these are quite simple. Easy to understand." He raises his finger, and I feel an act coming on. "Their drivers, not so much."

Even when I think he can't help himself to make attempts at humor, his diagnosis is serious, simple, and clear. Unfortunately, the distraction of his clarity is short-lived. I process the letters DWB through the few filters still clearly operating. It must be some joke or something, but this time I also want to call him out. Not everything is a joke, and especially when it's at someone else's expense.

"And what is this DWB thing you're talking about?"

I catch the seriousness on his face. I've again made a mistake, yet one I haven't identified. I face Malik with my hands on my hips. Whatever comes next, I'll just have to take it.

"You think you know me? You assume. Nah, you see a White man working on a truck and if that truck ain't there you, assume he's taken it on a test drive. But a Black man in the same situation is stealing, right, Brown? DWB means Driving While Black."

"Man, why are we back on race? Does it have to be infused into every conversation?"

"Until it's not infused into almost every waking moment of a Black man's life, then yes."

A period of verbal nothingness follows because nothing else needs to be said. I want to respect his honesty. His clarity. To be there 100 percent with him. For him to know that I hear him. And while not every action of mine would appear to reinforce it, I agree with him. *But what does agreeing with him even mean?* The ground still offers nothing to kick.

"You some teacher, Mr. Brown. What do you call that expression?" Malik moves his hands in a forward circular motion. "That's it. Yeah, it's called reading the room."

I ponder our circumstances, considering that we're no better than two idiots standing in the middle of an empty campground hundreds of miles from home because we can't deal with our own shit. When I told Malik I thought he stole my truck, he responded with how hard it is to drive when you're Black, and I think we're both about to accept a stalemate. Let bygones be as they are. That we're done talking. We're done arguing. Everything that could be said already has been, but I'm wrong.

"I'm shocked, or maybe I shouldn't be, at how surprised I still am when White people finally understand what Black people put up with everyday living in White society. And I said *finally*. You all have the same dumbfounded look. Part shock. Part embarrassment. Bigger part guilt for having not come to that conclusion sooner. And you're one of the good ones, Brown!"

"Is that what you told your boss at the auto shop? Just a test drive. C'mon, Malik. Taking a car from a shop. No license. No insurance. That's wrong."

"Yeah, absolutely, I borrowed a customer's car so I could take my auntie to see my grandma. Before. She. *Died*. Ain't no one gettin' their cars fixed in April and May 'cause of Covid, or corona, or whatever the fuck you call it, so that car just be sittin' there and I needed it. I'm feeling good 'cause I did something good for my family, and next thing you know, I'm gettin' pulled over for a busted taillight. Wrong? I had some weed in the car, and I'm thrown on the ground. Yous and I could buy the same bag of weed in a shop in yo neighborhood right now." Malik forcibly points his finger to the ground. "An hour after my auntie said goodbye to my grandmother, I'm on the ground with a gun in my face. I went from thinking I'd done something right for my family to thinking I'm the next funeral up."

Barely a breath of air is ingested before he continues.

"How many young twenty-something White kids get their license suspended for having weed in the car? A year before weed becomes legal?" he continues. "Shit, I remember this girl at the community college got pulled over for a busted brake light. She told the class that she purchased the textbook instead of replacing the light. It ain't all *fuck it*. White people get away with this stuff."

I look away from Malik because it's all I can do.

"Jamal used to tell me that at college, he had friends with fancy cars and they had cards to show if they got pulled over to share that their uncle or dad was a police officer. He'd tell us about driving with his friends, some of them all fucked up. A cop would pull them over and just make them switch drivers. Let them go. You believe that? Yeah, I know Jamal a storyteller and all, but he ain't making that shit up."

I lower my head for a break from Malik's social justice barrage and pull the phone from my pocket to check the time. 11:15. We need to move, but I do nothing to direct, sway, or infer this need to Malik. My eyes move between the ground, sky, and him. He's heated, and I get it. I just don't want it to continue.

"Wrong. Really, what part of that was wrong?"

I pull the phone out again. Not even a minute has passed.

"'Cause me, at the end of the day, when you take out the police incident for having a stupid taillight out and some weed in the car, I was onto something right for my family. All I know is that if this shit be happenin' to White people at the rate it be happenin' to Black people, there'd have been a cure a week ago."

I nod my head up and down. It's all I can think to do.

"COVID got my uncle dying alone in a hospital room, and I ain't in no way gonna let the same happen to my auntie. Sometimes you gotta do something wrong to do something right. And that something wrong, often, ain't even a problem for White people."

He's not breathing heavily, but with his hands on his hips, his breaths are noticeable. Charged with something that cannot be taken back.

"You know everything, huh," he says with an aggressiveness that exceeds its meaning. What we need to do remains nebulous, but it's clear his conversation is moving in the wrong direction. "So, what brilliant advice do you have for me, Mr. Brown?" With an unnecessarily heavy emphasis on my name, he strikes my hat off his head and whips it through the air, possibly swiping his thigh.

I don't get it. He and I know countless Black people who are very successful. He must know I'm aware of how extra hard they had to work for that success compared to White people with similar accomplishments, and I don't offer him this. I know that I know it, or at least in principle, but I also know I've done little to understand it.

"Oh, stop with that. Really. When does that get old? And I'm not saying it's an outdated reality or an unimportant conversation, but it doesn't need to be the only one." I raise my hand to swipe the hat off my head as he did, but not before realizing I'm not wearing one. I plow on. "Is there racism? Absolutely. Is the nation's history stained with it? Who's arguing that it's not?"

"For real?" he demands.

This really throws me for a loop. I thought I'd essentially agreed with him. Why's he still jabbing?

"How we gonna really talk about other stuff when we ain't figured this out?" He flips up the tailgate with unnecessary force and the frisbee rattles along the metal grooves of the bed.

It bothers me. For one, the use of force. Second, because I was just about to do that, and the shallowness of my thinking amplifies the brewing anger. With Malik for being with me. With

Terri for not telling me directly how I've been unable to provide her with the family she so wants. With Darren, for leaving me alone on the trail.

"I got ya. I got ya, Malik. You wanna get right down to it. You need to not go into a store with a big attitude. You need to not steal cars. You need to not sit in your car on the side of the road smoking weed."

"Oh, so that's what you think of me? Just another young Black man up to all kinds of no good. Ain't no good and who's gonna."

"Malik, stop that. Just stop that," I say, throwing my hands through the air at him like a football referee signaling an extra point kick gone wide.

He digs into his pocket with excessive and pointless drama. A task that shouldn't be the obstacle he makes it into. He exits his pant leg with a piece of paper and smoothes it over his thigh and holds it up for me to see. The receipt again.

"Okay, so you're forever validated," I declare with an unusual dose of sarcasm.

Malik checks to avoid the rust holes before resting his arms on the rim of the truck bed. The sun is almost directly overhead. Soon the metal will be too hot to touch. He returns the hat, my hat, to his head and turns it around, then opens the top buttons on my flannel, which I probably won't ask for back.

I grip the the truck's opposite sidewall, and there's nothing between us but space and metal. A forest surrounds us that stretches as far as man allows it. Beyond that a highway leading to our accomplishments and failures. Dreams and nightmares. To cities with rioters and protesters marching its streets. Most peacefully raising awareness to centuries of systemic injustice. Others denouncing a Black Lives Matter movement they see as an appetizer of a race war. Others just complaining about their lives as they always do. The faces of nearly everyone covered by masks. To different degrees, everyone is scared about catching a virus we know little about.

Beyond my own masks, a national and rational fear hides in plain sight. Fear of the patterns we've created and ones we've been fed by those with concealed intentions in pursuit of profits. White people in the city fearful of the random and consistent intimidation and violence they see from Black people in the streets, subways, and malls. Black people fearful of White gunmen methodically entering their churches or supermarkets. Rural racists stocking up on dried foods and ammunition. Directed by a misguided interpretation of modern times. Believing that a more level playing field isn't creating a more just society for all, but an arena where minorities who could never occupy their jobs and positions before, now are. The limited, accessible, and often restricted resources of our capitalism has uninvited guests ready to compete. There's many of them, and they all look different. The game is changing.

I've missed the individual stories. The lives of my students. Each carrying their own narrative about how racism impacts their life, while I've mastered crafting concepts at 30,000 feet. Summarizing our history into bullet points that describe wars, expansions, and advancements, continuously missing the stories right in front of me. And like the dozens of students who are continually late, missing work, unaware of expectations, and overwhelmingly clueless as to what their school needs from them, I also don't know what to do.

"You're right, Malik. This is a conversation that needs to happen, and again, and again."

Several minutes of silence carries us forward, though neither of us knows where. Possibly to just beyond where we were. All these years later and Malik's still a mystery to read. Maybe the most profound mysteries of a student I've had. He's paying attention to what I said while paying attention to his belief that he needs to appear as if he's paying attention to another White person telling him to move on. To be calm. If there's a third consideration, it avoids me, but another White person has probably said it to him.

"I'm not one you should be asking advice from. I'm just not." My words fade into the thick air.

After several days, he must know this to be the case. If not, then I've given him too much intellectual credit. "Well, let's start here. Why did you come to my house the other day?"

Malik chuckles. Maybe it's in response to me finally asking a direct question. Maybe because it's taken me this long to ask it.

"Funny you should ask." He looks inside the truck bed, rolling his eyes over the scattered camping gear sprawling throughout the metal surface. Maybe he's looking for something? Maybe an answer, or he's trying to distract me, or us both? He meets my eye again. "Well, funny you ask," he says again. "Not really funny, I guess. Ya really want to know why? Because there's another part of the story of my mother. Years ago, she started writing me these letters. Ya know, trying to explain why she wasn't with us. How she tried. How she…"

He takes a deep breath before continuing. "She wrote about sitting in the back of the police car and seeing this White man standing next to the police station with a large backpack. Said that it was at that moment she knew she'd have to teach her son that they still lived in a country where a White man could walk across the country, freely in and out of towns, while a Black one had to still watch every side of them wherever they went."

I let a new silence reinforce how real his words are to me, while being finally aware how no silence can convey this.

"Since high school you been meeting up with Jamal and Lewis. They been telling me about you coming out here, ya know. Me, I be piecing different stories together for a long time. When you showed us the trail pics in class years ago, someone asked if you'd do it again. You said something like 'the trail remains part of me,' or some shit like that, which really wasn't an answer at all. You the only person I knew who came out here. But there's more. My mother also wrote that—"

But Malik is cut off by the sound of another engine. One with a mechanical heartbeat far healthier than the one we're depending on to get us home.

The park ranger's truck enters the campsite loop, and it feels like a normal patrol. The ranger bends the curve and slows before stopping at our site. "Check out was eleven," he says and drives off. No nod or wave, and I think little of it. Maybe he'd prefer his campground to be empty rather than just one site used. Maybe Malik thinks this is racist because the man is White and looked at him. Maybe the ranger is racist because he's White and looked at us. Maybe.

The distraction is untimely. I grab my wallet from the cab and pat the pockets of my shirt, checking for my phone and keys. Checking to understand what Malik just shared is far more evasive.

"Hey, I want to hear the rest, I really do, Malik. But I got a phone call I need to take with Biko's principal in less than an hour. Terri has Covid, and she's not feeling well. We need to go. Let's grab some snacks in town and hit the road."

Malik nods, and we take the shortcut leading to the road with its wide shoulder. A sidewalk emerges within a few hundred feet and then the first colonial-era light post. The buildings display a decorative architecture, reflecting a town built with patience, intention, and resources. We pass several people, but something in the approaching couple captures our attention. Maybe it's their colorful attire or the loaf of bread swinging from the woman's hand. Maybe it's that they're the first people we see wearing masks. Maybe it's the letters I think I recognize under the woman's open sweatshirt. A beast of a clothing choice on a stifling hot day.

Malik greets them, and I'm caught off guard. "I like your shirt," he calmly says. His voice benign of accent or attitude, or is it ethnicity? The lady stops and then so does the man who accompanies her. I presume her husband. He takes a step backward, exposing graceless footwork.

"Why, thank you. I imagine you're referring to this?" She pulls on the corners of her zipper sweatshirt, fully exposing the familiar white Black Lives Matter logo on her black T-shirt. "Hold this," she says, gently pushing the loaf of bread into her husband's stomach. She takes off her sweatshirt, exposing her frail arms beneath the oversized shirt. "I'm still a bit chilly, but you're right. This message needs to be out there for all to see."

Malik extends a warm smile, building on the woman's friendliness. "I didn't really say all that," he replies.

"Oh, but your eyes and smile did, young man." She ties the sweatshirt around her waist and with the same gentleness, she retrieves the bread from her husband. "And I'm glad for it. If he didn't have this arthritis, we'd walk up and down Main Street all day with my new shirt for all to see."

We share a few seconds of a silence that's more comfortable than the others. Maybe all of us trying to absorb the moment and see how far this hopeful interaction can carry us forward when we all seem to be absorbing the country's hate and recklessness.

The man moves his head up and down several times before we hear his voice. "It's taking time." A not-so-subtle nudge from his wife connects their elbows. It's endearing, but then I realize it has greater meaning. "It's going to take more time," he corrects himself, his slow drawl filled with what New Englanders refer to as southern purity.

"Sadly, more time," the lady adds. Her smile is intended for Malik rather than the situation she describes. Over his white

T-shirt, the older man wears a tan vest like those worn by fish-ermen and small round pins cover each side of his chest. A local VFW chapter patch is sewn on his black mesh cap.

"What brings you to town, gentlemen?" the lady asks. "The trail, biking, fishing?"

Without missing a beat, Malik turns toward the elder cou-ple. "Little bit of each, but we're heading to the store for some snacks now."

"Well, we just returned from the market and said hello to one of my favorite former students. For some reason I remem-ber every moment of that class, my last year of a long teaching career." She turns her gaze upward, possibly looking for a sign that the years meant something to those young lives, but it's hard to see anything within the gray sheet of clouds that has overtaken the sky.

We take a step, but then Malik stops, pivoting back to the older couple. "What would you say was the most important lesson your former student learned from you?" he asks the woman.

Instantly, the old man who seemed lost in his static posture, straightens his back, reaching several inches taller into space he occupied years before. Malik's words sting. Then I realize this isn't his intent, though I'm no closer to what it really is.

The woman raises her chin, perhaps seeing her husband like she hadn't in years. She interlocks her fingers in front of her body, and I watch her eyelids lower and her skinny chest rise with a few good breaths. When she lowers her face, her eyes are open and something is different. The woman lands her gaze in the space between us, a clear intention on her part to occupy this benign area that is neither Malik or me.

"To find your voice," she answers quietly. "I'd say it's to find your voice." She nods as she repeats with even less confidence, understanding in her soul that teachers rarely see their work's long game.

"C'mon, they have a lot to do, Martha."

The older man gently taps his wife's elbow, using their own language sculptured by time and love. The ease with which their bodies communicate has limits, and he struggles to raise his hand beyond his hip to wave us on. The lady's smile deepens with authentic appreciation for the conversation. With little more to say in a moment that's already squeezing minutes from seconds, we smile and walk away.

The Damascus downtown is different from the other small Appalachian towns we've traveled through since Harpers Ferry. The main street has a vibrancy aided by the different colors of paint on the building's wood trim. While it wasn't my experience years earlier, from everything I've heard the town is a mecca for trail life. People committed to the land and their adventures within it, not to mention it being the trail's relative halfway point. Several people walk the wide sidewalks carrying large backpacks. Fast-moving hikers who started in early April are starting to arrive around now.

"That was cool," Malik says.

I look around for something out of the ordinary, but the only noticeable feature is the darkening clouds.

"What?"

"That lady and all. That was the last thing I expected, that's all." We cross the first and only intersection in town with a traffic light.

"Let's head over there. I'll prepare for this phone call while you get some snacks for the drive." I point to the small park and pavilion across the street, then hand him a ten-dollar bill, which he quickly moves into his pocket after thanking me.

Just as quickly he hands it back. "You paid for everything else so far, I got this. So, what's this call with the principal about, JB?"

"Let's just say this hasn't been the best year for me."

"You? Well, that might be the understatement of the year. I mean what *student* was this year good for?" His words trail into the thick heat with frustration and anxiety. "So, the principal is calling you to help plan next year 'cause you been there a long time or something?"

"Not exactly. Maybe even the exact opposite."

"Well, the exact opposite would be a call about what not to do, and that just seems like a waste of everyone's time, wouldn't ya say?"

"Alright, that's a bit of a literal interpretation." I need Malik to get food so we can leave, but he's standing over me. *Why? Of all that's happening, why does he want to know more about this?* "I've had some mess ups, or situations that she thinks are mess ups." Hopefully this will bore him into turning away, but he doesn't.

"Mess ups. I know what you mean, but I've never even heard that expression. Sounds like a White thing. Mess ups."

"Funny you say that, though nothing really feels funny. I think in some ways the call is about a White thing, like me." We move toward the bench a few feet from the wide sidewalk. My shallow confidence sinks with each step. I sit on the soft green panels and feel the old wood slightly bend under me.

"Now, you may not think so, but I'm no fool, JB. However, I have no clue what you're talking about."

I look up at Malik, wondering why he cares. Why he won't leave. "Listen, this call with the principal, it's complicated. She's doing a lot of work in our school on antiracism. I get the sense that she thinks I'm not up for it. Or because I didn't hand out computers or that I leave when the school day is over, or that, shoot, I don't know. Maybe she just feels I'm not doing enough. Not doing my part, but it's hard to know what this even means." I reach into the bag and grab the folder with my student letters and pen. "I get the sense that you care, and thanks, but we need to get out of here. Can you grab some snacks so we can leave?"

He mockingly salutes me before twisting his body on the rubber heels of his sneakers. Two or three wide steps follow like a changing of the guard presentation. His efforts to lighten the mood and accelerate our departure accomplish neither, but strangely, I appreciate them. My eyes follow him across the street, cringing that he doesn't look either way before entering the road, though recognizing there is nothing to stop for. I can't help but think he moves similarly back in the city.

He enters the market as my legs start to gently bounce on the balls of my feet. After a decade and a half of watching hundreds of students do the same, I wonder if I've seen my legs hop in place like this before. I slide the folder onto my lap, draw small circles in the corner of the page, and write some key words I want to use in the conversation.

- Apology – Start Here
- Commitment
- Community
-

These are the words she wants to hear, I tell myself. Neatly, I draw a fourth bullet point, but I can't think of a word to place next to it.

Suddenly, across the street a commotion punctures the air. A door smashes into a wall. Then Malik runs out and turns down the sidewalk. His knees pound up into his chest like an untrained athlete desperate for another chance, or that of a Black man running for his life.

Guided by shock, I intuitively stand and take a few steps, watching Malik sprint down the road. He skids to a stop and backtracks several feet as his hat, my hat, falls off his head. He gracefully scoops it up as his body bends into the small alley between the two-story buildings.

An overweight woman with an apron flapping off her body runs out of the store yelling, "Stop that man! Stop him! Stop him!"

Several people on the street stop and turn their attention.

I jog a few steps into the street as a huge gust of mountain wind whips down the concrete valley, drowning the woman's continued screams as two men stand in front of the alley where Malik ran, pointing. The sound of a flag whipping in the wind grabs my attention, but the large banner overhead isn't moving. That's not the source of what I'm hearing. My folder has blown open off the bench and all of my letters sail into the darkening sky.

As the circus of paper dances in the air, panic grabs my leg. It's pulling me in. I need the woman to stop yelling for the police. I look down the road, and my letters are flower petals in a drunk wind. Then back to the woman. Something vibrates in my pocket, and I pull out my phone.

Principal Becker.

14

WIDESPREAD PANIC. GUSTS OF wind transform the banner hanging across the road into a full parachute. The sign stand highlighting the "Hungry Hiker Sandwich with Chips for $4.99" skitters along the sidewalk before crashing to the ground. Wrappers and debris rip through the air. The last of my letters disappear in the maelstrom. Bright white letters on my phone read: Missed Call 12:01.

Shock runs through my body, and when I look up, I'm within two feet of the screaming lady. One might think that we'd all have an instinctive six-foot tape measure by now.

"Can I help? How can I help?" The words, or better yet, the pleas rush from my mouth.

"Go get that man. He stole from me!"

Her words are loud with conviction. No hesitation or doubt, like she's a woman with a clear history of suggestions as directions. Directions as demands. The clarity of her words overshadow what they describe, which feels less authentic. My deep panting interrupts analysis.

"Well," I say, swiveling in all directions, looking for something to say. "What did he steal? I mean. What was it?"

"What?" She bores into me. Stunned. How dare I. That I could ask something like this. "What are you talking about? He stole from me. You wanna help? Go get him," she yells into the wind. Someone new looking right through me. "Someone call the police! Call the sheriff!"

She slams her fists angrily into the space beside her hips and stomps the few steps back to her shop. The untied apron swings outward, following her. She shoves her face in the doorway and yells, "Laurie, bring me the phone!"

Within seconds a teenage girl exits holding a cell phone outward. The young girl's eyes grip the ground as the woman snatches the phone and spins back in my direction.

"Listen, I can pay for whatever he stole. No problem." I dig into my pants and then shift my hands to a rear pocket. I face the open old leather sleeve of my wallet toward her, showing her the edges of twenty something small bills that I can't fathom aren't enough to cover the cost for whatever Malik stole.

"What are you doing, sir? What in God's name are you doing?" she huffs.

Our maskless faces are much too close.

"I can pay for it. Whatever it is. How much was it? We don't need the police. Really, ma'am. We don't need to make this a big deal. C'mon, just tell me the cost."

She looks through me again.

Several people stand on the outer perimeter of a small circle that includes the woman, me, and the teenage girl. The faint sound of a siren cuts through the wind, and it's getting louder.

"Good, someone called the police. Thank God! We need law and order. Law and goddamn order," she declares. The woman forcefully turns away and hunches over the phone's small screen as I capture the back of the young girl fade beyond the closing store door. The wind captures the glass door as I slowly reopen it, forcing me to strain my arm to hold it in place. I walk past two of the three small aisles looking for her, but no one is around. I grab the door handle to exit as a faint sound from the back of the store touches the air.

"Wait."

I turn around. No one. I walk slowly toward the aisle closest to the register. The girl stands at the back of the store. Behind her is a library of domestic beer cans. We stare into each other, calculating the situation. Evaluating our pasts. Our futures. Unsure what the other wants. What the other needs. Our reservations become more prolific with every second. Both seeing another person deep in their own search. Roads and walkways leading to walls and blocked exits. But in her curled lips I also see something far braver. Something trying to make amends.

"He didn't steal anything. Quite the opposite. He was kind," she says, barely loud enough to be heard.

"What?"

"She didn't like the way he slid the money on the counter, so she slid it back. Told him to try again."

"That's it?" My chin juts forward and I hear myself almost yelling and immediately stop. *My tone can only deflate her*, I tell myself.

"No. He slid the money again, and she crumpled it up. Threw it at him. Accused him of stealing. Said she was calling the police. He picked up the money and tossed it on the counter. Some other words were said that I didn't hear. Then he ran out."

"What! That's what happened? That's ridiculous. You need to come outside and tell them." I abruptly shift my eyes from her to the door, and I can feel my intensity deepening her anxiety in the exact moment I need her clarity and conviction.

We're both distracted when red lights flash along the far wall of the store. Within seconds, the patrol car parks in front of the building. "You really need to tell this to them. That man can get in a lot of trouble with the police if they don't hear this. This has already gone too far," I plead with two extended arms, which I immediately realize have no purpose.

"No, you need to go. Please. Go now. I've already said too much. I know how this ends. I need this job." The young lady covers her face with both hands and turns away. She opens a cooler door and shakily rearranges a few six-packs, and the freezing air reaches the back of my legs as I exit the store. An overstuffed sheriff holds his hat on his head in defense of the warm wind. His deputy stands beside him.

"He was scary, Ronnie. Threatening. I know he had something in his pocket. I just know it."

"Really. What more can you tell me, Alice?" He removes his hand from his hat to flip over a page and scribbles in his small notepad.

"Excuse me, sir. I shared with her that I'm willing to pay, but according to the young lady inside, the young man did pay for the snacks. There's a crumpled ten-dollar bill on the counter. She said you threw it back at him." I direct my chin toward Alice.

"She said what? Laurie!" she roars into a wind that amplifies its range. "Listen, I don't know who you are, or if you're his—I don't even know what you people call it—but he had more in his pockets, I know it," she says with disgust, glancing away when something else becomes clear. She's counting on what's proven true over centuries of White people making accusations like this—an abundance of suspicion overshadowing evidence. "Heck, Sherriff. I swear I saw him stuff candy in his pocket."

The sheriff turns his unpleasant energy toward me. "Who are you? You with him?" He points off into a distance, unaware of precisely the direction Malik ran.

I don't answer. My lips forget how to move. Forget its sounds. How to respond. Am I with him?

The sheriff's face makes it apparent my silence is unappreciated. His hands shift to behind his back. "Okay, I see what's happening. Let's start here. Why or how is this your business, sir?"

The seconds build. With them a deepening and familiar insecurity. My mind is back in Principal Becker's office. Needing a story to keep kids safe. Keep me safe.

"You're not answering me, and I don't appreciate that," he says, barely leaving enough time between his rapid questions for a response. "You a through-hiker?"

"Me? No. Well, years ago. Just back for a visit, that's all."

He looks down on my tall frame. The jowls below his jawline shake from side to side. The small eyes in his big head demand to be taken seriously. "And what business is this to you?"

"I met that guy in the campground. He didn't seem like a guy that would steal, that's all."

"So, you know him? Know where he's headed, don't ya?" The sheriff's eyes widen. There's information in me. My annoyance may offer him something.

A vision of a joking Malik pops to mind. Another dramatic announcement. *If I ever come back here, I'm definitely going south to Freedom Cabin.* "Yeah, he's through-hiking. He's going, um, he's going north."

"You sure?"

I unintentionally look to the ground, where my eyes have sought safety for years. "Yeah. I mean, yes, I'm sure. That's what he told me."

The sheriff drills his eyes into me. "What's your name, son?"

"Brown. Jerry Brown. Everyone calls me JB."

"We'll take it from here, Mr. Brown."

"But, sir—"

"I've heard enough from you, Mr. Brown. We'll take it from here." His tone leaves little doubt about his expectations, and I take a few small steps backward. "Mr. Brown, I take crimes like this very seriously in my jurisdiction. This is a safe community. With good people. My patience for trouble, and those causing it, is thinning by the day. There's a lot of troublesome behavior happening in the big cities right now. I'm not about to tolerate it around here."

The deputy beside him turns away, shaking his head, and the smallest of reserve awareness I have leaves me wondering if it's because he so strongly agrees with his supervisor or something else. I remember the way Kent's brother spoke about the incident where his cronies beat up Walter. I know this vernacular code. Language intended to sound responsible and prolific that disguises layers of racism and bigotry.

Before his words curtail, I step backward and when I reach the center of the road, I swivel on my sneakers' thin soles and stop in front of the alley where Malik disappeared. Two people on the other side of the street point at me. *What just happened?* I pass the buildings feeling numb. I'm being watched.

My eyes rapid fire in all directions, certain I'll see Malik hiding behind a tree or somewhere out of sight. A bend in the trail hugs a small creek as I pass a large-group pavilion area that I hadn't noticed before. I freeze. A small arched bridge in the short distance. A few more steps, cautioned by confusion and the sense I'm walking into a trap. Those colors. I recognize a red streak. It's my flannel. Another few steps. The blue of my Expos cap. Both hang on a railing post at the bridge's edge. I frantically look in all directions. Malik isn't here either.

He clearly left my clothes here for a reason, but what? I lift the shirt and hat off the post and freeze again. The profoundly arched bridge over a small creek. Tree branches hanging over the sides of the slow-moving stream. Where have I seen this place before? I turn around and then back, thinking movement will spur a recollection. The sight is meaningful and close, yet distant and foreign. I'm unable to place anything beyond knowing I recognize this place. I slide the shirt under my arm and bend the hat's brim in my hand, watching the periphery for movements. Listening for sounds. Clues. I'm certain Malik will be at or near the campsite. Where we can rid ourselves of this mess. Hop in the truck and leave here forever.

But the campground is empty and quiet, though it doesn't feel that way. Someone is here, but it's unclear if I'll find the person I'm looking for or the people looking for him. At the site I scan the area for anything unusual. My eyes play tricks in every direction. In the middle of the truck bed, I see the lid not closed on the gear box. I slide the cover, instantly noticing what's missing. My pack. One headlamp has been removed from the old carabiner.

No. No. No. He really did go to the trail.

I turn the key to hear an engine in need of additional attention but without the scaling sound of a loose belt. Malik's repair worked. I slowly exit the campground and drive to the Appalachian Trail parking lot, and directed by an irrational sense for forward thinking planning and blind guidance, I restart the engine to pull out and back the truck in.

A high wind shakes the treetops. At ground level, it's barely enough breeze to feel on my skin, but the curly blond hair on my arms rise. Static electricity is in the air. My track record of people being where I needed them isn't great. Far worse for them having me where they needed. I should just drive back to the city.

Terri thinks I'll be home within a few hours. How many times can I let the same person down? What makes me think I'll find Malik here? If he's not at the cabin, and chances are he's not, I'm not sure what to do. I'll need to leave and head back. *Malik is damaged,* I tell myself. *This is not my fault.* Continued wheel taps. The sky darkens with late afternoon storm clouds. Another voice reminds me of something less obvious, contradicting nearly all my lies. I believe in him.

Knowing the woman's story at the store isn't adding up, I still didn't have the courage to stick up for Malik with the sheriff. I slam the creaky door and grab the remaining headlamp from the gearbox. I spread a green tarp over most of the gear in case it rains, or rather, when. I take my first steps as thunder roars in a neighboring valley. Like a beast being awoken in its cave.

Curving around the bends in the twisting trail, the imperfect connections of nature are comforting. Or maybe it's numbing. Another ten minutes like that around people and who could blame me for leaving everything behind again for the trail. Another switchback and a sheet of gray cloud darkens a sky made darker by the forest's denseness.

Each step takes me back in time. Two decades earlier to the days leading to Damascus. The first time in years I'd felt anything like pure life. Pumped into my veins by a heart longing for my brother. "I've got a lot to repair with you, JB. I need to show you how I've changed." I repeated his words over thousands of steps. I climbed mountains on them. "Thanks for giving me this chance, JB." His last words before hanging up. Before I could say, "I love you," which I'm not sure I could had time been endless. To know that he knew.

The trees overhead frantically sway under a dark sky that leaves one to wonder if the sun has set or if the storm's cover is this dark. After several hours of hiking, I'm still too scared to take out my phone. All the missed calls from Terri and texts I can't download to read, settle in. Something's wrong beyond the something wrong that's right in front of me. A sign points to a spur trail for the cabin, and I can't get the picture of where Malik left my flannel shirt and cap out of my head.

My mind reassures me I know this trail, but it's not true. I never went up this trail. Only down, and when I did I believed that I was heading toward the best day of my life. Where I'd call Darren and finalize our plan to reunite. Never again, I swore, would I deliberately take steps that were destined to lead to horror, and yet somehow, I'm back here. This time with a certain skepticism that I may finally be doing the right thing.

The outhouse sign means I'm close and electricity is in the air, both from the storm and my own nerves. The clouds hold their dimly sketched borders as multiple storms collide. Several footpaths lead to the tent sites that commonly border trail cabins. Walls and ceilings aren't for everyone, and some through-hikers never venture inside them. My feet slow upon first glance at the old wooden cabin, which appears empty. Lightning flashes. Two seconds later, thunder rips the valley. A twig cracks under my feet, sending me back to the cold autumn air, listening to my brother and the professor talk beside his trailer. But I'm wrong, because this time my presence is definitely detected as a dim light suddenly turns off inside.

My sneakers slide on the wet steps. My muscles tighten. My fingers grip the metal handle as thousands of hands had done before in search of shelter and rescue, but few like this. Confliction battles every part of my being. Absence or presence. I step inside and pause. The fear returns.

"Malik. Are you here?"

The words whisper their way around the cabin as a blast of lightning shocks the sky. It's overhead. In that flash of a dissected second, I see the outline of a vacant room, except for one familiar sight.

"Malik?"

"Yeah." A low but definitive whisper, but no sign of its origin.

"Are you okay?" *Would we be here if he was?* I skip the breath my body needs.

Another blast of thunder.

Another unfamiliar sound. "Shhhhhhhh. Shhhhhhhhh."

"It's just me, Malik. I know you didn't do anything wrong. I know it, Malik. People are cruel. I know you didn't do anything wrong." I turn on my headlamp and the room is empty.

Left. Right. Empty.

Several fingers then snake from under the table, gripping its side. Malik slides his body out between the table and bench and plops his backside down. His head lowers into his hands.

I remove the headlamp from my forehead and rest it facing upward on the table, illuminating the room. For a moment, I'm tempted to look for the same graffiti message on the ceiling of Freedom Cabin. Those words written in black marker have stained me for two decades. "None of us are Free."

I sit on the bench across from him and slide him a water bottle.

Malik doesn't move or notice. His cheeks look puffy with whatever makes a man's cheeks do this. I look into his eyes and then it hits me. Of all the misery that's consumed my attention for the last hour, the fact that Malik felt he had to run because he is a Black man hadn't entered my thoughts. It should have. Tap, tap, stop. Tap, tap, stop. Tap, tap, stop. His fingers on the table. His eyes and demeanor offer an expression that hides more than it shows.

"I spoke with the girl in the store. She said you did nothing wrong."

He digs his thumbs into the side of his temples, and I know there is no way to console him. Behind the silence in our heads, the maddening wind and thunder builds. Malik mumbles something under his breath that I can't hear. I want to reach out and grab his shoulder. To reinforce that I'm here for him, but I can't, though for the first time I know that I am.

"Malik, we need to leave. Put this behind us."

"I'm sick of being saved by other people. I don't want more bailouts from White people."

"I'm not bailing you out." The frustration evolves into anger. "Listen, even after all this time, I don't know what you're running from. But because of you, I'm sure as heck a whole lot clearer on what I've been running from. Have you been paying attention? I'm not helping you. You're helping me." I hear the words spill from my mouth, trying to understand the meaning of what I just said.

A sheet of rain sprints across the aluminum cabin roof.

"Maybe you thought I'd have some answers, but I don't. We're in a shitty situation because you ran into a racist lady, who in some way felt like you disrespected her. Shoot, maybe you did. But from what I think, what I heard from the girl in the shop, and from what I know about who you are, I know that you didn't do anything wrong. Maybe other than living in a country with a whole lot of fucking racist people. Got it. There it is."

Malik raises an eyebrow. Slightly. Neither of us has ever heard me speak with this kind of conviction. My hands start trembling. "We got to go."

"I'll just screw up somewhere else. It's what I do."

"Bullshit. Remember what you said? About making trouble while doing something right? Yeah, that's you. That's this."

Planks of rain whip the cabin walls.

"Malik, I'm not sure what kind of sense this makes, but I lived next door to this guy growing up on a farm. We called him the professor. He told my brother that you find maps and keys in the wounds. I didn't understand what he meant. He liked to phrase things in confusing ways. But I've thought more about that over the past two days with you than in the past twenty years, and you know what I've learned? He was wrong. You find *life* in the wounds! You can find how to *heal* in our wounds."

Lightning and thunder again smack the sky. Streaks of light zip through the cracks in the old wood cabin. I feel my body slumping. Zapped of energy and too afraid to make a decision. Stuck in my masks. My problems are narrow. Avoidable. Unworthy of healing. A small puddle forms near the center of the table. He's expressionless. Void of everything Malik, and I'm not sure if this is a good or bad thing. Unpredictability has never been my comfort zone. But I can't shake that the problems he's dealing with make me feel as if my own are inadequate.

"Malik, you can take all that pain and frame it with your White privilege stamp, and if it sticks, then so be it. But all this privilege, it doesn't mean that life has been without pain. Privilege doesn't mean prosperity." I sit with this, again unsure why I'm making it about me, as if it's a topic I know and understand. I'm unsure what he hears. Unsure how it's appropriate, but it's the only thing I can think to say. Mostly, unsure how this statement is going to get him moving.

Malik mumbles something else under his breath, and then, and only then do I really comprehend the trauma he's experienced today. A Black city boy—no, a man—caught in a fraudulent accusation from a racist shopkeeper in rural America. Followed by a racist sheriff. Running into the woods during a storm hundreds of miles from home on the slim understanding of where he's headed. Unsure if the former teacher he's been unintentionally traveling with cares enough beyond himself to help. Or even try.

I sit with it. Knowing what could or would have happened differently had we been somewhere else, been someone else, been something else. Walter's cosmic roll of the dice.

Malik's eyes are wide open, but I have no inclination of what they're seeing. What he's thinking. If he's even here with me. For what feels like an hour we sit across from each other because no words of muscles can move us, and then I find something.

"Listen, without you I would have sat in a stupid campground, but I needed to go to Harpers Ferry. I needed to come to Damascus. I needed to get back in the wounds. We leave our wounds open, they deepen. Sometimes, and I'm not sure if it's courage or foolishness or something I've never heard of or understood, but I'm learning that you need to get back into the wounds. So they can finally heal. And I think that's what we're both doing, but we need to get out of here, okay?"

Everything I could say has been said. I place my hand on Malik's wet forearm and swing my leg over the bench. I flip the daypack over my head. The straps lower on my shoulders. Malik slides off the bench, and while I'm in front, I feel like I'm following him as we head out into the wild. The night sky has darkened, and the rain has increased.

Malik is only noticeable because of the bouncing light stemming from his forehead. We walk in our thoughts, considering scenarios as to what happens next. His silence is deafening because I've never wanted to hear him speak more than now. To know how his brilliant and fractured mind is seeing this moment, or the ones that have passed.

After an hour, the trail levels and I know we're near the bottom. His silence is the most uncomfortable kind. Silence in darkness. The rain has let up, but our visibility is hindered by a thick fog. A parade of beeps ping from my phone. Another dozen or so missed calls and texts. Almost all from Terri, but I can't read them with the limited signal.

We approach the trailhead. Pause. It's later than I thought. One of the cars in the lot has its interior lights on. Strange, but not totally so and I think little of this. A few more steps. We're about ten feet behind the trail registry sign. Pause. Through the mist I can see writing on the vehicle's door. A few more steps. Pause. Clear Creek County Sheriff.

I reach for Malik's shoulder to push him downward to kneel on the ground, but there's no need for this. He's already there. More aware than me that we need to remain out of sight. He awkwardly fiddles with his forehead and his light disappears, and I do the same.

I deeply inhale. Moist, warm, post-storm forest air with a hint of bigotry and horror. Malik is still and silent. The focused calm of a man aware of how much is at stake. He can't know that for the first time since I almost ran him over that I'm 100 percent with him. I question what this means, and I want to see it. To see a feeling I know there's no light to see.

Our shoulders push against each other as our knees dig into the wet dirt, and my heavy breathing feels similar to when I watched the violent video in the truck we're now trying to reach. When I learned my lungs had gullies for air so painful that one might consider how necessary the next breath truly is. In my mind I replay the scene of Malik saving his friend from circumstances no friendship should have to endure. His eyes, now illuminated by the faint light cast from the nearby police car, scan the limited areas there are to see.

Maybe he's waiting for me to speak. To direct us onward. Expecting what he's experienced for most of the last three days. To be told of my plan. My direction. My view of how to make things better. None of these, I finally see, has gotten us anywhere safer. I've got nothing.

"A plan," I whisper, "got any ideas?" At first I think he's turned his head, but I realize quickly he's closed his eyes. "What should we do?" I whisper more urgently.

The ensuing silence lasts for metrics beyond measurement as we crouch behind the false safety of trees, the night's silence full of sounds. The blend of rain and cooling air casts a chill on my arms. I imagine him thinking to himself, This is the time you choose to ask me that question?

"Maybe we wait them out?" I offer.

Malik takes a deep breath and exhales slowly, his demeanor both calm and intense. "I got a plan, JB, and I need you to listen."

In the milliseconds following his demand to "listen," the articles Becker circulated spin throughout my mind. The ones I pretended not to read. The ones about how antiracist teaching starts with listening. How helping starts with listening.

"You gonna walk out there and talk to them. Tell 'em some shit. Anything. That's on you. Maybe an angel or three will help ya, and I'm gonna walk along the outside of the parking lot in the woods. Luckily for me, you backed into the lot and I can hide. If they leave, we split the other way and get outta here."

"Okay, okay. Right. Okay…" I respond. After several seconds Malik sighs. "Wait. Wait, wait, wait," I sputter. "What if they tell me I can go but they stay to watch me leave?"

"Good point," Malik says. "If they insist on watching you leave, I'll sneak into the back of the truck."

"Fuck no, Malik. That's crazy," and I feel his face inches from mine.

"You're finally right, JB. This is crazy. That after all these hours they ain't been told or figured out I did nothin' wrong. Or maybe they do know and they're still here. Yeah, this plan is crazy, but don't forget the crazy we be responding to." He leans in a little closer. "It's all crazy, but right now, I gotta trust myself, and I gotta trust you."

Two cars speed down the road. A distraction. No, a miracle. The sheriff will certainly pursue them, and my imagination hears the officer's motor shift into gear and peel out of the lot. The silence jars me back to reality. He passed on them, possibly an easy catch, to remain here for us.

"JB, when you get to the bottom of the trail you gonna turn on your head lamp and walk all normal. Remember, they're not after you," and more quietly he continues, "I don't think."

"Then what?"

"You remember I told you about Mr. Roberts working in a store that was always gettin' robbed? How he used crazy hand signals to tell the owner if he should call the cops or grab his gun? JB, you gotta go down there. You ain't done nothing wrong, and if they think you did, then this plan goes to shit quick, but we can't go down together. That's clear, right?" A second passes, then, "Right, JB?"

"Right, right," I blurt, finally realizing he can't see me nodding.

"I"ll be watching you. If they let you go but stay to watch, and you think it's clear for me to sneak into the truck, scratch your right ear. Remember, right means 'I'm alright.' If you think they're watching too closely and it's not safe for me, scratch your left ear. I'll sneak out to the road, and when you turn right I'll hop in. Got it?"

"Okay. Got it." All I can think of is that this plan is going from really fucking bad to really fucking worse, but Malik's conviction is the one worth following.

Malik briefly squeezes my shoulder, an action I know isn't all goodwill. "Trust me," he says, then pivots, rises, and disappears into the woods. After a deep breath, I twist on my headlamp and step onto the wet packed dirt of the parking lot.

The sheriff's car is in the exact spot of the couple who told me about planes crashing into the towers that morning. At first, I thought she meant the radio or weather tower fell, but then she corrected me. The whole building. Both of them. "Almost everyone inside is dead," were her exact words.

A few more steps and a round light shines on my feet, then slowly rises along my wet body.

An unwelcoming familiar voice. "If it isn't Mr. Brown, from Washington, DC again."

"Evenin', sheriff."

"Can I have a word with you? I was rather surprised when I noticed your truck in this lot when I drove by earlier. Then I became suspicious. Something's not adding up for me." The inside of the patrol car is dark.

Act like you've done nothing wrong, JB.

"What are you still doing here? Odd time for a hike in this weather. I was expecting someone, just not you."

"Trails are less crowded when it's like this."

Banter from the patrol car catches my ear. The sheriff isn't alone. Quieter dialogue is interrupted by the electronic zip of a window rising. A moment later, the same hum lowers the window.

The sheriff resumes like there was no gap in our exchange. "Hard to argue with that. Wait right there, son."

Then I wonder if Malik is hearing this. Wonder what the sheriff is thinking. Wonder if he knows Malik is nearby. Wonder what Malik is thinking.

"Here's what I'm gonna tell you, Mr. Brown. I think you should find some other trails to hike on. Do you hear what I'm saying?" A light turns on in the patrol car, and I see the same deputy from earlier. "Wouldn't you agree, Deputy Owens, that Mr. Brown should find another area for his hiking hobby?"

His partner looks at me and barely moves his head. An affirmation of compliance or disgust?

Frustrated by the lack of response, the sheriff turns back to his colleague and repeats himself.

Owens lowers his mask. "Yes, Sheriff. There are other places better suited for you, Mr. Brown."

I repeat what I've heard silently to myself. "I hear you both, gentlemen. I'm leaving now."

The window rises for what I hope is the final time, and as slow steps guide me toward the truck, I stretch my arm outward and scratch my right ear. When I'm a few steps from the truck, a ball of light cuts through the fog and encircles the ground around me.

"Little faster, Mr. Brown."

Awkwardly, I stretch my hand around my head as if reaching for the ear on the opposite side. He knows something's up. I frantically scratch my wet hair with both hands and realize the mixed signal I just sent. I walk a few feet to the center of the parking lot, avoiding the potholes I'm only able to see because of the obnoxious light cast from the patrol car window. I need to keep the light away from the back of the truck. I open the driver's side door, rest the bag on the seat and dig into the top pocket for the keys. I flip on the interior light.

"I'm good, sheriff. I've got my own light. Thank you."

I turn around, shocked at my nerve. Or was it a commonly acceptable thing to say? It doesn't matter as long as his light disappears. I think I feel the truck shift. Was that from the weight of Malik's body or my own movement? Why aren't they leaving? I get the sense the sheriff is about to shine his light again, or worse, approach the truck.

The patrol car roars to life, its crunching tires amplified by the thick air and silent forest. I lift the pack and dramatically toss it in the air above the bed. A short groan reassures me it's landed on something other than the metal surface. The patrol car exits toward town, and I turn right with a limited understanding of where the road leads in that direction, though aware that it leads away from town and the highway.

I swerve through the bends in the mountain road. Mostly sure, but not completely so that Malik is in the back. The GPS app on my phone atop the dash informs me that the interstate, which we need, is in the other direction. Then the signal is lost, again.

I pull over and take out the atlas, estimating that circling the mountains from here will add hours of travel. Time we can't afford. We're almost out of gas. Enraged with impulsivity, I shift gears to make a three-point turn in the middle of the road as a knock on the back window scares new life, and whatever comes with it, deeply into my core.

Malik's head pops in. "What are you doing, JB? You turning around?"

"I went the wrong way. We gotta turn around and get gas," I yell over the sound of a malnourished engine.

"You serious, JB? Really."

"We have to. Just stay down."

I repeat the words in my head, stunned that I can be in a place where something like this needs to be said. A deep breath fills my lungs with knowing Malik is safely in the back of the truck, and then I correct myself. No one is sure just how safe he is. Or any of us are.

"We get to the interstate and I'll pull over to get you inside," I yell, almost veering off the road. Another upshift as I rip off my jacket and stuff it through the window. "It's not much. Here."

Malik lowers his head. We pass the now empty trailhead parking lot and head toward town. My chest tightens at the sight of the faint light cast from the town's only traffic light, now blinking yellow. I slow to twenty on the dot, though every part of my body creeps forward even slower. From the corner of my eyes, nothing. Seconds later, or maybe minutes or hours, the town appears to be behind us. Then it really is, and the beautiful mountains engulf us. I slide the window again, and yell to Malik, asking if he's okay.

"No yelling," he responds.

"We're in good shape. We're out of here."

The mist turns into a drizzle, and as I roll up my window, the empty gas tank buzzer erupts in the small cab at stadium volume. It's relentless. Of all the annoying sounds sung by this sorry old truck, this is the most piercing. My irritation is forgotten when the most fearful sight I can imagine fills the chipped rearview mirror. Headlights pull out from the side of the road. Then the first spin of red and blue colored authority rotate into the night's obscurity.

15

THE ATTACKING LIGHTS ARE enough to imprison any soul and especially one, or is it two, in search of respite. The red and blue colors touch every part of me. Filling the space between what is real and a fear that reaches the unknown parts you're starting to know more and more by the second. My heart pumps blood into a foreign body. Arguably, not the one driving, but definitely the one Malik is stuck with. I pull into the same gas station we passed a day earlier after exiting the interstate, and now I know who visits in the middle of the night—someone who arguably doesn't want to. The fluorescent lights under the gas station canopy cast shine on the slick concrete from the rain. Cigarette and beer neon signs in the store window illuminate the cracks in its surface.

How does an officer approach a vehicle without walking by the back?

Out of necessity, I pull up to the filling pumps and the patrol car passes me.

What's happening?

I grab the door handle and stop, spying my other hand on the worn leather of the truck's steering wheel. My mind travels to the past and the last time I saw the truck's keys on the wobbly table by the door.

"Take 'em, JB." Father's last discernible words.

Months of rejuvenation followed Darren's recovery and then, in one day, it's all taken away. Of all the nights our father remained awake contemplating how Darren's life would end, ingrained in one of the deadliest days in American history was surely not one of them. Forever linked to people he'd never know. To events on a side of the world he'd never been to. For reasons he could never comprehend.

It had less than 17,000 miles. I grabbed the keys Darren had given him and minutes later, he lived alone in what was once our family's home.

As I paid every repair bill over two decades, I knew why I couldn't part with this senseless and impractical mistake of metal. It gave me hope. Made me feel connected to something that no longer existed. While the truck inhibited my life, it was an extension to a life I wanted redone. In the far depths of the mind that house our unrealistic hopes and dreams, I thought he'd come home for it.

But the truth is sadder. I've held onto the truck in place of doing the work to repair a damaged heart. It could have been the anchor from which I'd heal, but that part required courage. Mechanic bills were cheaper.

Several years after 9/11, I received a note from a man on Long Island who had worked with Darren. He wrote that they'd had breakfast that morning. Darren had told him all about Mountainbrook Farm and his upcoming trip on the trail with me. Afterward, he'd walked to the fruit stand for a banana. Darren opted to go back up to the office. Following a dark shadow overhead, he'd watched the plane hit the building and barely escaped himself. He was alive because he'd decided to get a banana.

Images race around my mind swirling with darkness, moving lights, and apprehension. Nothing else will fit within this ordinary moment in time. The interval of a second, the distance of an inch. Metrics made by man and the universe that create and swallow us. Continually evolving realities creating circumstances. If guided by luck or planning, circumstances into opportunity. Options. Decisions. Fate.

Mother keeping Darren beside us for birthday cake. The strong undertow alongside the only kid on the farm who didn't swim. The branch to grab just beyond Kami's reach. The patient sneezes infecting Terri with Covid. Walter's decision to not replace the headlight the night he was pulled over. The slow sperm of an infertile man.

I think of Malik. The folded square photo. His own broken truck in his rear pants pocket. A far less expensive token. In a haze of clarity, the decades flash offers of an unwelcome connection between who we are. Contemplating the coincidences of our worlds colliding at a moment that feels poised to define the lives we seek, as well as the ones we're running from.

Then the truck and picture are gone. Parked in some mystic junkyard. Framed atop a dusty mantle. But it's more than circumstances that Malik is contending with now. And like other moments of the last few days, it strikes me again that here and now, his fate is rarely distanced from being a Black man in a place chronically stained with racism.

My feet reach the ground that's dotted with dried circles of fuel. The patrol car is backed into the spot on the side of the lot directly facing the front of the truck. His headlights snap off, leaving us only under the dim light cast from the canopy's remaining bulbs. The steps to the gas tank door are slow. The nozzle clicks over the final ring of the tank, opening when a small flash reveals the patrol car's interior light and only one figure. A person who is clearly not the sheriff walks toward the truck. Deputy Owens. As the gas pumps itself, I walk a few feet toward the truck's hood. Moving our interaction away from Malik is goal number one.

"Good evening, Deputy. Just needing some gas. Then I'll be on my way."

His face is expressionless. "I wanted to have a word with you before you reached the interstate."

At the distance of an old-fashioned gun duel, we size each other up. Deputy Owens is about my height but fuller in all parts, though slimmer than the sheriff. Shoes the perfect shade of cleanliness without shining. Neatly pressed pants even after a long day. A small breeze blows through the station, making my soaked shirt feel cool on my body. My legs stiff from the soggy jean shorts. The uniform of law and order and me, an unknown. Can Malik hear us? Is he too far away? The silence is broken by the clunk of the automatic full-tank release.

"I'm gonna tell you something that ain't leaving this station, and I ain't never told this to no one. I'm not even sure why I'm telling you," he says.

What can he mean? Just tell me I'm free to go.

"I want you to know that we're not all like the sheriff out here." A subtle pause. "When he soon retires, well, then I'll be next in line."

I know I should be extending the officer my full attention, but I'm not.

"I've known Alice Whitaker at that store since I was a kid. Went to school with their son. Her, shall I say, less than righteous blood, flows thick." It looks like he taps his foot or maybe there was another movement, but something adjusts on his body, or maybe it's my eyes. "This here is a small town and my niece works at the store. Typically a quiet girl, she called me this afternoon."

A sound between static and voices of unrecognizable banter burst from his radio. He smoothly turns a few knobs on his belt to mute the airwaves and mumbles a comment about how being near the interstate picks up frequencies from passing truckers. All of this maneuvered without once looking down at this radio. "As I was saying. She saw the young man in the store. Said he didn't do anything wrong. To the contrary, she said he was polite and kind. She was scared to tell me."

We stand as only two men with nothing to lose can, then I realize he may have a lot to lose in telling me this. Neither of us knows how much I may lose. I contemplate yelling for Malik to come out from the truck, but it feels too risky. Then I hear a small shuffle in the bed, and it's instantly clear Owens hears it too. I take several steps backward to grab the nozzle, thinking it's both safe to do so and essential to distract our attention. He takes a step forward. His eyes rapidly move between me and the back of the truck.

The deputy turns the top part of his body back toward the patrol car as if someone's called for him. When he returns to face me, his jaw shuffles side to side several times. I slide the metal lever and hook the nozzle onto the pump holster.

"For what it's worth, word of what happened earlier today reached one of our residents, Mr. Rusty Hamilton. Aside from owning nearly half the buildings in town, he and his wife, Martha, mostly walk up and down Main Street a few dozen times a day holding hands. Very kind folks. Anyway, he owns the market building, and he told a few residents that this was the last straw from her. He's not renewing the woman's lease on the store. He's had enough of her racist ways."

He looks at me to say something. Anything. And I fathom that if Malik is hearing us, and I can't imagine he's not, he'd expect me to do the same. But I can't find the words and instead quietly say their name, "Rusty Hamilton. Martha."

Words sprint and then slow in my mind, and I'm not sure if they're as loud within my head or beyond it. *This is how it starts,* I tell myself. We stop accepting the hate. We disconnect from the hate. We act against the hate. Anything other than that enables the hate. I nod my head, sensing Owen has heard me.

"Like I said, I'm telling you more than I should," he continues, "but almost twenty years ago, on my first week on the force…" He stops talking and shuffles his feet while looking around. Maybe at nothing in particular. Contemplating what comes next. "It was a terrible week, really, but I won't go into that." He removes his hat and scratches his head. A balding head of short blond hair that may have been on the redder side as a child. It's the only time he moves his eyes away from me. "A really terrible week."

He seems lost in his declaration. If that's the story, I'm fine with it. Then he looks up, and I stare into him. Not his eyes. Into him, finally knowing that it's important for him to continue.

"We got a call from Ms. Whitaker. Alice. Yelling about having been robbed. Only fourteen dollars, but this was practically unheard of around here. When I filed the report with the sheriff, Alice told us the robber was a Black woman. I'll never forget the look on the faces of the two employees who gently but noticeably nodded their heads. I knew something was fishy. I knew deep down that something wasn't right. I pushed ahead anyway. I didn't stand up when I needed to. I've held onto that."

The officer looks past the light of the canopy to the station store. Neon lights for tobacco and commercial beer on one side. The backside of shelves lined with food that will outlive us all on the other. Beyond the building is the eternal concrete runway stretching from the ports of New Orleans to Canada.

"Long story short. The sheriff had me arrest a young Black lady at the gas station, who ironically had been in the store earlier that day as a paying customer. Kind young lady, that is, until she understandably wasn't. I'll never forget her. On a church retreat with her young child. Deep down, I believed every word she said, but like I said, I didn't stand up when I needed to."

The man keeps talking, albeit at a slower pace. Flashes of story, images, and history flicker at rapid speed, creating an old-fashioned moving picture. What? Who? When? Unwilling to ask why.

"It was awful timing when it happened," he continued. "The local court system was unexpectedly closed for a few days. Only released her when several employees fessed up about what they saw." The officer takes a deep breath and wipes his brow with his bare arm. "Not that it means anything to you, but I've sat with that, well, for all these years. Stings to know it happened on my watch, even now, that's all."

At the intersection between knowing what he's talking about, thinking I know what he's talking about, and not knowing anything about what he's talking about, I nod my head, unsure of what if any message it sends.

"Well, it took this incident today for Mr. Hamilton to do what should've been done a long time ago. Put her out of business." The officer checks his watch and then looks back at me. "Ah junk, I'm sorry for spewing this all out on you, sir. You've also had a long day. I just needed to clear my mind."

We face each other for several longer seconds, not knowing the protocol to break us apart. Still knowing that another human being is a few feet away, hiding, because it's the only way to be sure he's safe.

"Yeah, well, we hear you," I say, catching my blunder but possibly too late.

Deputy Owens stops his backward movement mid step and slowly shifts his hands to his hip and toward his gun belt. Slowly, he reverses his step.

"What do you mean 'we' hear you?" His passive affect dissolves into an intentional step forward. Nothing into everything.

The heavy breathing I hear from the back of the truck is not only in my mind. The fingers on the deputy's hands spread open from a restful hold on his hips as if he's ready to grip something.

Stay put just a little longer. Just a little longer.

16

FROZEN INTO MILLISECONDS THAT feel like they're shaping our future, my mind wanders to the farm, where everyone moved on, but not everyone moved forward. The steps we took were on the stones of buried memories too difficult to stand on alone. At a time when we collectively needed it most, we all learned in real time that Mountainbrook was a hostile place for stillness. For reflection. For healing. Mourning was integrated into work with the animals, harvests, and markets.

Dina said that everything on the farm was connected. A collection of small and then not-so-small ecosystems in balance with each other. Where we planted, harvested, and directed the animals to graze. Where we birthed life back into the areas trampled by footsteps and enriched the soil compromised by the shade of new trees. We nurtured the land and the animals in place of taking care of ourselves. Instead of talking about loss, love, and how to heal, we farmed.

Over time, I understood the farm to be an enigma. A contradiction. A blend of blinded privilege and radical disillusionment. It was also a rare vision. Someplace unique in a world where beyond it seemed like everything already existed. It was a place where you could grow, and help others grow, beyond the limitations of where most of us came from before. Where we laid down. Where we rose up every day to feel the earth under our fingers gripping the land until it became part of our bodies and souls.

But of all the days of life on Mountainbrook Farm, one moment and person is more deeply engrained than any other, and it's who I think about on the first day of school every year since I started teaching. Walter. Not his life-long story but the memory of an early Saturday morning during my senior year of high school. The story inspired the first lesson I always introduced to students.

After years of light farm tasks, I was assigned a job with Timmy loading trucks for the weekday market and again on Friday for the weekend city runs. Afterward, we'd unload the empty crates and coolers. One morning our job was different. We had to unload a market-bound truck that never left, and it became clear why when the professor's old Subaru wagon pulled into the lot. Walter and Professor Farace exited and purposefully walked in opposite directions. The professor to his trailer and Walter to his apartment beyond the back barn. The professor held his glasses in his hands, his wavy hair disheveled. One shoe untied. Some sort of stain on his pants. Walter walked too quickly for me to notice anything equally as unsettling.

A few minutes later a truck pulled into the lot and parked in the first available spot in front of the Mountainbrook Farm sign where anyone rarely parked. Out walked an oddly familiar man. Timmy lowered the crate of potatoes and hopped off the truck ramp. It was his uncle, Dale, and within seconds we heard yelling from inside the Farm Store. I asked Timmy what was happening.

Following a final burst of accusations, the door swung open and Dale exited, stopping within several feet to swing around and stab the air with his finger in Kent's direction. "I should not have to keep looking out for your people! My officers held restraint, but if that…" Dale stumbled his words, so clearly fighting a verbal temptation. His brother's arms moved to his hips, posturing the slight size advantage he had over his sibling. "If that *big* farmhand don't follow directions again, it'll be worse."

Kent took a large step toward his brother and then another. Suddenly, Timmy jumped in front of the 55-gallon blue plastic drum we hid behind. I was shocked. We were perfectly hidden. No one to my understanding needed our help. We were safe.

"Dad. Uncle Dale. Stop!" Timmy's words ripped through the perfect blue air, an abundance of care and unproven authority in his voice.

He had gained the attention of his father and uncle, yet possibly was unaware what to do with it. Now there were three people involved and one kneeling safely out of sight. We all expected something to follow, but the ensuing seconds failed to live up to expectations.

Kent turned his attention back to his brother and raised his finger inches from Dale's face. "He's no farmhand, and you know it. There's only one man to work this land as hard as Walter, and we called him Dad. When was the last time you worked that hard, Dale?"

Dale marched the remaining feet to his truck door and spun on his brother again, yelling louder than before. "And the boy, that's strike three. My blind eye over the summer was 100 years of hard time. Then the DEA, FBI, and Border Inspection Services on my ass for weeks. I'm done with him!" He slammed the truck's door, cranked the engine, and shifted into reverse in a fury.

His rear wheels spun hard, throwing gravel against the truck underside. He then let off the gas, and when the dust cleared, he calmly continued backing out and turned up Herb Ross Road. A subtle note of civility.

Kent watched the truck bend around the curve and then looked back to his younger son. I'll always remember that look. The eyes. Kent surrendered his stare first. He shook his head, though it was unclear if it was directed at his brother, who by then was on the interstate, or his son who he knew sided with him.

Walter walked past us and entered the store after Kent. I came out of hiding and stood by Timmy, who hadn't left where his feet were planted. We were silent. Not one single cloud above. An otherwise perfect farm day. Except for the truck full of food bound for Boston, the farm's largest market, but the professor who managed it was in his trailer.

"What happened, Timmy?"

He didn't answer, but something changed in Timmy that day. Maybe he found something. Something more than just his voice, which by my metrics was a monumental yet daring accomplishment. When Timmy turned around, I followed him and something changed with us as well. I felt like I was no longer his peer, that I was more of his subordinate, and when we returned to the truck to complete our tasks, he spoke with a new level of conviction.

"All I know is that the professor and Walter weren't here last night. We saw them pull in around an hour ago." He took a deep breath. "You probably know more than you're letting on, JB."

Per the course, I quietly returned his glare, unable to find anything to say.

Timmy continued. "Imre milked the cows last night, but some returned to the fields instead of the barn. Two calves were attacked by coyotes. One badly."

What did this have to do with his father and uncle yelling at each other in the parking lot? A long pause followed a story completely opposite from what I asked about. I wondered if Timmy had done that intentionally, but he had not. As Timmy saw it, this was the story. With every opportunity to ask more questions, to dig deeper, to press the one person who might respond, I chose not to. Timmy parked the truck, and we hopped out of the cab and went our separate ways. While I couldn't explain the friendship Timmy and I had before that morning, by the afternoon it was different.

The creaky Dairy House door swung open and Zoya emerged. It was rare to see her hands and arms unoccupied. She asked me about the commotion. The yelling.

Then the Farm Store door opened and Walter exited, carrying a long and narrow hard black case. The crackling dirt and crushed stone had a distinct sound under his well-worn boots. As he always did, Walter extended a brief lip smile and nodded. Then, a man almost constantly in motion did something I'd never seen him do. He stopped. Time stopped. His eyes still forward, locked in the direction of his body.

"How is the calf?" Zoya asked, but the apparent care in her words wasn't really directed at the animal.

I looked in the same direction as where Walter faced, thinking there was something there. The back barn, several trailers, endless fields after that. Beyond them the unsuspecting eye wouldn't know that it was there the river wrapped around the fields, and Walter was the only person to have a door leading directly to its bank. As he stood almost motionless over this broken and beautiful patch of earth, I realized how much more was happening than I understood.

Not just the incident between Kent and his brother. But also what happened to Tessa and my mother's relationship and leaving for Montreal. The mysteries around Kami and Darren. Years later, I suspected Zoya knew about all of this, or knew some of it. Had she not, no one could have imagined a situation as identical. The farm was vast, but the network of people living within it was small. A family, and one of its own had become ill. Sick with the disease of addiction and the dangerous symptoms that accompanied it. Walter and the professor were trying to help. His father, our father, was at that point frozen.

With Kent's blessing, Walter did everything he could to help Darren. News reached the farm quickly about the fights in rural bars where Darren baited racists and bigots until he could release his rage on people he felt worthy of it. Dale called his brother about the repeated offenses, and every time, Darren was let go. Privilege. Years later, I learned that the night before Timmy and I watched Walter and the professor pull into the lot that morning, Walter was stopped by the county police as he tried to rescue Darren from another harmful night. A light on the farm truck was out. They accused him of smuggling drugs from Canada, an ironic accusation considering the man Walter was trying to rescue was guilty of the charge. After Walter's run-in with the police, the professor insisted on driving. He knew the northern backroads near the desolate border were no place for a large Black man, and his best friend, to drive alone.

"The calf?" Zoya repeated, breaking the spell of silence.

After several seconds, Walter turned his body toward her and something was being surrendered. Something was being pulled away. First from his country, then into military servitude in another to hunt and kill for the price of his freedom. Walter's shoulders slunk on his large frame. "Not well." His words layered with exhaustion and possibly a fat lip.

Zoya absorbed the need to pause. "Too bad, my good friend. I am sorry," she finally said, softly.

Walter lowered the long black case to the ground. I tried to count the droplets of blood staining his tan shirt that, as it always did, remained neatly tucked behind the thick leather belt and brown pants.

I took a few steps backward to within inches of the barn's side wall. The ripped basketball net swung overhead from the day's first mountain wind, an autumn breeze. I saw more of Zoya's back and hairnet than her face.

They looked at each other, and I saw them with a new amazement, or was it a shallow revelation. Until that moment, I'd never thought about or realized they were both African. Then, that was all I could see. I watched their African eyes lock, suspecting in that moment that what they could know and knew of each other was its own galaxy. A bond formed by a land so beautiful and harsh and special and unforgiving that of course other men would try to harm it.

Now both stood proud and spiritually bruised in a valley on the other side of the world. In another land so beautiful and harsh and special and unforgiving that of course other men would try to harm it. Surrounded mostly by White people. Yet for this moment, they had the eyes of a friend to look into. Someone who knew just a little bit more than the rest of us. The moment was an ocean of silence and sadness. One separating two massive continents where they both left with children no longer their own. I pushed my back into the wall as fiercely as silence allowed. Wanting to disappear. The moment's purpose too powerful, sad, and real. Something had to break, and I'd soon learn that something well.

Then Walter spoke. "Who lives? Who dies? Where we're born. What happens after that? You know as I, Zoya. It's all one cosmic role of the dice."

He picked up the case and was soon out of sight. Minutes later, from several fields away, the echo of the rifle shot bounced off the mountain before fading over the river.

17

"WHAT I MEANT WAS, is that I hear you. And thanks." I dig my mind into Deputy Owens's thoughts. His understanding of where he is. Who he is. Where I am. The chance, in whatever form the world will allow it, that what he heard isn't what he believes. Officer Owens lowers his eyes and shifts his lower jaw several times. He's thinking, which turns into slight nods as his eyes raise back to my own.

"Thank you," I say softly.

He unceremoniously nods, exhales and turns around. Within seconds, he pulls left out of the lot, turning back toward town.

A young man, possibly the store clerk, stands in the doorway of the station, staring at me as I enter the truck and pull out from under the lit darkness and in the other direction where I immediately exit for Interstate 81 heading north. Several large rigs pass us as I keep our speed to a safe minimum. Within minutes, new neon lights offer hope. We veer into the roadstop and away from the arrow for car traffic and park alongside an orchestra of idling truck engines.

Before my door is fully open, I feel the truck bed raise several inches as Malik's shoes land on the pavement. I walk around to the back, and we face each other in the low light. It's not confrontational. It's not embracive. It's presence. He doesn't say anything, and neither do I. What words are left?

My arms feel clammy and raw from hours in a cold rain. I can't imagine how he feels. What he's heard. The feelings within and beyond him. We stare into each other, but our faces offer nothing. Everything has been spent. Wondering if what we see in the other, and ourselves, is something being redone, torn down, or something altogether different. Being rebuilt.

Malik balls up his fist and gently knocks twice on the metal rim of the truck bed. A clear message, and he walks to the passenger door. I ball my fist and knock on the rim of the opposite truck wall just as he did, but for no one to hear. As we pull away from the truck stop, the massive cloth of red and white stripes, blue background, and white stars chaotically blows in the darkness, sectionally lit by industrial light bulbs shining upward from the ground. The symbol of promise. The symbol of oppression. The great interpretation.

The truck's windows have been down for days and the constant wind is no longer recognizable. Malik is tilted away from me in the same way he was when we left several days ago. Massive trucks barrel by our left owning the road, leaving little room for horizontal misjudgment. North of Roanoke we pull into a rest stop. Far from the lights above the vending machines where gnats congregate, we pee into different sides of the same bush. Listening to the odd sound of urine trickling down the leaves and branches to the already moist soil.

Down the road, a series of beeps alert me to text messages just now downloading on my phone. All from Terri. The first sharing that she feels terrible. The next few that she's struggling to breathe. The following that she needs me to take her to the hospital. Then that she's been admitted. The next asking me where I am. If I'm okay. The last saying only that she needs me. New urgency infuses an existing fear and I push down on the old truck's accelerator to depths the pedal hasn't reached in years.

The exit for Front Royal, where we'll finally head east, is still 100 miles away. I think of Terri. About what she said. About helping the one who needs help when they need it. How I've continually missed that mark, and sadly how I may have missed it again. The extra pressure isn't producing faster speed.

I think about Malik. Not the Malik sitting next to me, but the one who sat in my classroom for two whole years of his life. I think about what it means to be a teacher. To be tasked with guiding a young person's learning. To help another person understand themselves in an overly complicated world I've not figured out myself. Questioning what it means to be a student. The experience of a twelve- and then fourteen-year-old Malik in my class. How much he left not knowing, though unwilling to ponder with what knowledge and understanding he arrived. Asking myself what I've learned as a teacher this year. Finally seeing that for close to an hour every day these evolving humans were directed to learn from me. To understand history. My history. At times, our history. Rarely, their history. Wondering how to guide others to learn where I haven't done so myself. A transient calmness briefly interrupts the mental madness. Then a flash on my phone. "The universe is in sync," the professor would say. I scroll the short message into the phone's full frame.

To: Jerry Brown
From: Tara Becker (she/her/hers)
Subject: Service to Biko Students Letter

Mr. Brown:
You did not attend our graduation last week.
Nor did you inform school leadership as to a
reason why. You also did not attend our meeting
yesterday, which was scheduled for noon.
These actions show that you are apparently
not interested in the lives of Biko students. This
letter is to inform you that these incidents are
grounds for...

But I stop reading and swipe Becker's email off the phone's screen. I've seen enough. Pathetically, I tell myself that we're different. I chalk it up to that. That adults always get in the way. I repeat the few words I read in my head more times than I should.

On the outskirts of Lexington, an oversized electronic screen flashes gas prices and the time and date, 2:17 a.m. June 19, 2020. Juneteenth. I think about the enslaved Black people in Galveston, Texas and when they learned of their freedom as slaves some two and a half years after the Emancipation Proclamation legally removed them from servitude. Naturally, my thoughts shift to the man next to me, who until right now I never would have admitted was who first pushed my understanding that I may have been misleading my students about the world in which we live.

It was during my Juneteenth lesson from Malik's tenth-grade year, and I was certain that the ears and brain above his slouched body wasn't paying attention. But then he uncovered his hands from his head before dropping them to his sides, whispering, but loud enough for the quiet roomful of students to hear, "Bad enough they made us beg and bleed for it. Then when we earned it, they didn't even bother to tell a bunch of niggas they was no longer slaves."

The whole class of tenth graders froze. All I could do was soften my pose and look at him. He'd again covered his face with his arms, but underneath I sensed sadness, anger, and education. Underneath my face, unfortunately uncovered, was also sadness and anger. I struggled to understand if my face showed what teaching is about. What learning is about.

I couldn't think how anyone in that room was less comfortable than me. Regrettably thankful that we were within minutes of the class bell, I suggested we wrap up. I didn't sleep for days after that. I also didn't tell anyone, ashamed that my class had pushed a student to say that, while overwhelmed with confusion because our students used that word all the time. But this felt different.

When I told another teacher about the incident years later, she asked if he got in trouble, stating that the student had used a highly offensive term and should have been reprimanded. She was shocked that this never crossed my mind. I thought the lesson sparked a primal response from a student. Wasn't that part of the goal? For years I thought about how one word could both be so inclusive and offensive. How it casually, or maybe intentionally, bonded the very people it was intended to offend. Maybe I was the reason so many students had a narrow view of American history.

And now. Now. Wherever now is, I can't help thinking about Juneteenth and its connection to the last twenty-four hours. What happens to a person's mind when they're kept from the truth? A person's heart? How can a person grow and become beneath the weight of injustice?

The final hills of Appalachia morph into suburbia. Empty parking lots in front of popular box stores line the road. The first Metro tracks hug an empty highway. A series of concrete loops mark the entrance to the capital region. A streak of sunlight invades the rear window, now cleaner from rain. Swirling helicopters coast in and out of view. Portable roadside signs identify detours around the capital because of protests and Covid. Other signs state the mask mandate. Another sign restricts non-essential visitors from entering the city. The flat water of the Potomac River offers an almost perfect reflection of the Washington Monument. Then a faint ripple reshapes it, transforming the monument's Klan-like mask into a Salvador Dali painting.

We park near the hospital and slam the doors shut in unison. Small things. Letting us know we're alive. Together. At least for now. Shoulder to shoulder, we stand in front of the metal signpost where three rectangle signs vertically hang, each declaring different permissible parking times. Two in direct contradiction of the third. Our eyes rotate around each sign's limited words. Rereading. Contemplating if we're delirious from the last twenty-four hours or that these signs don't make sense.

I toss the keys through the open window for what I tell myself is the final time. "They can take it," I mumble under my breath, and then without thought or consideration, I pat Malik's arm with the back of my hand. "You want it? It's yours."

He takes a long look at our transport companion and then shakes his head. "Nah, I've got other things to repair."

The sidewalks are empty except for people in scrubs of different faded colors. Everyone is wearing masks. Everyone avoiding eye contact. We stop at the top of the Metro escalator, and I think he's going to extend his hand, but neither of us does. I still can't find anything to say, nor can he. Maybe he's heard everything in his life that he needs to. Maybe he missed every word of it. Maybe the words, had they been heard, didn't mean anything at all.

Malik curls his lips into his mouth and places his hands on his hips. Maybe it's his way of saying that the real work is about to begin. Or maybe there's nothing he's trying to convey. He nods several times, and with each motion a world of emotion spins.

He turns away and slides his hands on the moving escalator handrail and lifts his legs, skipping over several exposed steps. For a few seconds, he sinks. He then turns around and tilts his head backward, and we catch each other's eyes for a long second. One that I know then and there that I'll always remember as having been longer.

Then Malik is gone. Sunk beneath my sightline into the underground concrete jungle. I wonder what will become of him. Where he'll go. The options he'll have. The choices he'll make.

Terri's words enter my mind. Not the part about helping the person who needs help now, but new words. Words she didn't say, but what's becoming clear. How life is also about learning to let others help us. To teach us what we're missing, and if we're lucky, to help show us the way forward. What it feels like Malik has done for me.

My thoughts shift to our journey into rural America. Was there rampant racism everywhere we turned? Or was it that we encountered exactly what we arrived with? A childhood trauma and life experience that created a Malik whose intuition is to react so quickly alongside a childhood trauma and life experience that created a me so often too scared to act at all.

My hand slides over the blotch of black ink stain at the bottom of my short's pocket to what remains of the pen from the letters. Letters written with so much love and hopefulness that they were destined to find their true home in the mountain breeze. I toss the shards of cracked plastic into an already over-flowing garbage and start running down the road.

Several feet before where I think my presence would be detected, a gust of artificially chilled air strikes my body through the automatic doors. The hospital is a frenzy of chaotic signs, brightness, and disease. My temperature is checked after a box of face masks is shoved into my chest. My identification is scanned and multiple forms are signed.

I enter Terri's room among the frantic rush of beeps, anxious movements, and good intentions as the sliding red pyramids on the screen start to reflect the western horizon. I sit beside her as she extends her hand, and I grip her bony knuckles, feeling radiant life, but then something else.

We're back in the countryside having driven halfway through the mountains. The windows are down and the view from the roadside pull-off shows a setting sun with endless beauty and no promises of tomorrow.

Through her subtle smile, Terri whispers to me through her blinking eyes. "Yeah you. Flawed, scarred, and scared. I'll take on this mystery with you." Then she tells me what I've long been searching for. "Find that sound, JB. You got it? Now, together, just this once."

Life is people.
Life is people.

Acknowledgments

Writing TAUGHT started as an exercise to better understand the antiracist journey and the microaggressions of racism—two topics I am continually studying as an educator. For me, this type of learning is messy and patriotic.

A literary agent who was interested in the manuscript for TAUGHT asked me, "Are you concerned about being canceled?" Appreciative of the feedback, the question confirmed what I already knew: TAUGHT could spark the argument that a writer should not write about and from the perspective of someone they are not. When pursued without authenticity and respect, I couldn't agree more.

While writing TAUGHT, I worked closely with teachers and students of different racial and cultural backgrounds and sexual orientations for one reason—to make me a more informed educator and writer. Not only was this cohort of former teachers and students deeply instrumental in how I approached the story, they have been my professional community for more than two decades. First as an educator in Washington, DC public schools and then as an education nonprofit leader.

My deepest gratitude extends to this large but tight knit community of current and former teachers and students. This novel exists because of you.

The novel would also not be possible without the extraordinary support of several other people. The first is my editing and creative partner, Crystal Adaway, whose mind and heart elevated each page since the first revision. The proofreading expertise of Debra Hartmann and the technical support of Ken Mackel were invaluable. Clare Berke, Grace Katabaruki, Jessica Haber, and Nicole Burton all went beyond my feedback requests and I could not have completed the novel without the unwavering support of Kate Douglass.

Ultimately, I wrote TAUGHT to explore the fragility of our lives and to create a springboard to meaningful dialogue about race, education, and healing. For every student that felt misunderstood and for every teacher that struggled to understand the young lives before them, TAUGHT is dedicated to you.

Thank you for reading the book.

Eric F. Goldstein
January 1, 2026